Conrad L. Wilson.
July 1954.

Everyman, I will go with thee, and be thy guide,
In thy most need to go by thy side.

EVERYMAN'S LIBRARY

No. 912

FICTION

THE TURN OF THE SCREW
& THE ASPERN PAPERS
BY HENRY JAMES

HENRY JAMES, born in New York on 15th April 1843, the elder brother of William James, the philosopher. Educated at Harvard and in England, France, and Switzerland. Visited Europe 1869–75; settled in London 1876 onwards, and at Rye, Sussex, from 1896. Naturalized as a British subject, 1915; awarded Order of Merit, January 1916. Died on 28th February 1916.

THE TURN OF THE SCREW

THE ASPERN PAPERS

HENRY JAMES

LONDON: J. M. DENT & SONS LTD.

INTRODUCTORY NOTE

THE two stories by Henry James in this volume show him in his characteristic personal manner of tale-telling, but to entirely different effect, the one leading to tragedy, the other to subtle and delicate comedy. The scene of the first, *The Turn of the Screw*, is laid in an English country house, and the characters are two tragic children, two intermediary grown-ups (one the narrator of the tale), and two ghosts. We must remember that Henry James, like his master Balzac, had a taste for mystery and the macabre which he did not often indulge so cruelly. The second story, *The Aspern Papers*, has its scene in Venice, that Venice to which he often returned in his real and fictive European wanderings. One may recall a letter of his, dated from Palazzo Barbaro, Venice, 23rd June 1907, in which he wrote: '. . . For myself, in this paradise of great household spaces, I kind of feel that even the bribe of the Canal Grande and a *giardinetto* together wouldn't quite reconcile me to the purgatory of a very small, *really* (and not merely relatively) small house. . . .' The fact is, he had every inclination to be housed in a palace, if not one quite so forlorn as that of *The Aspern Papers*. The chief characters there, the two derelict American ladies, and their very alert fellow-countryman with 'the literary heart' who wants to get hold of Jasper Aspern's relics, are perfectly conceived to suit the purpose or plot of the story and educe the other character—the old palace itself! For James was a master in depicting the power, or, if you will, the spirit, of place. Places to him were as significant as the people who lived in them; he was an epicure in old cities, in palaces, and in American, English, or foreign vistas.

In the year when *The Aspern Papers* was written, James was writing a series of critical appreciations of his favourite novelists and tale-tellers, especially the

French, among them Balzac, Flaubert, Stendhal, and Guy de Maupassant. Those who are curious about literary affinities and artistic derivations may find it worth while to trace the influence on him of these masters and follow up the clues afforded by his studies of Balzac, 'that Benedictine of the actual,' and Flaubert, 'the profane anchorite.' Beside that French evidence, we can gain reminders from nearer home. The personal style of the governess's tale in *The Turn of the Screw* recalls that of Dickens's Esther in *Bleak House*, and there are pages in *The Aspern Papers* that have a savour both of Thackeray (in his more intimate vein) and of the Russian master Turgenev. Fielding, Dickens, Thackeray, George Eliot, and his own countryman Hawthorne are cited by him in his Balzac study among 'the living painters of a living time,' 'painters of manners and fashions,' genuine historians even if they do not 'don the uniform.' In that respect Henry James was a true historian too, first among those who lived and wrote as Anglo-American authors. Indeed, he holds a place of his own in the chart of the Modern Novel, which is now making a concerted entry into *Everyman's Library* —a chart he outlined critically as long ago as 1914.[1]

E. R.

---

[1] See his essay on 'The New Novel,' printed in *The Times Literary Supplement* and reprinted in his book, *Notes on Novelists*, that same year

LIST OF THE CHIEF WORKS OF HENRY JAMES

A Passionate Pilgrim and Other Tales, 1875; *Transatlantic Sketches*, 1875; *Roderick Hudson*, 1875 (rev. ed. 1879); *The American*, 1877; *Watch and Ward*, 1878; *French Poets and Novelists*, 1878; *The Europeans*, 1878; *Daisy Miller*, 1879; *An International Episode*, 1879; *Four Meetings*, 1879 (published with the two previous works in a two-volume edition); *Hawthorne*, 1879 (English Men of Letters); *The Madonna of the Future and Other Tales*, 1879; *The Diary of a Man of Fifty and A Bundle of Letters*, 1880 (the first of these had appeared in the preceding collection); *Confidence*, 1880; *Washington Square, The Pension Beaurepas*, etc., 1881; *The Portrait of a Lady*, 1881 (dramatized 1883); *The Siege of London, The Point of View*, etc., 1883; *Portraits of Places*, 1883; *Notes on a Collection of Drawings by George Du Maurier*, 1884; *Tales of Three Cities*, 1884; *A Little Tour in France*, 1885; *Stories Revised*, 3 vols., 1885; *The Bostonians*, 1886; *The Princess Casamassima*, 1886; *Partial Portraits*, 1888; *The Aspern Papers, Louisa Pallant, The Modern Warning*, 1888; *The Reverberator*, 1888; *A London Life, The Patagonia, The Lion, Mrs. Temperley*, 1889; *The Tragic Muse*, 1890; *The Lesson of the Master, The Marriages, The Pupil, Brooksmith, The Solution, Sir Edmund Orme*, 1892; *The Private Life, Lord Beaupré, The Visits*, 1893; *The Wheel of Time, Collaboration, Owen Wingrave*, 1893; *The Real Thing and Other Tales*, 1893; *Picture and Text*, 1893; *Essays in London and Elsewhere*, 1893; Theatricals (two comedies): *Tenants Disengaged*, 1894; Second Series, *The Album, The Reprobate* (and *Theatricals*), 1895; *Terminations, The Death of the Lion, The Coxon Fund, The Middle Years, The Altar of the Dead*, 1895; *Embarrassments, The Figure in the Carpet, Glasses, The Next Time, The Way it came*, 1896; *The Other House*, 1896; *The Spoils of Poynton*, 1897; *What Maisie knew*, 1897; *The Two Magics, The Turn of the Screw, Covering End*, 1898; *In the Cage*, 1898; *The Awkward Age*, 1899; *The Soft Side*, 1900; *The Sacred Fount*, 1901; *The Wings of the Dove*, 1902; *William Wetmore*, 1903; *The Better Sort*, 1903; *The Ambassadors*, 1903; *The Golden Bowl*, 1904; *The Question of Our Speech, The Lesson of Balzac*, 1905; *English Hours*, 1905; *The American Scene*, 1907; *Views and Reviews*, 1908 (a collection of early literary studies); *Julia Bride*, 1909; *Italian Hours*, 1909; *The Finer Grain*, 1910; *The Outcry*, 1911; *A Small Boy and Others*, 1913; *Notes on Novelists*, 1914 (literary studies, chiefly of the nineties); *Notes of a Son and Brother*, 1914; *The Ivory Tower*, 1917; *The Sense of the Past*, 1917; *The Middle Years*, 1917; *Within the Rim and Other Essays*, 1918; *Gabrielle de Bergerac*, 1918 (*Atlantic Monthly*, 1869); *Travelling Companions*, etc., 1919 (early stories); *Notes and Reviews* (early literary notes), 1921.

Practically all the above first appeared in periodical form shortly before their reappearance in book form. The journals to which James chiefly contributed were *The North American Review, The Atlantic Monthly, The Nation, The Galaxy, New York Tribune, The*

Cornhill Magazine, Macmillan's Magazine, Harper's Magazine and Weekly, The Century Magazine, The Parisian, and *Longman's Magazine*.

LETTERS, AND NOTE BOOKS

The Letters of Henry James, selected and edited by Percy Lubbock, (2 vols.), 1920; *Henry James: Letters to A. C. Benson and Auguste Monod*, edited by E. F. Benson, 1930; *Theatre and Friendship*, with a commentary by Elizabeth Robins, 1932.

The Note Books of Henry James, edited by Prof. F. O. Matthiessen, 1948.

COLLECTED EDITIONS. The New York edition, for which James extensively revised the novels and stories and wrote new critical prefaces, appeared from 1907–17; the London Edition (35 vols.), 1921–3.

SOME WRITINGS ABOUT HENRY JAMES.

Rebecca West: *Henry James*, 1916; Joseph Warren Beach: *The Method of Henry James*, 1918; Theodora Bosanquet: *Henry James at Work*, 1924; Van Wyck Brooks: *The Pilgrimage of Henry James*, 1925; Pelham Edgar: *Henry James: Man and Author*, 1927; Ralph Barton Perry: *The Thought and Character of Henry James*, 1935; F. O. Matthiessen: *Henry James: The Major Phase*, 1946; *The Question of Henry James* (essays by Max Beerbohm, T. S. Eliot, Ford M. Ford, F. O. Matthiessen, and others), 1947; *The Legend of the Master* (*Henry James*) (biographical impressions by many writers, compiled by Simon Nowell-Smith), 1947. Many important studies of James and his writings are found in other works, e.g. *The Craft of Fiction* by Percy Lubbock, *Portraits* by Desmond Mac-Carthy, etc.

THE TURN OF THE SCREW

THE story has held us, round the fire, sufficiently
breathless, but except the obvious remark that it
was gruesome, as on Christmas Eve in an old house a
strange tale should essentially be, I remember no
comment uttered till somebody happened to note it
as the only case he had met in which such a visitation
had fallen on a child. The case, I may mention,
was that of an apparition in just such an old house
as had gathered us for the occasion—an appearance,
of a dreadful kind, to a little boy sleeping in the room
with his mother and waking her up in the terror of
it; waking her not to dissipate his dread and soothe
him to sleep again, but to encounter also herself,
before she had succeeded in doing so, the same sight
that had shocked him. It was this observation that
drew from Douglas—not immediately, but later in
the evening—a reply that had the interesting consequence to which I call attention. Someone else told
a story not particularly effective, which I saw he was
not following. This I took for a sign that he had
himself something to produce and that we should
only have to wait. We waited in fact till two nights
later; but that same evening, before we scattered,
he brought out what was in his mind.

'I quite agree—in regard to Griffin's ghost, or
whatever it was—that its appearing first to the
little boy, at so tender an age, adds a particular touch. But it's not the first occurrence of
its charming kind that I know to have been

3

concerned with a child. If the child gives the effect
another turn of the screw, what do you say to *two*
children——?'

'We say, of course,' somebody exclaimed, 'that
two children give two turns! Also that we want to
hear about them.'

I can see Douglas there before the fire, to which
he had got up to present his back, looking down
at this converser with his hands in his pockets.
'Nobody but me, till now, has ever heard. It's
quite too horrible.' This was naturally declared
by several voices to give the thing the utmost
price, and our friend, with quiet art, prepared his
triumph by turning his eyes over the rest of us and
going on: 'It's beyond everything. Nothing at all
that I know touches it.'

'For sheer terror?' I remember asking.

He seemed to say it wasn't so simple as that; to
be really at a loss how to qualify it. He passed his
hand over his eyes, made a little wincing grimace.
'For dreadful—dreadfulness!'

'Oh, how delicious!' cried one of the women.

He took no notice of her; he looked at me, but
as if, instead of me, he saw what he spoke of. 'For
general uncanny ugliness and horror and pain.'

'Well, then,' I said, 'just sit right down and
begin.'

He turned round to the fire, gave a kick to a log,
watched it an instant. Then as he faced us again:
'I can't begin. I shall have to send to town.'
There was a unanimous groan at this, and much
reproach; after which, in his preoccupied way, he
explained. 'The story's written. It's in a locked
drawer—it has not been out for years. I could

write to my man and enclose the key; he could
send down the packet as he finds it.' It was to
me in particular that he appeared to propound this
—appeared almost to appeal for aid not to hesitate.
He had broken a thickness of ice, the formation of
many a winter; had had his reasons for a long silence.
The others resented postponement, but it was just
his scruples that charmed me. I adjured him to
write by the first post and to agree with us for an
early hearing; then I asked him if the experience in
question had been his own. To this his answer was
prompt. 'Oh, thank God, no!'

'And is the record yours? You took the thing
down?'

'Nothing but the impression. I took that *here*'
—he tapped his heart. 'I 've never lost it.'

'Then your manuscript——?'

'Is in old faded ink and in the most beautiful
hand.' He hung fire again. 'A woman's. She has
been dead these twenty years. She sent me the
pages in question before she died.' They were all
listening now, and of course there was somebody to
be arch, or at any rate to draw the inference. But
if he put the inference by without a smile it was
also without irritation. 'She was a most charming
person, but she was ten years older than I. She
was my sister's governess,' he quietly said. 'She
was the most agreeable woman I 've ever known
in her position; she would have been worthy of any
whatever. It was long ago, and this episode was
long before. I was at Trinity, and I found her at
home on my coming down the second summer. I
was much there that year—it was a beautiful one;
and we had, in her off-hours, some strolls and talks

in the garden—talks in which she struck me as awfully clever and nice. Oh, yes; don't grin: I liked her extremely and am glad to this day to think she liked me too. If she hadn't she wouldn't have told me. She had never told any one. It wasn't simply that she said so, but that I knew she hadn't. I was sure; I could see. You'll easily judge why when you hear.'

'Because the thing had been such a scare?'

He continued to fix me. 'You'll easily judge,' he repeated; '*you* will.'

I fixed him too. 'I see. She was in love.'

He laughed for the first time. 'You *are* acute. Yes, she was in love. That is, she *had* been. That came out—she couldn't tell her story without its coming out. I saw it, and she saw I saw it; but neither of us spoke of it. I remember the time and the place—the corner of the lawn, the shade of the great beeches and the long hot summer afternoon. It wasn't a scene for a shudder; but oh——!' He quitted the fire and dropped back into his chair.

'You'll receive the packet Thursday morning?' I said.

'Probably not till the second post.'

'Well then; after dinner——'

'You'll all meet me here?' He looked us round again. 'Isn't anybody going?' It was almost the tone of hope.

'Everybody will stay!'

'*I* will—and *I* will!' cried the ladies whose departure had been fixed. Mrs. Griffin, however, expressed the need for a little more light. 'Who was it she was in love with?'

'The story will tell,' I took upon myself to reply.

'Oh, I can't wait for the story!'

'The story *won't* tell,' said Douglas; 'not in any literal, vulgar way.'

'More's the pity then. That's the only way I ever understand.'

'Won't *you* tell, Douglas?' somebody else inquired.

He sprang to his feet again. 'Yes—to-morrow. Now I must go to bed. Good night.' And, quickly catching up a candlestick, he left us slightly bewildered. From our end of the great brown hall we heard his step on the stair; whereupon Mrs. Griffin spoke. 'Well, if I don't know who she was in love with I know who *he* was.'

'She was ten years older,' said her husband.

'*Raison de plus*—at that age! But it's rather nice, his long reticence.'

'Forty years!' Griffin put in.

'With this outbreak at last.'

'The outbreak,' I returned, 'will make a tremendous occasion of Thursday night'; and every one so agreed with me that in the light of it we lost all attention for everything else. The last story, however incomplete and like the mere opening of a serial, had been told; we handshook and 'candlestuck,' as somebody said, and went to bed.

I knew the next day that a letter containing the key had, by the first post, gone off to his London apartments; but in spite of—or perhaps just on account of—the eventual diffusion of this knowledge we quite let him alone till after dinner, till such an hour of the evening in fact as might best accord with the kind of emotion on which our hopes were fixed. Then he became as communicative as we could desire, and indeed gave us his best reason for being so. We had it from him again before the fire in the hall, as we had had our mild wonders of the previous night. It appeared that the narrative he had promised to read us really required for a proper intelligence a few words of prologue. Let me say here distinctly, to have done with it, that this narrative, from an exact transcript of my own made much later, is what I shall presently give. Poor Douglas, before his death—when it was in sight —committed to me the manuscript that reached him on the third of these days and that, on the same spot, with immense effect, he began to read to our hushed little circle on the night of the fourth. The departing ladies who had said they would stay didn't, of course, thank heaven, stay: they departed, in consequence of arrangements made, in a rage of curiosity, as they professed, produced by the touches with which he had already worked us up. But that only made his little final auditory more compact and select, kept it round the hearth subject to a common thrill.

The first of these touches conveyed that the written statement took up the date at a point after it had, in a manner, begun. The fact to be in possession of was therefore that his old friend, the youngest of several daughters of a poor country parson, had at the age of twenty, on taking service for the first time in the schoolroom, come up to London, in trepidation, to answer in person an advertisement that had already placed her in brief correspondence with the advertiser. This person proved, on her presenting herself for judgment at a house in Harley Street that impressed her as vast and imposing—this prospective patron proved a gentleman, a bachelor in the prime of life, such a figure as had never risen, save in a dream or an old novel, before a fluttered, anxious girl out of a Hampshire vicarage. One could easily fix his type; it never, happily, dies out. He was handsome and bold and pleasant, off-hand and gay and kind. He struck her, inevitably, as gallant and splendid, but what took her most of all and gave her the courage she afterwards showed was that he put the whole thing to her as a favour, an obligation he should gratefully incur. She figured him as rich, but as fearfully extravagant—saw him all in a glow of high fashion, of good looks, of expensive habits, of charming ways with women. He had for his town residence a big house filled with the spoils of travel and the trophies of the chase; but it was to his country home, an old family place in Essex, that he wished her immediately to proceed.

He had been left, by the death of their parents in India, guardian to a small nephew and a small niece, children of a younger, a military brother whom he had lost two years before. These children were, by the strangest of chances for a man in his position—a lone man without the right sort of experience or a grain of patience—very heavy on his hands. It had all been a great worry and, on his own part doubtless, a series of blunders, but he immensely pitied the poor chicks and had done all he could; had in particular sent them down to his other house, the proper place for them being of course the country, and kept them there from the first with the best people he could find to look after them, parting even with his own servants to wait on them and going down himself, whenever he might, to see how they were doing. The awkward thing was that they had practically no other relations and that his own affairs took up all his time. He had put them in possession of Bly, which was healthy and secure, and had placed at the head of their little establishment—but belowstairs only—an excellent woman, Mrs. Grose, whom he was sure his visitor would like and who had formerly been maid to his mother. She was now housekeeper and was also acting for the time as superintendent to the little girl, of whom, without children of her own, she was by good luck extremely fond. There were plenty of people to help, but of course the young lady who should go down as governess would be in supreme authority. She would also have, in holidays, to look after the small boy, who had been for a term at school—young as he was to be sent, but what else could be done?—and who, as the holidays were about to begin, would be back from one day to the other. There had been for the two children at first a young lady whom they had had the misfortune to lose. She had done for them quite beautifully—she was a most respectable person—till her death, the great awkwardness of which had, precisely, left no alternative but the school for little Miles. Mrs. Grose, since then, in the way of manners and things, had done as she could for Flora; and there were further, a cook, a housemaid, a dairy-woman, an old pony, an old groom and an old gardener, all likewise thoroughly respectable.

So far had Douglas presented his picture when someone put a question. 'And what did the former governess die of? Of so much respectability?'

Our friend's answer was prompt. 'That will come out. I don't anticipate.'

'Pardon me—I thought that was just what you *are* doing.'

'In her successor's place,' I suggested, 'I should have wished to learn if the office brought with it:'

'Necessary danger to life?' Douglas completed my thought. 'She did wish to learn, and she did learn. You shall hear to-morrow what she learnt. Meanwhile of course the prospect struck her as slightly grim. She was young, untried, nervous: it was a vision of serious duties and little company, of really great loneliness. She hesitated—took a couple of days to consult and consider. But the salary offered much exceeded her modest measure, and on a second interview she faced the music, she engaged.' And Douglas, with this, made a pause that, for the benefit of the company, moved me to throw in:

'The moral of which was of course the seduction exercised by the splendid young man. She succumbed to it.'

He got up and, as he had done the night before, went to the fire gave a stir to a log with his foot, then stood a moment with his back to us. 'She saw him only twice.'

'Yes, but that's just the beauty of her passion.'

A little to my surprise, on this, Douglas turned round to me. 'It *was* the beauty of it. There were others,' he went on, 'who hadn't succumbed. He told her frankly all his difficulty—that for several applicants the conditions had been prohibitive. They were somehow simply afraid. It sounded dull—it sounded strange; and all the more so because of his main condition.'

'Which was——?'

'That she should never trouble him—but never, never: neither appeal nor complain nor write about anything; only meet all questions herself, receive all moneys from his solicitor, take the whole thing over and let him alone. She promised to do this, and she mentioned to me that when, for a moment, disburdened, delighted, he held her hand, thanking her for the sacrifice, she already felt rewarded.'

'But was that all her reward?' one of the ladies asked.

'She never saw him again.'

'Oh!' said the lady; which, as our friend immediately again left us, was the only other word of importance contributed to the subject till, the next night, by the corner of the hearth, in the best chair, he opened the faded red cover of a thin, old-fashioned, gilt-edged album. The whole thing took indeed more nights than one, but on the first occasion the same lady put another question. 'What's your title?'

'I haven't one.'

'Oh, *I* have!' I said. But Douglas, without heeding me, had begun to read with a fine clearness that was like a rendering to the ear of the beauty of his author's hand.

I REMEMBER the whole beginning as a succession of flights and drops, a little see-saw of the right throbs and the wrong. After rising, in town, to meet his appeal I had at all events a couple of very bad days —found all my doubts bristle again, felt indeed sure I had made a mistake. In this state of mind I spent the long hours of bumping swinging coach that carried me to the stopping-place at which I was to be met by a vehicle from the house. This convenience, I was told, had been ordered, and I found, toward the close of the June afternoon, a commodious fly in waiting for me. Driving at that hour, on a lovely day, through a country the summer sweetness of which served as a friendly welcome, my fortitude revived and, as we turned into the avenue, took a flight that was probably but a proof of the point to which it had sunk. I suppose I had expected, or had dreaded, something so dreary that what greeted me was a good surprise. I remember as a thoroughly pleasant impression the broad, clear front, its open windows and fresh curtains and the pair of maids looking out; I remember the lawn and the bright flowers and the crunch of my wheels on the gravel and the clustered tree-tops over which the rooks circled and cawed in the golden sky. The scene had a greatness that made it a different affair from my own scant home, and there immediately appeared at the door, with a little girl in her hand, a civil person who dropped me as decent a curtsy as if I had been the mistress or a distinguished visitor. I had received in Harley Street a narrower notion of the place, and that, as I recalled it, made me think the proprietor still more of a gentleman, suggested that what I was to enjoy might be a matter beyond his promise.

I had no drop again till the next day, for I was carried triumphantly through the following hours by my introduction to the younger of my pupils. The little girl who accompanied Mrs. Grose affected me on the spot as a creature too charming not to make it a great fortune to have to do with her. She was the most beautiful child I had ever seen, and I afterwards wondered why my employer hadn't made more of a point to me of this. I slept little that night—I was too much excited; and this astonished me too, I recollect, remained with me, adding to my sense of the liberality with which I was treated. The large, impressive room, one of the best in the house, the great state bed as I almost felt it, the figured full draperies, the long glasses in which, for the first time, I could see myself from head to foot, all struck me—like the wonderful appeal of my small charge—as so many things thrown in. It was thrown in as well, from the first moment, that I should get on with Mrs. Grose in a relation over which, on my way, in the coach, I fear I had rather brooded. The one appearance indeed that in this early outlook might have made me shrink again was that of her being so inordinately glad to see me. I felt within half an hour that she was so glad— stout, simple, plain, clean, wholesome woman—as to be positively on her guard against showing it too much. I wondered even then a little why she should wish *not* to show it, and that, with reflection, with suspicion, might of course have made me uneasy.

But it was a comfort that there could be no uneasiness in a connection with anything so beatific as the radiant image of my little girl, the vision of whose angelic beauty had probably more than anything else to do with the restlessness that, before morning, made me several times rise and wander about my room to take in the whole picture and prospect; to watch from my open window the faint summer dawn, to look at such stretches of the rest of the house as I could catch, and to listen, while in the fading dusk the first birds began to twitter, for the possible recurrence of a sound or two, less natural and not without but within, that I had fancied I heard. There had been a moment when I believed I recognized, faint and far, the cry of a child; there had been another when I found myself just consciously starting as at the passage, before my door, of a light footstep. But these fancies were not marked enough not to be thrown off, and it is only in the light, or the gloom, I should rather say, of other and subsequent matters that they now come back to me. To watch, teach, 'form' little Flora would too evidently be the making of a happy and useful life. It had been agreed between us downstairs that after this first occasion I should have her as a matter of course at night, her small white bed being already arranged, to that end, in my room. What I had undertaken was the whole care of her, and she had remained just this last time with Mrs. Grose only as an effect of our consideration for my

inevitable strangeness and her natural timidity. In
spite of this timidity—which the child herself, in the
oddest way in the world, had been perfectly frank
and brave about, allowing it, without a sign of
uncomfortable consciousness, with the deep, sweet
serenity indeed of one of Raphael's holy infants,
to be discussed, to be imputed to her and to de-
termine us—I felt quite sure she would presently
like me. It was part of what I already liked Mrs.
Grose herself for, the pleasure I could see her feel
in my admiration and wonder as I sat at supper
with four tall candles and with my pupil, in a high
chair and a bib, brightly facing me between them
over bread and milk. There were naturally things
that in Flora's presence could pass between us only
as prodigious and gratified looks, obscure and roundabout allusions.

'And the little boy—does he look like her? Is
he, too, so very remarkable?'

One wouldn't, it was already conveyed between
us, too grossly flatter a child. 'Oh, miss, *most*
remarkable. If you think well of this one!'—and
she stood there with a plate in her hand, beaming
at our companion, who looked from one of us to
the other with placid, heavenly eyes that contained
nothing to check us.

'Yes; if I do——?'

'You *will* be carried away by the little gentleman!'

'Well, that, I think, is what I came for—to be
carried away. I'm afraid, however,' I remember
feeling the impulse to add, 'I'm rather easily carried
away. I was carried away in London!'

I can still see Mrs. Grose's broad face as she took
this in. 'In Harley Street?'

'In Harley Street.'

'Well, miss, you 're not the first—and you won't be the last.'

'Oh, I 've no pretensions,' I could laugh, 'to being the only one. My other pupil, at any rate, as I understand, comes back to-morrow?'

'Not to-morrow—Friday, miss. He arrives, as you did, by the coach, under care of the guard, and is to be met by the same carriage.'

I forthwith wanted to know if the proper as well as the pleasant and friendly thing wouldn't therefore be that on the arrival of the public conveyance I should await him with his little sister; a proposition to which Mrs. Grose assented so heartily that I somehow took her manner as a kind of comforting pledge — never falsified, thank heaven! — that we should on every question be quite at one. Oh, she was glad I was there!

What I felt the next day was, I suppose, nothing that could be fairly called a reaction from the cheer of my arrival; it was probably at the most only a slight oppression produced by a fuller measure of the scale, as I walked round them, gazed up at them, took them in, of my new circumstances. They had, as it were, an extent and mass for which I had not been prepared and in the presence of which I found myself, freshly, a little scared not less than a little proud. Regular lessons, in this agitation, certainly suffered some wrong; I reflected that my first duty was, by the gentlest arts I could contrive, to win the child into the sense of knowing me. I spent the day with her out of doors; I arranged with her, to her great satisfaction, that it should be she, she only, who might show me the place. She showed

it step by step and room by room and secret by
secret, with droll, delightful, childish talk about it,
and with the result, in half an hour, of our becoming
tremendous friends. Young as she was I was struck,
throughout our little tour, with her confidence and
courage, with the way, in empty chambers and dull
corridors, on crooked staircases that made me pause,
and even on the summit of an old machicolated
square tower that made me dizzy, her morning
music, her disposition to tell me so many more
things than she asked, rang out and led me on.
I have not seen Bly since the day I left it, and I
dare say that to my present older and more informed
eyes it would show a very reduced importance. But
as my little conductress, with her hair of gold and her
frock of blue, danced before me round corners and
pattered down passages, I had the view of a castle
of romance inhabited by a rosy sprite, such a place
as would somehow, for diversion of the young idea,
take all colour out of story-books and fairy-tales.
Wasn't it just a story-book over which I had fallen
a-doze and a-dream? No; it was a big, ugly, antique
but convenient house, embodying a few features of a
building still older, half-displaced and half-utilized,
in which I had the fancy of our being almost as
lost as a handful of passengers in a great drifting ship.
Well, I was strangely at the helm!

II

THIS came home to me when, two days later, I drove over with Flora to meet, as Mrs. Grose said, the little gentleman; and all the more for an incident that, presenting itself the second evening, had deeply disconcerted me. The first day had been, on the whole, as I have expressed, reassuring; but I was to see it wind up to a change of note. The postbag that evening—it came late—contained a letter for me which, however, in the hand of my employer, I found to be composed but of a few words enclosing another, addressed to himself, with a seal still unbroken. 'This, I recognize, is from the head master, and the head master's an awful bore. Read him, please; deal with him; but mind you don't report. Not a word. I'm off!' I broke the seal with a great effort—so great a one that I was a long time coming to it; took the unopened missive at last up to my room and only attacked it just before going to bed. I had better have let it wait till morning, for it gave me a second sleepless night. With no counsel to take, the next day, I was full of distress; and it finally got so the better of me that I determined to open myself at least to Mrs. Grose.

'What does it mean? The child's dismissed his school.'

She gave me a look that I remarked at the moment; then, visibly, with a quick blankness, seemed to try to take it back. 'But aren't they all——?'

'Sent home—yes. But only for the holidays. Miles may never go back at all.'

Consciously, under my attention, she reddened. 'They won't take him?'

'They absolutely decline.'

At this she raised her eyes, which she had turned from me; I saw them fill with good tears. 'What has he done?'

I cast about; then I judged best simply to hand her my document—which, however, had the effect of making her, without taking it, simply put her hands behind her. She shook her head sadly. 'Such things are not for me, miss.'

My counsellor couldn't read! I winced at my mistake, which I attenuated as I could, and opened the letter again to repeat it to her; then, faltering in the act and folding it up once more, I put it back in my pocket. 'Is it really *bad*?'

The tears were still in her eyes. 'Do the gentlemen say so?'

'They go into no particulars. They simply express their regret that it should be impossible to keep him. That can have but one meaning.' Mrs. Grose listened with dumb emotion; she forbore to ask me what this meaning might be; so that, presently, to put the thing with some coherence and with the mere aid of her presence to my own mind, I went on: 'That he's an injury to the others.'

At this, with one of the quick turns of simple folk, she suddenly flamed up. 'Master Miles!—*him* an injury?'

There was such a flood of good faith in it that, though I had not yet seen the child, my very fears made me jump to the absurdity of the idea. I found myself, to meet my friend the better, offering it, on the spot, sarcastically. 'To his poor little innocent mates!'

'It's too dreadful,' cried Mrs. Grose, 'to say such cruel things! Why, he's scarce ten years old.'

'Yes, yes; it would be incredible.'

She was evidently grateful for such a profession. 'See him, miss, first. *Then* believe it!' I felt forthwith a new impatience to see him; it was the beginning of a curiosity that, all the next hours, was to deepen almost to pain. Mrs. Grose was aware, I could judge, of what she had produced in me, and she followed it up with assurance. 'You might as well believe it of the little lady. Bless her,' she added the next moment—'*look* at her!'

I turned and saw that Flora, whom, ten minutes before, I had established in the schoolroom with a sheet of white paper, a pencil and a copy of nice 'round O's,' now presented herself to view at the open door. She expressed in her little way an extraordinary detachment from disagreeable duties, looking at me, however, with a great childish light that seemed to offer it as a mere result of the affection she had conceived for my person, which had rendered necessary that she should follow me. I needed nothing more than this to feel the full force of Mrs. Grose's comparison, and, catching my pupil in my arms, covered her with kisses in which there was a sob of atonement.

None the less, the rest of the day, I watched for further occasion to approach my colleague, especially as, toward evening, I began to fancy she rather sought to avoid me. I overtook her, I remember, on the staircase; we went down together and at the

bottom I detained her, holding her there with a
hand on her arm. 'I take what you said to me at
noon as a declaration that *you've* never known him
to be bad.'

She threw back her head; she had clearly by
this time, and very honestly, adopted an attitude.
'Oh, never known him—I don't pretend *that*!'

I was upset again. 'Then you *have* known
him——?'

'Yes indeed, miss, thank God!'

On reflection I accepted this. 'You mean that a
boy who never is——?'

'Is no boy for *me*!'

I held her tighter. 'You like them with the
spirit to be naughty?' Then, keeping pace with
her answer, 'So do I!' I eagerly brought out. 'But
not to the degree to contaminate——'

'To contaminate?'—my big word left her at a loss.
I explained it. 'To corrupt.'

She stared, taking my meaning in; but it produced in her an odd laugh. 'Are you afraid he'll
corrupt *you*?' She put the question with such a
fine bold humour that with a laugh, a little silly
doubtless, to match her own, I gave way for the
time to the apprehension of ridicule.

But the next day, as the hour for my drive
approached, I cropped up in another place. 'What
was the lady who was here before?'

'The last governess? She was also young and
pretty—almost as young and almost as pretty, miss,
even as you.'

'Ah, then I hope her youth and her beauty helped
her!' I recollect throwing off. 'He seems to like
us young and pretty!'

'Oh, he *did*,' Mrs. Grose assented; 'It was the way he liked every one!' She had no sooner spoken, indeed, than she caught herself up. 'I mean that's *his* way—the master's.'

I was struck. 'But of whom did you speak first?'

She looked blank, but she coloured. 'Why, of *him*.'

'Of the master?'

'Of who else?'

There was so obviously no one else that the next moment I had lost my impression of her having accidentally said more than she meant; and I merely asked what I wanted to know. 'Did *she* see anything in the boy——?'

'That wasn't right: She never told me.'

I had a scruple, but I overcame it. 'Was she careful—particular?'

Mrs. Grose appeared to try to be conscientious. 'About some things—yes.'

'But not about all?'

Again she considered. 'Well, miss—she's gone. I won't tell tales.'

'I quite understand your feeling,' I hastened to reply; but I thought it after an instant not opposed to this concession to pursue: 'Did she die here?'

'No—she went off.'

I don't know what there was in this brevity of Mrs. Grose's that struck me as ambiguous. 'Went off to die?' Mrs. Grose looked straight out of the window, but I felt that, hypothetically, I had a right to know what young persons engaged for Bly were expected to do. 'She was taken ill, you mean, and went home?

'She was not taken ill, so far as appeared, in this house. She left it, at the end of the year, to go home, as she said, for a short holiday, to which the time she had put in had certainly given her a right. We had then a young woman—a nursemaid who had stayed on and who was a good girl and clever; and *she* took the children altogether for the interval. But our young lady never came back, and at the very moment I was expecting her I heard from the master that she was dead.'

I turned this over. 'But of what?'

'He never told me! But please, miss,' said Mrs. Grose, 'I must get to my work.'

III

HER thus turning her back on me was fortunately not, for my just preoccupations, a snub that could check the growth of our mutual esteem. We met, after I had brought home little Miles, more intimately than ever on the ground of my stupefaction, my general emotion: so monstrous was I then ready to pronounce it that such a child as had now been revealed to me should be under an interdict. I was a little late on the scene of his arrival, and I felt, as he stood wistfully looking out for me before the door of the inn at which the coach had put him down, that I had seen him on the instant, without and within, in the great glow of freshness, the same positive fragrance of purity, in which I had from the first moment seen his little sister. He was incredibly beautiful, and Mrs. Grose had put her finger on it: everything but a sort of passion of tenderness for him was swept away by his presence. What I then and there took him to my heart for was something divine that I have never found to the same degree in any child—his indescribable little air of knowing nothing in the world but love. It would have been impossible to carry a bad name with a greater sweetness of innocence, and by the time I had got back to Bly with him I remained merely bewildered—so far, that is, as I was not outraged—by the sense of the horrible letter locked up in one of the drawers in my room. As soon as I could compass a private word with Mrs. Grose I declared to her that it was grotesque.

She promptly understood me. 'You mean the cruel charge——?'

'It doesn't live an instant. My dear woman, *look* at him!'

She smiled at my pretension to have discovered his charm. 'I assure you, miss, I do nothing else! What will you say then?' she immediately added.

'In answer to the letter?' I had made up my mind. 'Nothing at all.'

'And to his uncle?'

I was incisive. 'Nothing at all.'

'And to the boy himself?'

I was wonderful. 'Nothing at all.'

She gave with her apron a great wipe to her mouth. 'Then I'll stand by you. We'll see it out.'

'We'll see it out!' I ardently echoed, giving her my hand to make it a vow.

She held me there a moment, then whisked up her apron again with her detached hand. 'Would you mind, miss, if I used the freedom——'

'To kiss me? No!' I took the good creature in my arms and, after we had embraced like sisters, felt still more fortified and indignant.

This, at all events, was for the time: a time so full that as I recall the way it went it reminds me of all the art I now need to make it a little distinct. What I look back at with amazement is the situation I accepted. I had undertaken, with my companion, to see it out, and I was under a charm apparently that could smooth away the extent and the far and difficult connections of such an effort.

I was lifted aloft on a great wave of infatuation and pity. I found it simple, in my ignorance, my confusion and perhaps my conceit, to assume that I could deal with a boy whose education for the world was all on the point of beginning. I am unable even to remember at this day what proposal I framed for the end of his holidays and the resumption of his studies. Lessons with me indeed, that charming summer, we all had a theory that he was to have; but I now feel that for weeks the lessons must have been rather my own. I learnt something—at first certainly—that had not been one of the teachings of my small, smothered life; learnt to be amused, and even amusing, and not to think for the morrow. It was the first time, in a manner, that I had known space and air and freedom, all the music of summer and all the mystery of nature. And then there was consideration—and consideration was sweet. Oh, it it was a trap—not designed but deep—to my imagination, to my delicacy, perhaps to my vanity; to whatever in me was most excitable. The best way to picture it all is to say that I was off my guard. They gave me so little trouble—they were of a gentleness so extraordinary. I used to speculate—but even this with a dim disconnectedness—as to how the rough future (for all futures are rough!) would handle them and might bruise them. They had the bloom of health and happiness; and yet, as if I had been in charge of a pair of little grandees, of princes of the blood, for whom everything, to be right, would have to be fenced about and ordered and arranged, the only form that in my fancy the after-years could take for them was that of a romantic, a really royal extension of the garden and the park. It may be

of course above all what suddenly broke into this
gives the previous time a charm of stillness—that
hush in which something gathers or crouches. The
change was actually like the spring of a beast.

In the first weeks the days were long; they often,
at their finest, gave me what I used to call my own
hour, the hour when, for my pupils, tea-time and
bed-time having come and gone, I had before my
final retirement a small interval alone. Much as I
liked my companions this hour was the thing in the
day I liked most; and I liked it best of all when, as
the light faded—or rather, I should say, the day
lingered and the last calls of the last birds sounded,
in a flushed sky, from the old trees—I could take a
turn into the grounds and enjoy, almost with a sense
of property that amused and flattered me, the beauty
and dignity of the place. It was a pleasure at these
moments to feel myself tranquil and justified; doubtless perhaps also to reflect that by my discretion,
my quiet good sense and general high propriety, I
was giving pleasure—if he ever thought of it!—to
the person to whose pressure I had yielded. What
I was doing was what he had earnestly hoped and
directly asked of me, and that I *could*, after all, do
it proved even a greater joy that I had expected.
I dare say I fancied myself, in short, a remarkable
young woman and took comfort in the faith that
this would more publicly appear. Well, I needed
to be remarkable to offer a front to the remarkable
things that presently gave their first sign.

It was plump, one afternoon, in the middle of
my very hour: the children were tucked away and
I had come out for my stroll. One of the thoughts
that, as I don't in the least shrink now from noting,

used to be with me in these wanderings was that it would be as charming as a charming story suddenly to meet someone. Someone would appear there at the turn of a path and would stand before me and smile and approve. I didn't ask more than that—I only asked that he should *know*; and the only way to be sure he knew would be to see it, and the kind light of it, in his handsome face. That was exactly present to me—by which I mean the face was—when, on the first of these occasions, at the end of a long June day, I stopped short on emerging from one of the plantations and coming into view of the house. What arrested me on the spot—and with a shock much greater than any vision had allowed for—was the sense that my imagination had, in a flash, turned real. He did stand there!—but high up, beyond the lawn and at the very top of the tower to which, on that first morning, little Flora had conducted me. This tower was one of a pair—square, incongruous, crenellated structures—that were distinguished, for some reason, though I could see little difference, as the new and the old. They flanked opposite ends of the house and were probably architectural absurdities, redeemed in a measure, indeed, by not being wholly disengaged nor of a height too pretentious, dating, in their ginger-bread antiquity, from a romantic revival that was already a respectable past. I admired them, had fancies about them, for we could all profit in a degree, especially when they loomed through the dusk, by the grandeur of their actual battlements; yet it was not at such an elevation that the figure I had so often invoked seemed most in place.

It produced in me, this figure, in the clear twilight, I remember, two distinct gasps of emotion, which were, sharply, the shock of my first and that of my second surprise. My second was a violent perception of the mistake of my first: the man who met my eyes was not the person I had precipitately supposed. There came to me thus a bewilderment of vision of which, after these years, there is no living view that I can hope to give. An unknown man in a lonely place is a permitted object of fear to a young woman privately bred; and the figure that faced me was—a few more seconds assured me—as little any one else I knew as it was the image that had been in my mind. I had not seen it in Harley Street—I had not seen it anywhere. The place, moreover, in the strangest way in the world, had on the instant and by the very fact of its appearance become a solitude. To me at least, making my statement here with a deliberation with which I have never made it, the whole feeling of the moment returns. It was as if, while I took in what I did take in, all the rest of the scene had been stricken with death. I can hear again, as I write, the intense hush in which the sounds of evening dropped. The rooks stopped cawing in the golden sky and the friendly hour lost for the unspeakable minute all its voice. But there was no other change in nature, unless indeed it were a change that I saw with a stranger sharpness. The gold was still in the sky, the clearness in the air, and the man who looked at me over the battlements was as definite as a picture in a frame. That's how I thought, with extraordinary quickness, of each person he might have been and that he wasn't. We were confronted across

our distance quite long enough for me to ask myself
with intensity who then he was and to feel, as an
effect of my inability to say, a wonder that in a few
seconds more became intense.

The great question, or one of these, is afterwards,
I know, with regard to certain matters, the question
of how long they have lasted. Well, this matter of
mine, think what you will of it, lasted while I caught
at a dozen possibilities, none of which made a difference for the better, that I could see, in there having
been in the house—and for how long, above all?—
a person of whom I was in ignorance. It lasted
while I just bridled a little with the sense of how
my office seemed to require that there should be no
such ignorance and no such person. It lasted while
this visitant, at all events—and there was a touch
of the strange freedom, as I remember, in the sign
of familiarity of his wearing no hat—seemed to
fix me, from his position, with just the question,
just the scrutiny through the fading light, that his
own presence provoked. We were too far apart to
call to each other, but there was a moment at which,
at shorter range, some challenge between us, breaking the hush, would have been the right result of
our straight mutual stare. He was in one of the
angles, the one away from the house, very erect, as
it struck me, and with both hands on the ledge.
So I saw him as I see the letters I form on this page;
then, exactly, after a minute, as if to add to the
spectacle, he slowly changed his place — passed,
looking at me hard all the while, to the opposite
corner of the platform. Yes, it was intense to me
that during this transit he never took his eyes from
me, and I can see at this moment the way his hand

as he went, moved from one of the crenellations to
the next. He stopped at the other corner, but less
long, and even as he turned away still markedly
fixed me. He turned away; that was all I
knew.

IV

It was not that I didn't wait, on this occasion, for more, since I was as deeply rooted as shaken. Was there a 'secret' at Bly—a mystery of Udolpho or an insane, an unmentionable relative kept in unsuspected confinement? I can't say how long I turned it over, or how long, in a confusion of curiosity and dread, I remained where I had had my collision; I only recall that when I re-entered the house darkness had quite closed in. Agitation, in the interval, certainly had held me and driven me, for I must, in circling about the place, have walked three miles; but I was to be later on so much more overwhelmed that this mere dawn of alarm was a comparatively human chill. The most singular part of it, in fact—singular as the rest had been—was the part I became, in the hall, aware of in meeting Mrs. Grose. This picture comes back to me in the general train—the impression, as I received it on my return, of the wide white panelled space, bright in the lamplight and with its portraits and red carpets, and of the good surprised look of my friend, which immediately told me she had missed me. It came to me straightway, under her contact, that, with plain heartiness, mere relieved anxiety at my appearance, she knew nothing whatever that could bear upon the incident I had there ready for her. I had not suspected in advance that her comfortable face would pull me up, and I somehow measured the importance

33

of what I had seen by my thus finding myself hesitate to mention it.   Scarce anything in the whole history seems to me so odd as this fact that my real beginning of fear was one, as I may say, with the instinct of sparing my companion.   On the spot, accordingly, in the pleasant hall and with her eyes on me, I, for a reason that I couldn't then have phrased, achieved an inward revolution—offered a vague pretext for my lateness and, with the idea of the beauty of the night and of the heavy dew and wet feet, went as soon as possible to my room.

Here it was another affair; here, for many days after, it was a queer affair enough.   There were hours, from day to day—or at least there were moments, snatched even from clear duties—when I had to shut myself up to think.   It wasn't so much yet that I was more nervous than I could bear to be as that I was remarkably afraid of becoming so; for the truth I had now to turn over was simply and clearly the truth that I could arrive at no account whatever of the visitor with whom I had been so inexplicably and yet, as it seemed to me, so intimately concerned.   It took me little time to see that I might easily sound, without forms of inquiry and without exciting remark, any domestic complication.   The shock I had suffered must have sharpened all my senses; I felt sure, at the end of three days and as the result of mere closer attention, that I had not been practised upon by the servants nor made the object of any 'game.'   Of whatever it was that I knew nothing was known around me. There was but one sane inference: someone had taken a liberty rather monstrous.   That was what, repeatedly, I dipped into my room and locked the door to say to myself. We had been, collectively, subject to an intrusion; some unscrupulous traveller, curious in old houses, had made his way in unobserved, enjoyed the prospect from the best point of view and then stolen out as he came. If he had given me such a bold, hard stare, that was but a part of his indiscretion. The good thing, after all, was that we should surely see no more of him.

This was not so good a thing, I admit, as not to leave me to judge that what, essentially, made nothing else much signify was simply my charming work. My charming work was just my life with Miles and Flora, and through nothing could I so like it as through feeling that to throw myself into it was to throw myself out of my trouble. The attraction of my small charges was a constant joy, leading me to wonder afresh at the vanity of my original fears, the distaste I had begun by entertaining for the probable grey prose of my office. There was to be no grey prose, it appeared, and no long grind; so how could work not be charming that presented itself as daily beauty? It was all the romance of the nursery and the poetry of the schoolroom. I don't mean by this, of course, that we studied only fiction and verse; I mean that I can express no otherwise the sort of interest my companions inspired. How can I describe that except by saying that instead of growing deadly used to them—and it 's a marvel for a governess: I call the sisterhood to witness!—I made constant fresh discoveries. There was one direction, assuredly, in which these discoveries stopped: deep obscurity continued to cover the region of the boy's conduct at school. It had been promptly given me, I have noted, to face that mystery without a pang. Perhaps even it would be nearer the truth to say that —without a word—he himself had cleared it up. He had made the whole charge absurd. My conclusion bloomed there with the real rose-flush of his innocence: he was only too fine and fair for the little horrid, unclean school-world, and he had paid a price for it. I reflected acutely that the sense of such individual differences, such superiorities of quality, always, on the part of the majority—which could include even stupid sordid head masters— turns infallibly to the vindictive.

Both the children had a gentleness—it was their only fault, and it never made Miles a muff—that kept them (how shall I express it?) almost impersonal and certainly quite unpunishable. They were like those cherubs of the anecdote who had—morally, at any rate—nothing to whack! I remember feeling with Miles in especial as if he had had, as it were, nothing to call even an infinitesimal history. We expect of a small child scant enough 'antecedents,' but there was in this beautiful little boy something extraordinarily sensitive, yet extraordinarily happy, that, more than in any creature of his age I have seen, struck me as beginning anew each day. He had never for a second suffered. I took this as a direct disproof of his having really been chastised. If he had been wicked he would have 'caught' it, and I should have caught it by the rebound— I should have found the trace, should have felt the wound and the dishonour. I could reconstitute nothing at all, and he was therefore an angel. He never spoke of his school, never mentioned a comrade or a master; and I, for my part, was quite too

much disgusted to allude to them. Of course I was
under the spell, and the wonderful part is that, even
at the time, I perfectly knew I was. But I gave
myself up to it; it was an antidote to any pain, and
I had more pains than one. I was in receipt in these
days of disturbing letters from home, where things
were not going well. But with this joy of my
children what things in the world mattered? That
was the question I used to put to my scrappy retire-
ments. I was dazzled by their loveliness.

There was a Sunday—to get on—when it rained
with such force and for so many hours that there
could be no procession to church; in consequence
of which, as the day declined, I had arranged with
Mrs. Grose that, should the evening show improve-
ment, we would attend together the late service.
The rain happily stopped, and I prepared for our
walk, which, through the park and by the good road
to the village, would be a matter of twenty minutes.
Coming downstairs to meet my colleague in the
hall, I remembered a pair of gloves that had required three stitches and that had received them—
with a publicity perhaps not edifying—while I sat
with the children at their tea, served on Sundays,
by exception, in that cold clean temple of mahogany
and brass, the 'grown-up' dining-room. The gloves
had been dropped there, and I turned in to recover
them. The day was grey enough, but the afternoon
light still lingered, and it enabled me, on crossing
the threshold, not only to recognize, on a chair near
the wide window, then closed, the articles I wanted,
but to become aware of a person on the other side of
the window and looking straight in. One step into
the room had sufficed; my vision was instantaneous;

it was all there. The person looking straight in was the person who had already appeared to me. He appeared thus again with I won't say greater distinctness, for that was impossible, but with a nearness that represented a forward stride in our intercourse and made me, as I met him, catch my breath and turn cold. He was the same—he was the same, and seen, this time, as he had been seen before, from the waist up, the window, though the dining-room was on the ground-floor, not going down to the terrace on which he stood. His face was close to the glass, yet the effect of this better view was, strangely, just to show me how intense the former had been. He remained but a few seconds—long enough to convince me he also saw and recognized; but it was as if I had been looking at him for years and had known him always. Something, however, happened this time that had not happened before; his stare into my face, through the glass and across the room, was as deep and hard as then, but it quitted me for a moment during which I could still watch it, see it fix successively several other things. On the spot there came to me the added shock of a certitude that it was not for me he had come. He had come for someone else.

The flash of this knowledge—for it was knowledge in the midst of dread—produced in me the most extraordinary effect, starting, as I stood there, a sudden vibration of duty and courage. I say courage because I was beyond all doubt already far gone. I bounded straight out of the door again, reached that of the house, got in an instant upon the drive and, passing along the terrace as fast as I could rush, turned a corner and came full in sight. But it

was in sight of nothing now—my visitor had vanished.
I stopped, almost dropped, with the real relief of
this; but I took in the whole scene—I gave him time
to reappear. I call it time, but how long was it?
I can't speak to the purpose to-day of the duration
of these things. That kind of measure must have
left me: they couldn't have lasted as they actually
appeared to me to last. The terrace and the whole
place, the lawn and the garden behind it, all I could
see of the park, were empty with a great emptiness.
There were shrubberies and big trees, but I remember
the clear assurance I felt that none of them concealed him. He was there or was not there: not
there if I didn't see him. I got hold of this; then,
instinctively, instead of returning as I had come,
went to the window. It was confusedly present to
me that I ought to place myself where he had stood.
I did so; I applied my face to the pane and looked,
as he had looked, into the room. As if, at this
moment, to show me exactly what his range had
been, Mrs. Grose, as I had done for himself just
before, came in from the hall. With this I had the
full image of a repetition of what had already
occurred. She saw me as I had seen my own
visitant; she pulled up short as I had done; I
gave her something of the shock that I had received.
She turned white, and this made me ask myself
if I had blanched as much. She stared, in short, and
retreated just on *my* lines, and I knew she had then
passed out and come round to me and that I should
presently meet her. I remained where I was, and
while I waited I thought of more things than one.
But there 's only one I take space to mention. I
wondered why *she* should be scared.

V

OH, she let me know as soon as, round the corner of the house, she loomed again into view. 'What in the name of goodness is the matter——?' She was now flushed and out of breath.

I said nothing till she came quite near. 'With me?' I must have made a wonderful face. 'Do I show it?'

'You're as white as a sheet. You look awful.'

I considered; I could meet on this, without scruple, any degree of innocence. My need to respect the bloom of Mrs. Grose's had dropped, without a rustle, from my shoulders, and if I wavered for the instant it was not with what I kept back. I put out my hand to her and she took it; I held her hard a little, liking to feel her close to me. There was a kind of support in the shy heave of her surprise. 'You came for me for church, of course, but I can't go.'

'Has anything happened?'

'Yes. You must know now. Did I look very queer?'

'Through this window? Dreadful!'

'Well,' I said, 'I've been frightened.' Mrs. Grose's eyes expressed plainly that *she* had no wish to be, yet also that she knew too well her place not to be ready to share with me any marked inconvenience. Oh, it was quite settled that she *must* share! 'Just what you saw from the dining-room a minute ago was the effect of that. What *I* saw—just before—was much worse.'

Her hand tightened. 'What was it?'

'An extraordinary man. Looking in.'

'What extraordinary man?'

'I haven't the least idea.'

Mrs. Grose gazed round us in vain. 'Then where is he gone?'

'I know still less.'

'Have you seen him before?'

'Yes—once. On the old tower.'

She could only look at me harder. 'Do you mean he's a stranger?'

'Oh, very much!'

'Yet you didn't tell me?'

'No — for reasons. But now that you've guessed——'

Mrs. Grose's round eyes encountered this charge. 'Ah, I haven't guessed!' she said very simply. 'How can I if *you* don't imagine?'

'I don't in the very least.'

'You've seen him nowhere but on the tower?'

'And on this spot just now.'

Mrs. Grose looked round again. 'What was he doing on the tower?'

'Only standing there and looking down at me.'

She thought a minute. 'Was he a gentleman?'

I found I had no need to think. 'No.' She gazed in deeper wonder. 'No.'

'Then nobody about the place? Nobody from the village?'

'Nobody—nobody I didn't tell you, but I made sure.'

She breathed a vague relief: this was, oddly, so

much to the good.   It only went indeed a little way.
'But if he isn't a gentleman——'

'What *is* he?   He 's a horror.'

'A horror?'

'He 's—God help me if I know *what* he is!'

Mrs. Grose looked round once more; she fixed her
eyes on the duskier distance and then, pulling herself
together, turned to me with full inconsequence.
'It 's time we should be at church.'

'Oh, I 'm not fit for church!'

'Won't it do you good?'

'It won't do *them*——!'   I nodded at the house.

'The children?'

'I can't leave them now.'

'You 're afraid——?'

I spoke boldly.   'I 'm afraid of *him.*'

Mrs. Grose's large face showed me, at this, for
the first time, the far-away faint glimmer of a consciousness more acute: I somehow made out in it
the delayed dawn of an idea I myself had not given
her and that was as yet quite obscure to me.   It
comes back to me that I thought instantly of this
as something I could get from her; and I felt it to
be connected with the desire she presently showed
to know more.   'When was it—on the tower?'

'About the middle of the month.   At this same
hour.'

'Almost at dark,' said Mrs. Grose.

'Oh, no, not nearly.   I saw him as I see you.'

'Then how did he get in?'

'And how did he get out?'   I laughed.   'I had
no opportunity to ask him!   This evening, you see,'
I pursued, 'he has not been able to get in.'

'He only peeps?'

'I hope it will be confined to that!' She had now let go my hand; she turned away a little. I waited an instant; then I brought out: 'Go to church. Good-bye. I must watch.'

Slowly she faced me again. 'Do you fear for them?'

We met in another long look. 'Don't *you*?' Instead of answering she came nearer to the window and, for a minute, applied her face to the glass. 'You see how he could see,' I meanwhile went on.

She didn't move. 'How long was he here?'

'Till I came out. I came to meet him.'

Mrs. Grose at last turned round, and there was still more in her face. '*I* couldn't have come out.'

'Neither could I!' I laughed again. 'But I did come. I've my duty.'

'So have I mine,' she replied; after which she added: 'What's he like?'

'I've been dying to tell you. But he's like nobody.'

'Nobody?' she echoed.

'He has no hat.' Then seeing in her face that she already, in this, with a deeper dismay, found a touch of picture, I quickly added stroke to stroke. 'He has red hair, very red, close-curling, and a pale face, long in shape, with straight, good features and little, rather queer whiskers that are as red as his hair. His eyebrows are somehow darker; they look particularly arched and as if they might move a good deal. His eyes are sharp, strange—awfully; but I only know clearly that they're rather small and very fixed. His mouth's wide and his lips are thin, and except for his little whiskers he's quite clean-shaven. He gives me a sort of sense of looking like an actor.'

'An actor!' It was impossible to resemble one less, at least, than Mrs. Grose at that moment.

'I've never seen one, but so I suppose them. He's tall, active, erect,' I continued, 'but never— no, never!—a gentleman.'

My companion's face had blanched as I went on; her round eyes started and her mild mouth gaped. 'A gentleman?' she gasped, confounded, stupefied: 'a gentleman *he*?'

'You know him then?'

She visibly tried to hold herself. 'But he *is* handsome?'

I saw the way to help her. 'Remarkably!'

'And dressed——?'

'In somebody's clothes. They're smart, but they're not his own.'

She broke into a breathless affirmative groan. 'They're the master's!'

I caught it up. 'You *do* know him?'

She faltered but a second. 'Quint!' she cried.

'Quint?'

'Peter Quint—his own man, his valet, when he was here!'

'When the master was?'

Gaping still, but meeting me, she pieced it all together. 'He never wore his hat, but he did wear —well, there were waistcoats missed! They were both here—last year. Then the master went, and Quint was alone.'

I followed, but halting a little. 'Alone?'

'Alone with *us*.' Then as from a deeper depth, 'In charge,' she added.

'And what became of him?'

She hung fire so long that I was still more mystified. 'He went too,' she brought out at last.

'Went where?'

Her expression, at this, became extraordinary. 'God knows where! He died.'

'Died?' I almost shrieked.

She seemed fairly to square herself, plant herself more firmly to express the wonder of it. 'Yes. Mr. Quint's dead.'

VI

IT took of course more than that particular passage to place us together in presence of what we had now to live with as we could, my dreadful liability to impressions of the order so vividly exemplified, and my companion's knowledge henceforth—a knowledge half consternation and half compassion — of that liability. There had been this evening, after the revelation that left me for an hour so prostrate— there had been for either of us no attendance on any service but a little service of tears and vows, of prayers and promises, a climax to the series of mutual challenges and pledges that had straightway ensued on our retreating together to the schoolroom and shutting ourselves up there to have everything out. The result of our having everything out was simply to reduce our situation to the last rigour of its elements. She herself had seen nothing, not the shadow of a shadow, and nobody in the house but the governess was in the governess's plight; yet she accepted without directly impugning my sanity the truth as I gave it to her, and ended by showing me on this ground an awestricken tenderness, a deference to my more than questionable privilege, of which the very breath has remained with me as that of the sweetest of human charities.

What was settled between us accordingly that night was that we thought we might bear things together; and I was not even sure that in spite of her exemption it was she who had the best of the burden. I knew at this hour, I think, as well as I knew later, what I was capable of meeting to shelter my pupils; but it took me some time to be wholly sure of what my honest comrade was prepared for to keep terms with so stiff an agreement. I was queer company enough — quite as queer as the company I received; but as I trace over what we went through I see how much common ground we must have found in the one idea that, by good fortune, *could* steady us. It was the idea, the second movement, that led me straight out, as I may say, of the inner chamber of my dread. I could take the air in the court, at least, and there Mrs. Grose could join me. Perfectly can I recall now the particular way strength came to me before we separated for the night. We had gone over and over every feature of what I had seen.

'He was looking for someone else, you say—someone who was not you?'

'He was looking for little Miles.' A portentous clearness now possessed me. '*That's* whom he was looking for.'

'But how do you know?'

'I know, I know, I know!' My exaltation grew. 'And *you* know, my dear!'

She didn't deny this, but I required, I felt, not even so much telling as that. She took it up again in a moment. 'What if *he* should see him?'

'Little Miles? That's what he wants!'

She looked immensely scared again. 'The child?'

'Heaven forbid! The man. He wants to appear to *them*.' That he might was an awful conception, and yet somehow I could keep it at bay; which moreover, as we lingered there, was what I succeeded in practically proving. I had an absolute certainty that I should see again what I had already seen, but something within me said that by offering myself bravely as the sole subject of such experience, by accepting, by inviting, by surmounting it all, I should serve as an expiatory victim and guard the tranquillity of the rest of the household. The children in especial I should thus fence about and absolutely save. I recall one of the last things I said that night to Mrs. Grose.

'It does strike me that my pupils have never mentioned——!'

She looked at me hard as I musingly pulled up. 'His having been here and the time they were with him?'

'The time they were with him, and his name, his presence, his history, in any way. They 've never alluded to it.'

'Oh, the little lady doesn't remember. She never heard or knew.'

'The circumstances of his death?' I thought with some intensity. 'Perhaps not. But Miles would remember—Miles would know.'

'Ah, don't try him!' broke from Mrs. Grose.

I returned her the look she had given me. 'Don't be afraid.' I continued to think. 'It *is* rather odd.'

'That he has never spoken of him?'

'Never by the least reference. And you tell me they were "great friends"?'

'Oh, it wasn't *him*!' Mrs. Grose with emphasis declared. 'It was Quint's own fancy. To play with him, I mean—to spoil him.' She paused a moment; then she added: 'Quint was much too free.'

This gave me, straight from my vision of his face—*such* a face!—a sudden sickness of disgust. 'Too free with *my* boy?'

'Too free with every one!'

I forbore for the moment to analyse this description further than by the reflection that a part of it applied to several of the members of the household, of the half-dozen maids and men who were still of our small colony. But there was everything, for our apprehension, in the lucky fact that no discomfortable legend, no perturbation of scullions, had ever, within any one's memory, attached to the kind old place. It had neither bad name nor ill fame, and Mrs. Grose, most apparently, only desired to cling to me and to quake in silence. I even put her, the very last thing of all, to the test. It was when, at midnight, she had her hand on the schoolroom door to take leave. 'I *have* it from you, then—for it's of great importance—that he was definitely and admittedly bad?'

'Oh, not admittedly. *I* knew it—but the master didn't.'

'And you never told him?'

'Well, he didn't like tale-bearing—he hated complaints. He was terribly short with anything of that kind, and if people were all right to *him*——'

'He wouldn't be bothered with more?' This squared well enough with my impression of him: he was not a trouble-loving gentleman, nor so very particular perhaps about some of the company he himself kept. All the same, I pressed my informant. 'I promise you *I* would have told!'

She felt my discrimination. 'I dare say I was wrong. But really I was afraid.'

'Afraid of what?'

'Of things that man could do. Quint was so clever—he was so deep.'

I took this in still more than I probably showed. 'You weren't afraid of anything else? Not of his effect——?'

'His effect?' she repeated with a face of anguish and waiting while I faltered.

'On innocent little precious lives. They were in your charge.'

'No, they weren't in mine!' she roundly and distressfully returned. 'The master believed in him and placed him here because he was supposed not to be quite in health and the country air so good for him. So he had everything to say. Yes'—she let me have it—'even about *them*.'

'Them—that creature?' I had to smother a kind of howl. 'And you could bear it?'

'No. I couldn't—and I can't now!' And the poor woman burst into tears.

A rigid control, from the next day, was, as I have said, to follow them; yet how often and how passionately, for a week, we came back together to the subject! Much as we had discussed it that Sunday night, I was, in the immediate later hours in especial —for it may be imagined whether I slept—still haunted with the shadow of something she had not told me. I myself had kept back nothing, but there was a word Mrs. Grose had kept back. I was sure, moreover, by morning that this was not from a failure of frankness, but because on every side there were fears. It seems to me indeed, in raking it all over, that by the time the morrow's sun was high I had restlessly read into the facts before us almost all the

meaning they were to receive from subsequent and
more cruel occurrences. What they gave me, above
all, was just the sinister figure of the living man—
the dead one would keep awhile!—and of the months
he had continuously passed at Bly, which, added
up, made a formidable stretch. The limit of this
evil time had arrived only when, on the dawn of a
winter's morning, Peter Quint was found, by a
labourer going to early work, stone dead on the
road from the village: a catastrophe explained—
superficially at least—by a visible wound to his
head; such a wound as might have been produced
(and as, on the final evidence, *had* been) by a fatal
slip, in the dark and after leaving the public-house,
on the steepish icy slope, a wrong path altogether,
at the bottom of which he lay. The icy slope, the
turn mistaken at night and in liquor, accounted for
much—practically, in the end and after the inquest
and boundless chatter, for everything; but there had
been matters in his life—strange passages and perils,
secret disorders, vices more than suspected, that
would have accounted for a good deal more.

I scarce know how to put my story into words
that shall be a credible picture of my state of mind;
but I was in these days literally able to find a joy
in the extraordinary flight of heroism the occasion
demanded of me. I now saw that I had been asked
for a service admirable and difficult; and there would
be a greatness in letting it be seen—oh, in the right
quarter!—that I could succeed where many another
girl might have failed. It was an immense help to
me—I confess I rather applaud myself as I look
back!—that I saw my response so strongly and so
simply. I was there to protect and defend the little

creatures in the world the most bereaved and the most lovable, the appeal of whose helplessness had suddenly become only too explicit, a deep, constant ache of one's own engaged affection. We were cut off, really, together; we were united in our danger. They had nothing but me, and I—well, I had *them*. It was, in short, a magnificent chance. This chance presented itself to me in an image richly material. I was a screen—I was to stand before them. The more I saw the less they would. I began to watch them in a stifled suspense, a disguised tension, that might well, had it continued too long, have turned to something like madness. What saved me, as I now see, was that it turned to another matter altogether. It didn't last as suspense—it was superseded by horrible proofs. Proofs, I say, yes—from the moment I really took hold.

This moment dated from an afternoon hour that I happened to spend in the grounds with the younger of my pupils alone. We had left Miles indoors, on the red cushion of a deep window-seat; he had wished to finish a book, and I had been glad to encourage a purpose so laudable in a young man whose only defect was a certain ingenuity of restlessness. His sister, on the contrary, had been alert to come out, and I strolled with her half an hour, seeking the shade, for the sun was still high and the day exceptionally warm. I was aware afresh with her, as we went, of how, like her brother, she contrived —it was the charming thing in both children—to let me alone without appearing to drop me and to accompany me without appearing to oppress. They were never importunate and yet never listless. My attention to them all really went to seeing them

amuse themselves immensely without me: this was
a spectacle they seemed actively to prepare and
that employed me as an active admirer. I walked
in a world of their invention—they had no occasion
whatever to draw upon mine; so that my time was
taken only with being for them some remarkable
person or thing that the game of the moment required
and that was merely, thanks to my superior, my
exalted stamp, a happy and highly distinguished
sinecure. I forget what I was on the present occasion; I only remember that I was something very
important and very quiet and that Flora was playing
very hard. We were on the edge of the lake, and,
as we had lately begun geography, the lake was the
Sea of Azof.

Suddenly, amid these elements, I became aware
that on the other side of the Sea of Azof we had
an interested spectator. The way this knowledge
gathered in me was the strangest thing in the world—
the strangest, that is, except the very much stranger
in which it quickly merged itself. I had sat
down with a piece of work—for I was something
or other that could sit—on the old stone bench
which overlooked the pond; and in this position I
began to take in with certitude and yet without
direct vision the presence, a good way off, of a third
person. The old trees, the thick shrubbery, made
a great and pleasant shade, but it was all suffused
with the brightness of the hot, still hour. There
was no ambiguity in anything; none whatever, at
least, in the conviction I from one moment to another found myself forming as to what I should
see straight before me and across the lake as a consequence of raising my eyes. They were attached

at this juncture to the stitching in which I was engaged, and I can feel once more the spasm of my effort not to move them till I should so have steadied myself as to be able to make up my mind what to do. There was an alien object in view—a figure whose right of presence I instantly and passionately questioned. I recollect counting over perfectly the possibilities, reminding myself that nothing was more natural, for instance, than the appearance of one of the men about the place, or even of a messenger, a postman or a tradesman's boy, from the village. That reminder had as little effect on my practical certitude as I was conscious — still even without looking — of its having upon the character and attitude of our visitor. Nothing was more natural than that these things should be the other things they absolutely were not.

Of the positive identity of the apparition I would assure myself as soon as the small clock of my courage should have ticked out the right second; meanwhile, with an effort that was already sharp enough, I transferred my eyes straight to little Flora, who, at the moment, was about ten yards away. My heart had stood still for an instant with the wonder and terror of the question whether she too would see; and I held my breath while I waited for what a cry from her, what some sudden innocent sign either of interest or of alarm, would tell me. I waited, but nothing came; then in the first place —and there is something more dire in this, I feel, than in anything I have to relate—I was determined by a sense that within a minute all spontaneous sounds from her had dropped; and in the second by the circumstance that also within the minute

she had, in her play, turned her back to the water.
This was her attitude when I at last looked at her
—looked with the confirmed conviction that we were
still, together, under direct personal notice. She had
picked up a small, flat piece of wood which happened
to have in it a little hole that had evidently suggested
to her the idea of sticking in another fragment that
might figure as a mast and make the thing a boat.
This second morsel, as I watched her, she was very
markedly and intently attempting to tighten in its
place. My apprehension of what she was doing
sustained me so that after some seconds I felt I
was ready for more. Then I again shifted my eyes
—I faced what I had to face.

VII

I GOT hold of Mrs. Grose as soon after this as I could;
and I can give no intelligible account of how I fought
out the interval. Yet I still hear myself cry as I
fairly threw myself into her arms: 'They *know*—it's
too monstrous: they know, they know!'

'And what on earth———?' I felt her incredulity
as she held me.

'Why, all that *we* know—and heaven knows what
more besides!' Then as she released me I made it
out to her, made it out perhaps only now with
full coherency even to myself. 'Two hours ago,
in the garden'—I could scarce articulate—'Flora
saw!'

Mrs. Grose took it as she might have taken a
blow in the stomach. 'She has told you?' she
panted.

'Not a word—that's the horror. She kept it to
herself! The child of eight, *that* child!' Unutterable
still for me was the stupefaction of it.

Mrs. Grose of course could only gape the wider.
'Then how do you know?'

'I was there—I saw with my eyes: saw she was
perfectly aware.'

'Do you mean aware of *him*?'

'No—of *her*.' I was conscious as I spoke that I
looked prodigious things, for I got the slow reflection
of them in my companion's face. 'Another person
—this time; but a figure of quite as unmistakable

horror and evil: a woman in black, pale and dreadful
—with such an air also, and such a face!—on the
other side of the lake. I was there with the child—
quiet for the hour; and in the midst of it she
came.'

'Came how—from where?'

'From where they come from! She just appeared
and stood there—but not so near.'

'And without coming nearer?'

'Oh, for the effect and the feeling she might have
been as close as you!'

My friend, with an odd impulse, fell back a step.
'Was she someone you 've never seen?'

'Never. But someone the child has. Someone
you have.' Then to show how I had thought it all
out: 'My predecessor—the one who died.'

'Miss Jessel?'

'Miss Jessel. You don't believe me?' I pressed.

She turned right and left in her distress. 'How
can you be sure?'

This drew from me, in the state of my nerves, a
flash of impatience. 'Then ask Flora—*she 's* sure!'
But I had no sooner spoken than I caught myself
up. 'No, for God's sake, *don't*. She 'll say she
isn't—she 'll lie!'

Mrs. Grose was not too bewildered instinctively
to protest. 'Ah, how *can* you?'

'Because I 'm clear. Flora doesn't want me to
know.'

'It 's only then to spare you.'

'No, no—there are depths, depths! The more I
go over it the more I see in it, and the more I see in
it the more I fear. I don't know what I *don't* see
—what I *don't* fear!'

Mrs. Grose tried to keep up with me. 'You mean you're afraid of seeing her again?'

'Oh, no; that's nothing—now!' Then I explained. 'It's of *not* seeing her.'

But my companion only looked wan. 'I don't understand.'

'Why, it's that the child may keep it up—and that the child assuredly *will*—without my knowing it.'

At the image of this possibility Mrs. Grose for a moment collapsed, yet presently to pull herself together again as from the positive force of the sense of what, should we yield an inch, there would really be to give way to. 'Dear, dear—we must keep our heads! And after all, if she doesn't mind it——!' She even tried a grim joke. 'Perhaps she likes it!'

'Like *such* things—a scrap of an infant!'

'Isn't it just a proof of her blest innocence?' my friend bravely inquired.

She brought me, for the instant, almost round. 'Oh, we must clutch at *that*—we must cling to it! If it isn't a proof of what you say, it's a proof of —God knows what! For the woman's a horror of horrors.'

Mrs. Grose, at this, fixed her eyes a minute on the ground; then at last raising them, 'Tell me how you know,' she said.

'Then you admit it's what she was?' I cried.

'Tell me how you know,' my friend simply repeated.

'Know? By seeing her! By the way she looked.'

'At you, do you mean—so wickedly?'

'Dear me, no—I could have borne that. She gave me never a glance. She only fixed the child.'

Mrs. Grose tried to see it. 'Fixed her?'

'Ah, with such awful eyes!'

She stared at mine as if they might really have resembled them. 'Do you mean of dislike?'

'God help us, no. Of something much worse.'

'Worse than dislike?' — this left her indeed at a loss.

'With a determination—indescribable. With a kind of fury of intention.'

I made her turn pale. 'Intention?'

'To get hold of her.' Mrs. Grose—her eyes just lingering on mine—gave a shudder and walked to the window; and while she stood there looking out I completed my statement. '*That's* what Flora knows.'

After a little she turned round. 'The person was in black, you say?'

'In mourning—rather poor, almost shabby. But —yes—with extraordinary beauty.' I now recognized to what I had at last, stroke by stroke, brought the victim of my confidence, for she quite visibly weighed this. 'Oh, handsome—very, very,' I insisted; 'wonderfully handsome. But infamous.'

She slowly came back to me. 'Miss Jessel— *was* infamous.' She once more took my hand in both her own, holding it as tight as if to fortify me against the increase of alarm I might draw from this disclosure. 'They were both infamous,' she finally said.

So for a little we faced it once more together; and I found absolutely a degree of help in seeing it now so straight. 'I appreciate,' I said, 'the great decency of your not having hitherto spoken; but the time has certainly come to give me the whole thing.' She appeared to assent to this, but still only in silence; seeing which I went on: 'I must have it now. Of what did she die? Come, there was something between them.'

'There was everything.'

'In spite of the difference——?'

'Oh, of their rank, their condition'—she brought it woefully out. '*She* was a lady.'

I turned it over; I again saw. 'Yes—she was a lady.'

'And he so dreadfully below,' said Mrs. Grose.

I felt that I doubtless needn't press too hard, in such company, on the place of a servant in the scale; but there was nothing to prevent an acceptance of my companion's own measure of my predecessor's abasement. There was a way to deal with that, and I dealt; the more readily for my full vision—on the evidence—of our employer's late good-looking 'own' man; impudent, assured, spoiled, depraved. 'The fellow was a hound.'

Mrs. Grose considered as if it were perhaps a little a case for a sense of shades. 'I've never seen one like him. He did what he wished.'

'With *her*?'

'With them all.'

It was as if now in my friend's own eyes Miss Jessel had again appeared. I seemed at any rate for an instant to trace their evocation of her as distinctly as I had seen her by the pond; and I brought out with decision: 'It must have been also what *she* wished!'

Mrs. Grose's face signified that it had been indeed, but she said at the same time: 'Poor woman—she paid for it!'

'Then you do know what she died of?' I asked.

'No—I know nothing. I wanted not to know; I was glad enough I didn't; and I thanked heaven she was well out of this!'

'Yet you had then your idea——'

'Of her real reason for leaving? Oh, yes—as to that. She couldn't have stayed. Fancy it here—for a governess! And afterwards I imagined—and I still imagine. And what I imagine is dreadful.'

'Not so dreadful as what *I* do,' I replied; on which I must have shown her—as I was indeed but too conscious—a front of miserable defeat. It brought out again all her compassion for me, and at the renewed touch of her kindness my power to resist broke down. I burst, as I had the other time made her burst, into tears; she took me to her motherly breast, and my lamentation overflowed. 'I don't do it!' I sobbed in despair; 'I don't save or shield them! It's far worse than I dreamed. They're lost!'

VIII

WHAT I had said to Mrs. Grose was true enough.
there were in the matter I had put before her depths
and possibilities that I lacked resolution to sound,
so that when we met once more in the wonder of it
we were of a common mind about the duty of resistance to extravagant fancies. We were to keep our
heads if we should keep nothing else—difficult indeed
as that might be in the face of all that, in our prodigious experience, seemed least to be questioned.
Late that night, while the house slept, we had another talk in my room; when she went all the way
with me as to its being beyond doubt that I had
seen exactly what I had seen. I found that to keep
her thoroughly in the grip of this I had only to ask
her how, if I had 'made it up,' I came to be able to
give, of each of the persons appearing to me, a picture
disclosing, to the last detail, their special marks—
a portrait on the exhibition of which she had instantly
recognized and named them. She wished, of course
—small blame to her!—to sink the whole subject;
and I was quick to assure her that my own interest
in it had now violently taken the form of a search
for the way to escape from it. I closed with her
cordially on the article of the likelihood that with
recurrence—for recurrence we took for granted—
I should get used to my danger; distinctly professing
that my personal exposure had suddenly become the
least of my discomforts. It was my new suspicion

that was intolerable; and yet even to this complication the later hours of the day had brought a little ease.

On leaving her, after my first outbreak, I had of course returned to my pupils, associating the right remedy for my dismay with that sense of their charm which I had already recognized as a resource I could positively cultivate and which had never failed me yet. I had simply, in other words, plunged afresh into Flora's special society and there become aware—it was almost a luxury!—that she could put her little conscious hand straight upon the spot that ached. She had looked at me in sweet speculation and then had accused me to my face of having 'cried.' I had supposed the ugly signs of it brushed away; but I could literally—for the time, at all events —rejoice, under this fathomless charity, that they had not entirely disappeared. To gaze into the depths of blue of the child's eyes and pronounce their loveliness a trick of premature cunning was to be guilty of a cynicism in preference to which I naturally preferred to abjure my judgment and, so far as might be, my agitation. I couldn't abjure for merely wanting to, but I could repeat to Mrs. Grose—as I did there, over and over, in the small hours—that with our small friends' voices in the air, their pressure on one's heart and their fragrant faces against one's cheek, everything fell to the ground but their incapacity and their beauty. It was a pity that, somehow, to settle this once for all, I had equally to re-enumerate the signs of subtlety that, in the afternoon, by the lake, had made a miracle of my show of self-possession. It was a pity to be obliged to reinvestigate the certitude of the moment itself and repeat how it had come to me as a revelation that the inconceivable communion I then surprised must have been for both parties a matter of habit. It was a pity I should have had to quaver out again, the reasons for my not having, in my delusion, so much as questioned that the little girl saw our visitant even as I actually saw Mrs. Grose herself, and that she wanted, by just so much as she did thus see, to make me suppose she didn't, and at the same time, without showing anything, arrive at a guess as to whether I myself did! It was a pity I needed to recapitulate the portentous little activities by which she sought to divert my attention—the perceptible increase of movement, the greater intensity of play, the singing, the gabbling of nonsense and the invitation to romp.

Yet if I had not indulged, to prove there was nothing in it, in this review, I should have missed the two or three dim elements of comfort that still remained to me. I shouldn't, for instance, have been able to asseverate to my friend that I was certain —which was so much to the good—that *I* at least had not betrayed myself. I shouldn't have been prompted, by stress of need, by desperation of mind —I scarce know what to call it—to invoke such further aid to intelligence as might spring from pushing my colleague fairly to the wall. She had told me, bit by bit, under pressure, a great deal; but a small shifty spot on the wrong side of it all still sometimes brushed my brow like the wing of a bat; and I remember how on this occasion—for the sleeping house and the concentration alike of our danger and our watch seemed to help—I felt the importance of giving the last jerk to the curtain. 'I don't believe anything so horrible,' I recollect saying; 'no, let us

put it definitely, my dear, that I don't. But if I
did, you know, there's a thing I should require now,
just without sparing you the least bit more—oh, not
a scrap, come!—to get out of you. What was it
you had in mind when, in our distress, before Miles
came back, over the letter from his school, you said,
under my insistence, that you didn't pretend for him
he hadn't literally *ever* been "bad"? He has *not*,
truly, "ever," in these weeks that I myself have
lived with him and so closely watched him; he has
been an imperturbable little prodigy of delightful,
lovable goodness. Therefore you might perfectly
have made the claim for him if you had not, as it
happened, seen an exception to take. What was
your exception, and to what passage in your personal
observation of him did you refer?'

It was a straight question enough, but levity was
not our note, and in any case I had before the grey
dawn admonished us to separate got my answer.
What my friend had had in mind proved immensely
to the purpose. It was neither more nor less than
the particular fact that for a period of several months
Quint and the boy had been perpetually together.
It was, indeed, the very appropriate item of evidence
of her having ventured to criticize the propriety, to
hint at the incongruity, of so close an alliance, and
even to go so far on the subject as a frank overture
to Miss Jessel would take her. Miss Jessel had, with
a very high manner about it, requested her to mind
her business, and the good woman had on this
directly approached little Miles. What she had said
to him, since I pressed, was that *she* liked to see
young gentlemen not forget their station.

I pressed again, of course, the closer for that.

'You reminded him that Quint was only a base menial?'

'As you might say! And it was his answer, for one thing, that was bad.'

'And for another thing?' I waited. 'He repeated your words to Quint?'

'No, not that. It's just what he *wouldn't*!' she could still impress on me. 'I was sure, at any rate,' she added, 'that he didn't. But he denied certain occasions.'

'What occasions?'

'When they had been about together quite as if Quint were his tutor—and a very grand one—and Miss Jessel only for the little lady. When he had gone off with the fellow, I mean, and spent hours with him.'

'He then prevaricated about it—he said he hadn't?' Her assent was clear enough to cause me to add in a moment: 'I see. He lied.'

'Oh!' Mrs. Grose mumbled. This was a suggestion that it didn't matter; which indeed she backed up by a further remark. 'You see, after all, Miss Jessel didn't mind. She didn't forbid him.'

I considered. 'Did he put that to you as a justification?'

At this she dropped again. 'No, he never spoke of it.'

'Never mentioned her in connection with Quint?'

She saw, visibly flushing, where I was coming out. 'Well, he didn't show anything. He denied,' she repeated; 'he denied.'

Lord, how I pressed her now! 'So that you could see he knew what was between the two wretches?'

'I don't know—I don't know!' the poor woman wailed.

'You do know, you dear thing,' I replied; 'only you haven't my dreadful boldness of mind, and you keep back, out of timidity, and modesty and delicacy, even the impression that in the past, when you had, without my aid, to flounder about in silence, most of all made you miserable. But I shall get it out of you yet! There was something in the boy that suggested to you,' I continued, 'his covering and concealing their relation.'

'Oh, he couldn't prevent——'

'Your learning the truth? I dare say! But, heavens,' I fell, with vehemence, a-thinking, 'what it shows that they must, to that extent, have succeeded in making of him!'

'Ah, nothing that's not nice *now*!' Mrs. Grose lugubriously pleaded.

'I don't wonder you looked queer,' I persisted, 'when I mentioned to you the letter from his school!'

'I doubt if I looked as queer as you!' she retorted with homely force. 'And if he was so bad then as that comes to, how is he such an angel now?'

'Yes, indeed—and if he was a fiend at school! How, how, how? Well,' I said in my torment, 'you must put it to me again, though I shall not be able to tell you for some days. Only put it to me again!' I cried in a way that made my friend stare. 'There are directions in which I mustn't for the present let myself go.' Meanwhile I returned to her first example—the one to which she had just previously referred—of the boy's happy capacity for an occasional slip. 'If Quint—on your remonstrance at the time you speak of—was a base menial, one of the things Miles said to you, I find myself guessing, was that you were another.' Again her admission was so adequate that I continued: 'And you forgave him that?'

'Wouldn't *you*?'

'Oh, yes!' And we exchanged there, in the stillness, a sound of the oddest amusement. Then I went on: 'At all events, while he was with the man——'

'Miss Flora was with the woman. It suited them all!'

It suited me too, I felt, only too well; by which I mean that it suited exactly the particular deadly view I was in the very act of forbidding myself to entertain. But I so far succeeded in checking the expression of this view that I will throw, just here, no further light on it than may be offered by the mention of my final observation to Mrs. Grose. 'His having lied and been impudent are, I confess, less engaging specimens than I had hoped to have from you of the outbreak in him of the little natural man. Still,' I mused, 'they must do, for they make me feel more than ever that I must watch.'

It made me blush, the next minute, to see in my friend's face how much more unreservedly she had forgiven him than her anecdote struck me as pointing out to my own tenderness any way to do. This was marked when, at the schoolroom door, she quitted me. 'Surely you don't accuse *him*——'

'Of carrying on an intercourse that he conceals from me? Ah, remember that, until further evidence, I now accuse nobody.' Then before shutting her out to go by another passage to her own place. 'I must just wait,' I wound up.

IX

I waited and waited, and the days took as they elapsed something from my consternation. A very few of them, in fact, passing, in constant sight of my pupils, without a fresh incident, sufficed to give to grievous fancies and even to odious memories a kind of brush of the sponge. I have spoken of the surrender to their extraordinary childish grace as a thing I could actively promote in myself, and it may be imagined if I neglected now to apply at this source for whatever balm it would yield. Stranger than I can express, certainly, was the effort to struggle against my new lights. It would doubtless have been a greater tension still, however, had it not been so frequently successful. I used to wonder how my little charges could help guessing that I thought strange things about them; and the circumstance that these things only made them more interesting was not by itself a direct aid to keeping them in the dark. I trembled lest they should see that they *were* so immensely more interesting. Putting things at the worst, at all events, as in meditation I so often did, any clouding of their innocence could only be—blameless and foredoomed as they were— a reason the more for taking risks. There were moments when I knew myself to catch them up by an irresistible impulse and press them to my heart. As soon as I had done so I used to wonder: 'What will they think of that? Doesn't it betray too

much?' It would have been easy to get into a sad,
wild tangle about how much I might betray; but
the real account, I feel, of the hours of peace I could
still enjoy was that the immediate charm of my companions was a beguilement still effective even under
the shadow of the possibility that it was studied.
For if it occurred to me that I might occasionally
excite suspicion by the little outbreaks of my sharper
passion for them, so too I remember asking if I
mightn't see a queerness in the traceable increase
of their own demonstrations.

They were at this period extravagantly and preternaturally fond of me; which, after all, I could reflect,
was no more than a graceful response in children
perpetually bowed down over and hugged. The
homage of which they were so lavish succeeded in
truth for my nerves quite as well as if I never
appeared to myself, as I may say, literally to catch
them at a purpose in it. They had never, I think,
wanted to do so many things for their poor pro-
tectress; I mean—though they got their lessons
better and better, which was naturally what would
please her most—in the way of diverting, entertaining, surprising her; reading her passages, telling her
stories, acting her charades, pouncing out at her,
in disguises, as animals and historical characters,
and above all, astonishing her by the 'pieces' they
had secretly got by heart and could interminably
recite. I should never get to the bottom—were I
to let myself go even now—of the prodigious private
commentary, all under still more private correction,
with which I in these days overscored their full
hours. They had shown me from the first a facility
for everything, a general faculty which, taking a

fresh start, achieved remarkable flights. They got
their little tasks as if they loved them; they indulged, from the mere exuberance of the gift, in the
most unimposed little miracles of memory. They
not only popped out at me as tigers and as Romans,
but as Shakespearians, astronomers, and navigators.
This was so singularly the case that it had presumably
much to do with the fact as to which, at the present
day, I am at a loss for a different explanation: I allude
to my unnatural composure on the subject of another
school for Miles. What I remember is that I was
content for the time not to open the question, and
that contentment must have sprung from the sense
of his perpetually striking show of cleverness. He
was too clever for a bad governess, for a parson's
daughter, to spoil; and the strangest if not the
brightest thread in the pensive embroidery I just
spoke of was the impression I might have got, if I
had dared to work it out, that he was under some
influence operating in his small intellectual life as a
tremendous incitement.

If it was easy to reflect, however, that such a boy
could postpone school, it was at least as marked
that for such a boy to have been 'kicked out' by
a schoolmaster was a mystification without end.
Let me add that in their company now—and I was
careful almost never to be out of it—I could follow
no scent very far. We lived in a cloud of music
and affection and success and private theatricals.
The musical sense in each of the children was of
the quickest, but the elder in especial had a marvellous
knack of catching and repeating. The schoolroom
piano broke into all gruesome fancies; and when
that failed there were confabulations in corners, with

a sequel of one of them going out in the highest
spirits in order to 'come in' as something new. I had
had brothers myself, and it was no revelation to me
that little girls could be slavish idolaters of little
boys. What surpassed everything was that there
was a little boy in the world who could have for the
inferior age, sex, and intelligence so fine a consideration. They were extraordinarily at one, and to say
that they never either quarrelled or complained is
to make the note of praise coarse for their quality
of sweetness. Sometimes perhaps indeed (when I
dropped into coarseness) I came across traces of
little understandings between them by which one
of them should keep me occupied while the other
slipped away. There is a naïf side, I suppose, in
all diplomacy; but if my pupils practised upon me
it was surely with the minimum of grossness. It
was all in the other quarter that, after a lull, the
grossness broke out.

I find that I really hang back; but I must take
my horrid plunge. In going on with the record
of what was hideous at Bly I not only challenge
the most liberal faith—for which I little care; but
(and this is another matter) I renew what I myself
suffered, I again push my dreadful way through it
to the end. There came suddenly an hour after
which, as I look back, the business seems to me to
have been all pure suffering; but I have at least
reached the heart of it, and the straightest road
out is doubtless to advance. One evening—with
nothing to lead up or prepare it—I felt the cold
touch of the impression that had breathed on me the
night of my arrival and which, much lighter then
as I have mentioned, I should probably have made

little of in memory had my subsequent sojourn been less agitated. I had not gone to bed; I sat reading by a couple of candles. There was a roomful of old books at Bly—last-century fiction some of it, which, to the extent of a distinctly deprecated renown, but never to so much as that of a stray specimen, had reached the sequestered home and appealed to the unavowed curiosity of my youth. I remember that the book I had in my hand was Fielding's *Amelia*; also that I was wholly awake. I recall further both a general conviction that it was horribly late and a particular objection to looking at my watch. I figure finally that the white curtain draping, in the fashion of those days, the head of Flora's little bed, shrouded, as I had assured myself long before, the perfection of childish rest. I recollect in short that though I was deeply interested in my author I found myself, at the turn of a page and with his spell all scattered, looking straight up from him and hard at the door of my room. There was a moment during which I listened, reminded of the faint sense I had had, the first night, of there being something undefinably astir in the house, and noted the soft breath of the open casement just move the half-drawn blind. Then, with all the marks of a deliberation that must have seemed magnificent had there been any one to admire it, I laid down my book, rose to my feet and, taking a candle, went straight out of the room and, from the passage, on which my light made little impression, noiselessly closed and locked the door.

I can say now neither what determined nor what guided me, but I went straight along the lobby, holding my candle high, till I came within sight of

the tall window that presided over the great turn
of the staircase. At this point I precipitately found
myself aware of three things. They were practically
simultaneous, yet they had flashes of succession.
My candle, under a bold flourish, went out, and I
perceived, by the uncovered window, that the yielding dusk of earliest morning rendered it unnecessary.
Without it, the next instant, I knew that there was
a figure on the stair. I speak of sequences, but I
required no lapse of seconds to stiffen myself for a
third encounter with Quint. The apparition had
reached the landing half-way up and was therefore
on the spot nearest the window, where, at sight of
me, it stopped short and fixed me exactly as it had
fixed me from the tower and from the garden. He
knew me as well as I knew him; and so, in the cold,
faint twilight, with a glimmer in the high glass and
another on the polish of the oak stair below, we
faced each other in our common intensity. He was
absolutely, on this occasion, a living, detestable,
dangerous presence. But that was not the wonder
of wonders; I reserve this distinction for quite another circumstance: the circumstance that dread had
unmistakably quitted me and that there was nothing
in me unable to meet and measure him.

I had plenty of anguish after that extraordinary
moment, but I had, thank God, no terror. And
he knew I hadn't—I found myself at the end of
an instant magnificently aware of this. I felt, in
a fierce rigour of confidence, that if I stood my
ground a minute I should cease—for the time at
least—to have him to reckon with; and during the
minute, accordingly, the thing was as human and
hideous as a real interview: hideous just because

it *was* human, as human as to have met alone, in
the small hours, in a sleeping house, some enemy,
some adventurer, some criminal. It was the dead
silence of our long gaze at such close quarters that
gave the whole horror, huge as it was, its only note
of the unnatural. If I had met a murderer in such a
place and at such an hour we still at least would
have spoken. Something would have passed, in
life, between us; if nothing had passed one of us
would have moved. The moment was so prolonged
that it would have taken but little more to make
me doubt if even *I* were in life. I can't express what
followed it save by saying that the silence itself—
which was indeed in a manner an attestation of my
strength—became the element into which I saw the
figure disappear; in which I definitely saw it turn,
as I might have seen the low wretch to which it
had once belonged turn on receipt of an order, and
pass, with my eyes on the villainous back that no
hunch could have more disfigured, straight down the
staircase and into the darkness in which the next
bend was lost.

X

I REMAINED awhile at the top of the stair, but with
the effect presently of understanding that when my
visitor had gone, he had gone; then I returned to
my room. The foremost thing I saw there by the
light of the candle I had left burning was that
Flora's little bed was empty; and on this I caught
my breath with all the terror that, five minutes
before, I had been able to resist. I dashed at the
place in which I had left her lying and over which
—for the small silk counterpane and the sheets were
disarranged—the white curtains had been deceivingly
pulled forward; then my step, to my unutterable
relief, produced an answering sound: I noticed an
agitation of the window-blind, and the child, ducking
down, emerged rosily from the other side of it. She
stood there in so much of her candour and so little
of her night-gown, with her pink bare feet and the
golden glow of her curls. She looked intensely grave,
and I had never had such a sense of losing an
advantage acquired (the thrill of which had just
been so prodigious) as on my consciousness that she
addressed me with a reproach: 'You naughty: where
have you been?' Instead of challenging her own
irregularity I found myself arraigned and explaining.
She herself explained, for that matter, with the
loveliest, eagerest simplicity. She had known suddenly, as she lay there, that I was out of the room,
and had jumped up to see what had become of me.

I had dropped, with the joy of her reappearance, back into my chair—feeling then, and then only, a little faint; and she had pattered straight over to me, thrown herself upon my knee, given herself to be held with the flame of the candle full in the wonderful little face that was still flushed with sleep. I remember closing my eyes an instant, yieldingly, consciously, as before the excess of something beautiful that shone out of the blue of her own. 'You were looking for me out of the window?' I said. 'You thought I might be walking in the grounds?'

'Well, you know, I thought someone was'—she never blanched as she smiled out that at me.

Oh, how I looked at her now! 'And did you see any one?'

'Ah, no!' she returned almost (with the full privilege of childish inconsequence) resentfully, though with a long sweetness in her little drawl of the negative.

At the moment, in the state of my nerves, I absolutely believed she lied; and if I once more closed my eyes it was before the dazzle of the three or four possible ways in which I might take this up. One of these for a moment tempted me with such singular force that, to resist it, I must have gripped my little girl with a spasm that, wonderfully, she submitted to without a cry or a sign of fright. Why not break out at her on the spot and have it all over?—give it to her straight in her lovely little lighted face? 'You see, you see, you *know* that you do and that you already quite suspect I believe it; therefore why not frankly confess it to me, so that we may at least live with it together and learn perhaps, in the strangeness of our fate, where

we are and what it means?' This solicitation
dropped, alas, as it came: if I could immediately
have succumbed to it I might have spared myself
—well, you'll see what. Instead of succumbing
I sprang again to my feet, looked at her bed and
took a helpless middle way. 'Why did you pull
the curtain over the place to make me think you
were still there?'

Flora luminously considered; after which, with
her little divine smile: 'Because I don't like to
frighten you!'

'But if I had, by your idea, gone out——?'

She absolutely declined to be puzzled; she turned
her eyes to the flame of the candle as if the question
were as irrelevant, or at any rate as impersonal, as
Mrs. Marcet or nine-times-nine. 'Oh, but you know,'
she quite adequately answered, 'that you might
come back, you dear, and that you *have*!' And
after a little, when she had got into bed, I had, a
long time, by almost sitting on her for the retention
of her hand, to show how I recognized the pertinence
of my return.

You may imagine the general complexion, from
that moment, of my nights. I repeatedly sat up
till I didn't know when; I selected moments when
my room-mate unmistakably slept, and, stealing
out, took noiseless turns in the passage. I even
pushed as far as to where I had last met Quint.
But I never met him there again, and I may as
well say at once that I on no other occasion saw
him in the house. I just missed, on the staircase,
nevertheless, a different adventure. Looking down
it from the top I once recognized the presence of
a woman seated on one of the lower steps with

her back presented to me, her body half-bowed and
her head, in an attitude of woe, in her hands.   I had
been there but an instant, however, when she vanished
without looking round at me.   I knew, for all that,
exactly what dreadful face she had to show; and I
wondered whether, if instead of being above I had
been below, I should have had the same nerve for
going up that I had lately shown Quint.   Well,
there continued to be plenty of call for nerve.   On
the eleventh night after my latest encounter with
that gentleman—they were all numbered now—I had
an alarm that perilously skirted it and that indeed,
from the particular quality of its unexpectedness,
proved quite my sharpest shock.   It was precisely
the first night during this series, that, weary with
vigils, I had conceived I might again without laxity
lay myself down at my old hour.   I slept immediately
and, as I afterwards knew, till about one o'clock; but
when I woke it was to sit straight up as completely
roused as if a hand had shaken me.   I had left a
light burning, but it was now out, and I felt an
instant certainty that Flora had extinguished it.
This brought me to my feet and straight, in the
darkness, to her bed which I found she had left.
A glance at the window enlightened me further,
and the striking of a match completed the picture.

The child had again got up—this time blowing out
the taper, and had again, for some purpose of observation or response, squeezed in behind the blind and
was peering out into the night.   That she now saw
as she had not, I had satisfied myself, the previous
time—was proved to me by the fact that she was
disturbed neither by my re-illumination nor by the
haste I made to get into slippers and into a wrap.

Hidden, protected, absorbed, she evidently rested on the sill—the casement opened forward—and gave herself up. There was a great still moon to help her, and this fact had counted in my quick decision. She was face to face with the apparition we had met at the lake, and could now communicate with it as she had not then been able to do. What I, on my side, had to care for was, without disturbing her, to reach, from the corridor, some other window turned to the same quarter. I got to the door without her hearing me; I got out of it, closed it, and listened from the other side for some sound from her. While I stood in the passage I had my eyes on her brother's door, which was but ten steps off and which, indescribably, produced in me a renewal of the strange impulse that I lately spoke of as my temptation. What if I should go straight in and march to *his* window?—what if, by risking to his boyish bewilderment a revelation of my motive, I should throw across the rest of the mystery the long halter of my boldness?

This thought held me sufficiently to make me cross to his threshold and pause again. I preternaturally listened; I figured to myself what might portentously be; I wondered if his bed were also empty and he also secretly at watch. It was a deep soundless minute, at the end of which my impulse failed. He was quiet; he might be innocent; the risk was hideous; I turned away. There was a figure in the grounds—a figure prowling for a sight, the visitor with whom Flora was engaged; but it wasn't the visitor most concerned with my boy. I hesitated afresh, but on other grounds and only a few seconds; then I had made my choice. There were empty rooms enough at Bly, and it was only a question of choosing the right one. The right one suddenly presented itself to me as the lower one—though high above the gardens—in the solid corner of the house that I have spoken of as the old tower. This was a large, square chamber, arranged with some state as a bedroom, the extravagant size of which made it so inconvenient that it had not for years, though kept by Mrs. Grose in exemplary order, been occupied. I had often admired it and I knew my way about in it; I had only, after just faltering at the first chill gloom of its disuse, to pass across it and unbolt in all quietness one of the shutters. Achieving this transit I uncovered the glass without a sound and, applying my face to the pane, was able, the darkness without being much less than within, to see that I commanded the right direction. Then I saw something more. The moon made the night extraordinarily penetrable and showed me on the lawn a person, diminished by distance, who stood there motionless and as if fascinated, looking up to where I had appeared—looking, that is, not so much straight at me as at something that was apparently above me. There was clearly another person above me—there was a person on the tower; but the presence on the lawn was not in the least what I had conceived and had confidently hurried to meet. The presence on the lawn—I felt sick as I made it out—was poor little Miles himself.

XI

It was not till late next day that I spoke to Mrs.
Grose; the rigour with which I kept my pupils in
sight making it often difficult to meet her privately;
the more as we each felt the importance of not
provoking—on the part of the servants quite as much
as on that of the children—any suspicion of a secret
flurry or of a discussion of mysteries. I drew a great
security in this particular from her mere smooth
aspect. There was nothing in her fresh face to pass
on to others the least of my horrible confidences.
She believed me, I was sure, absolutely: if she hadn't
I don't know what would have become of me, for
I couldn't have borne the strain alone. But she was
a magnificent monument to the blessing of a want
of imagination, and if she could see in our little
charges nothing but their beauty and amiability,
their happiness and cleverness, she had no direct
communication with the sources of my trouble. If
they had been at all visibly blighted or battered she
would doubtless have grown, on tracing it back,
haggard enough to match them; as matters stood,
however, I could feel her, when she surveyed them
with her large white arms folded and the habit of
serenity in all her look, thank the Lord's mercy that
if they were ruined the pieces would still serve.
Flights of fancy gave place, in her mind, to a steady
fireside glow, and I had already begun to perceive
how, with the development of the conviction that—

as time went on without a public accident—our
young things could, after all, look out for themselves,
she addressed her greatest solicitude to the sad
case presented by their deputy-guardian. That, for
myself, was a sound simplification: I could engage
that, to the world, my face should tell no tales, but
it would have been, in the conditions, an immense
added worry to find myself anxious about hers.

At the hour I now speak of she had joined me,
under pressure, on the terrace, where, with the lapse
of the season, the afternoon sun was now agreeable;
and we sat there together while before us and at a
distance, yet within call if we wished, the children
strolled to and fro in one of their most manageable
moods. They moved slowly, in unison, below us,
over the lawn, the boy, as they went, reading aloud
from a story-book and passing his arm round his
sister to keep her quite in touch. Mrs. Grose watched
them with positive placidity; then I caught the
suppressed intellectual creak with which she conscientiously turned to take from me a view of the
back of the tapestry. I had made her a receptacle
of lurid things, but there was an odd recognition of
my superiority—my accomplishments and my func-
tion—in her patience under my pain. She offered
her mind to my disclosures as, had I wished to mix
a witch's broth and proposed it with assurance, she
would have held out a large, clean saucepan. This
had become thoroughly her attitude by the time that,
in my recital of the events of the night, I reached
the point of what Miles had said to me when, after
seeing him, at such a monstrous hour, almost on the
very spot where he happened now to be, I had gone
down to bring him in; choosing then, at the window.

with a concentrated need of not alarming the house, rather that method than any noisier process. I had left her meanwhile in little doubt of my small hope of representing with success even to her actual sympathy my sense of the real splendour of the little inspiration with which, after I had got him into the house, the boy met my final articulate challenge. As soon as I appeared in the moonlight on the terrace he had come to me as straight as possible; on which I had taken his hand without a word and led him, through the dark spaces, up the staircase where Quint had so hungrily hovered for him, along the lobby where I had listened and trembled, and so to his forsaken room.

Not a sound, on the way, had passed between us, and I had wondered—oh, *how* I had wondered! —if he were groping about in his dreadful little mind for something plausible and not too grotesque. It would tax his invention certainly, and I felt, this time, over his real embarrassment, a curious thrill of triumph. It was a sharp trap for any game hitherto successful. He could play no longer at perfect propriety, nor could he pretend to it; so how the deuce would he get out of the scrape? There beat in me indeed, with the passionate throb of this question, an equal dumb appeal as to how the deuce *I* should. I was confronted at last, as never yet, with all the risk attached even now to sounding my own horrid note. I remember, in fact, that as we pushed into his little chamber, where the bed had not been slept in at all and the window, uncovered to the moonlight, made the place so clear that there was no need of striking a match— I remember how I suddenly dropped, sank upon the

edge of the bed from the force of the idea that he
must know how he really, as they say, 'had' me.
He could do what he liked, with all his cleverness
to help him, so long as I should continue to defer to
the old tradition of the criminality of those care-
takers of the young who minister to superstitions
and fears. He 'had' me indeed, and in a cleft
stick; for who would ever absolve me, who would
consent that I should be unhung, if, by the faintest
tremor of an overture, I were the first to introduce
into our perfect intercourse an element so dire? No,
no: it was useless to attempt to convey to Mrs.
Grose, just as it is scarcely less so to attempt to
suggest here, how, during our short, stiff brush
there in the dark, he fairly shook me with admiration.
I was of course thoroughly kind and merciful; never,
never yet had I placed on his small shoulders hands
of such tenderness as those with which, while I
rested against the bed, I held him there well under
fire. I had no alternative but, in form at least, to
put it to him.

'You must tell me now—and all the truth. What
did you go out for? What were you doing there?'

I can still see his wonderful smile, the whites of
his beautiful eyes and the uncovering of his clear
teeth, shine to me in the dusk. 'If I tell you why,
will you understand?' My heart, at this, leaped
into my mouth. *Would* he tell me why? I found
no sound on my lips to press it, and I was aware
of answering only with a vague, repeated, grimacing
nod. He was gentleness itself, and while I wagged
my head at him he stood there more than ever a
little fairy prince. It was his brightness indeed
that gave me a respite. Would it be so great if

he were really going to tell me? 'Well,' he said at last, 'just exactly in order that you should do this.'

'Do what?'

'Think me—for a change—*bad*!' I shall never forget the sweetness and gaiety with which he brought out the word, nor how, on top of it, he bent forward and kissed me. It was practically the end of everything. I met his kiss and I had to make, while I folded him for a minute in my arms, the most stupendous effort not to cry. He had given exactly the account of himself that permitted least my going behind it, and it was only with the effect of confirming my acceptance of it that, as I presently glanced about the room, I could say:

'Then you didn't undress at all?'

He fairly glittered in the gloom. 'Not at all. I sat up and read.'

'And when did you go down?'

'At midnight. When I'm bad I *am* bad!'

'I see, I see—it's charming. But how could you be sure I should know it?'

'Oh, I arranged that with Flora.' His answers rang out with a readiness! 'She was to get up and look out.'

'Which is what she did do.' It was I who fell into the trap!

'So she disturbed you, and, to see what she was looking at, you also looked—you saw.'

'While you,' I concurred, 'caught your death in the night air!'

He literally bloomed so from this exploit that he could afford radiantly to assent. 'How otherwise should I have been bad enough?' he asked. Then, after another embrace, the incident and our interview closed on my recognition of all the reserves of goodness that, for his joke, he had been able to draw upon.

XII

THE particular impression I had received proved in the morning light, I repeat, not quite successfully presentable to Mrs. Grose, though I re-enforced it with the mention of still another remark that he had made before we separated. 'It all lies in half a dozen words,' I said to her, 'words that really settle the matter. "Think, you know, what I *might* do!" He threw that off to show me how good he is. He knows down to the ground what he "might do." That's what he gave them a taste of at school.'

'Lord, you do change!' cried my friend.

'I don't change—I simply make it out. The four, depend upon it, perpetually meet. If on either of these last nights you had been with either child you'd clearly have understood. The more I've watched and waited the more I've felt that if there were nothing else to make it sure it would be made so by the systematic silence of each. *Never*, by a slip of the tongue, have they so much as alluded to either of their old friends, any more than Miles has alluded to his expulsion. Oh, yes, we may sit here and look at them, and they may show off to us there to their fill; but even while they pretend to be lost in their fairy-tale they're steeped in their vision of the dead restored to them. He's not reading to her,' I declared; 'they're talking of *them*—they're talking horrors! I go on, I know, as if I were crazy; and it's a wonder I'm not. What I've seen would

have made *you* so; but it has only made me more
lucid, made me get hold of still other things.'

My lucidity must have seemed awful, but the
charming creatures who were victims of it, passing
and repassing in their interlocked sweetness, gave
my colleague something to hold on by; and I felt
how tight she held as, without stirring in the breath
of my passion, she covered them still with her eyes.
'Of what other things have you got hold?'

'Why, of the very things that have delighted,
fascinated and yet, at bottom, as I now so strangely
see, mystified and troubled me. Their more than
earthly beauty, their absolutely unnatural goodness. It's a game,' I went on; 'it's a policy and
a fraud!'

'On the part of little darlings——?'

'As yet mere lovely babies? Yes, mad as that
seems!' The very act of bringing it out really
helped me to trace it—follow it all up and piece it
all together. 'They haven't been good—they've
only been absent. It has been easy to live with
them because they're simply leading a life of their
own. They're not mine—they're not ours. They're
his and they're hers!'

'Quint's and that woman's?'

'Quint's and that woman's. They want to get
to them.'

Oh, how, at this, poor Mrs. Grose appeared to
study them! 'But for what?'

'For the love of all the evil that, in those dreadful
days, the pair put into them. And to ply them
with that evil still, to keep up the work of demons,
is what brings the others back.'

'Laws!' said my friend under her breath. The

exclamation was homely, but it revealed a real acceptance of my further proof of what, in the bad time—for there had been a worse even than this!—must have occurred. There could have been no such justification for me as the plain assent of her experience to whatever depth of depravity I found credible in our brace of scoundrels. It was in obvious submission of memory that she brought out after a moment: 'They *were* rascals! But what can they now do?' she pursued.

'Do?' I echoed so loud that Miles and Flora, as they passed at their distance, paused an instant in their walk and looked at us. 'Don't they do enough?' I demanded in a lower tone, while the children, having smiled and nodded and kissed hands to us, resumed their exhibition. We were held by it a minute; then I answered: 'They can destroy them!' At this my companion did turn, but the appeal she launched was a silent one, the effect of which was to make me more explicit. 'They don't know as yet quite how—but they're trying hard. They're seen only across, as it were, and beyond—in strange places and on high places, the top of towers, the roof of houses, the outside of windows, the further edge of pools; but there's a deep design on either side, to shorten the distance and overcome the obstacle: so the success of the tempters is only a question of time. They've only to keep to their suggestions of danger.'

'For the children to come?'

'And perish in the attempt!' Mrs. Grose slowly got up, and I scrupulously added: 'Unless, of course, we can prevent!'

Standing there before me while I kept my seat, she

visibly turned things over. 'Their uncle must do the preventing. He must take them away.'

'And who's to make him?'

She had been scanning the distance, but she now dropped on me a foolish face. 'You, miss.'

'By writing to him that his house is poisoned and his nephew and niece mad?'

'But if they *are*, miss?'

'And if I am myself, you mean? That's charming news to be sent him by a person enjoying his confidence and whose prime undertaking was to give him no worry.'

Mrs. Grose considered, following the children again. 'Yes, he do hate worry. That was the great reason——'

'Why those fiends took him in so long? No doubt, though his indifference must have been awful. As I'm not a fiend, at any rate, I shouldn't take him in.'

My companion, after an instant and for all answer, sat down again and grasped my arm. 'Make him at any rate come to you.'

I stared. 'To *me*?' I had a sudden fear of what she might do. '"Him?"'

'He ought to *be* here—he ought to help.'

I quickly rose and I think I must have shown her a queerer face than ever yet. 'You see me asking him for a visit?' No, with her eyes on my face she evidently couldn't. Instead of it even—as a woman reads another—she could see what I myself saw: his derision, his amusement, his contempt for the breakdown of my resignation at being left alone and for the fine machinery I had set in motion to attract his attention to my slighted charms. She didn't

know—no one knew—how proud I had been to serve
him and to stick to our terms; yet she none the less
took the measure, I think, of the warning I now
gave her. 'If you should so lose your head as to
appeal to him for me——'

She was really frightened. 'Yes, miss?'

'I would leave, on the spot, both him and you.'

XIII

IT was all very well to join them, but speaking to
them proved quite as much as ever an effort beyond
my strength—offered, in close quarters, difficulties
as insurmountable as before. This situation continued a month, and with new aggravations and
particular notes, the note above all, sharper and
sharper, of the small ironic consciousness on the part
of my pupils. It was not, I am as sure to-day as I
was sure then, my mere infernal imagination: it was
absolutely traceable that they were aware of my
predicament and that this strange relation made, in
a manner, for a long time, the air in which we moved.
I don't mean that they had their tongues in their
cheeks or did anything vulgar, for that was not one
of their dangers: I do mean, on the other hand, that
the element of the unnamed and untouched became,
between us, greater than any other, and that so
much avoidance couldn't have been made successful
without a great deal of tacit arrangement. It was
as if, at moments, we were perpetually coming into
sight of subjects before which we must stop short,
turning suddenly out of alleys that we perceived to
be blind, closing with a little bang that made us
look at each other—for, like all bangs, it was something louder than we had intended—the doors we
had indiscreetly opened. All roads lead to Rome,
and there were times when it might have struck us

that almost every branch of study or subject of
conversation skirted forbidden ground. Forbidden
ground was the question of the return of the dead in
general and of whatever, in especial, might survive,
for memory, of the friends little children had lost.
There were days when I could have sworn that one
of them had, with a small invisible nudge, said to
the other: 'She thinks she'll do it this time—but
she *won't*!' To 'do it' would have been to indulge,
for instance—and for once in a way—in some direct
reference to the lady who had prepared them for my
discipline. They had a delightful endless appetite
for passages in my own history to which I had again
and again treated them; they were in possession of
everything that had ever happened to me, had had,
with every circumstance, the story of my smallest
adventures and of those of my brothers and sisters
and of the cat and the dog at home, as well as many
particulars of the whimsical bent of my father, of
the furniture and arrangement of our house and of
the conversation of the old women of our village.
There were things enough, taking one with another,
to chatter about, if one went very fast and knew
by instinct when to go round. They pulled with an
art of their own the strings of my invention and
my memory; and nothing else perhaps, when I
thought of such occasions afterwards, gave me so
the suspicion of being watched from under cover.
It was in any case over *my* life, *my* past and *my*
friends alone that we could take anything like our
ease; a state of affairs that led them sometimes
without the least pertinence to break out into sociable
reminders. I was invited — with no visible connection—to repeat afresh Goody Gosling's celebrated

mot or to confirm the details already supplied as to
the cleverness of the vicarage pony.

It was partly at such junctures as these and partly
at quite different ones that, with the turn my matters
had now taken, my predicament, as I have called it,
grew most sensible. The fact that the days passed
for me without another encounter ought, it would
have appeared, to have done something toward
soothing my nerves Since the light brush, that
second night on the upper landing, of the presence
of a woman at the foot of the stair, I had seen
nothing, whether in or out of the house, that one
had better not have seen. There was many a corner
round which I expected to come upon Quint, and
many a situation that, in a merely sinister way,
would have favoured the appearance of Miss Jessel.
The summer had turned, the summer had gone; the
autumn had dropped upon Bly and had blown out
half our lights. The place, with its grey sky and
withered garlands, its bared spaces and scattered
dead leaves, was like a theatre after the performance
—all strewn with crumpled playbills. There were
exactly states of the air, conditions of sound and of
stillness, unspeakable impressions of the *kind* of
ministering moment, that brought back to me, long
enough to catch it, the feeling of the medium in
which, that June evening out of doors, I had had
my first sight of Quint, and in which too, at those
other instants, I had, after seeing him through the
window, looked for him in vain in the circle of
shrubbery. I recognized the signs, the portents—
I recognized the moment, the spot. But they
remained unaccompanied and empty, and I continued unmolested; if unmolested one could call a

young woman whose sensibility had, in the most extraordinary fashion, not declined but deepened. I had said in my talk with Mrs. Grose on that horrid scene of Flora's by the lake—and had perplexed her by so saying—that it would from that moment distress me much more to lose my power than to keep it. I had then expressed what was vividly in my mind: the truth that, whether the children really saw or not—since, that is, it was not yet definitely proved—I greatly preferred, as a safeguard, the fullness of my own exposure. I was ready to know the very worst that was to be known. What I had then had an ugly glimpse of was that my eyes might be sealed just while theirs were most opened. Well, my eyes *were* [sealed, it appeared, at present—a consummation for which it seemed blasphemous not to thank God. There was, alas, a difficulty about that: I would have thanked Him with all my soul had I not had in a proportionate measure this conviction of the secret of my pupils.

How can I retrace to-day the strange steps of my obsession? There were times of our being together when I would have been ready to swear that, literally, in my presence, but with my direct sense of it closed, they had visitors who were known and were welcome. Then it was that, had I not been deterred by the very chance that such an injury might prove greater than the injury to be averted, my exaltation would have broken out. 'They're here, they're here, you little wretches,' I would have cried, 'and you can't deny it now!' The little wretches denied it with all the added volume of their sociability and their tenderness, just in the crystal depths of which —like the flash of a fish in a stream—the mockery of their advantage peeped up. The shock had in truth sunk into me still deeper than I knew on the night when, looking out either for Quint or for Miss Jessel under the stars, I had seen there the boy over whose rest I watched and who had immediately brought in with him—had straightway there turned on me—the lovely upward look with which, from the battlements above us, the hideous apparition of Quint had played. If it was a question of a scare my discovery on this occasion had scared me more than any other, and it was essentially in the scared state that I drew my actual conclusions. They harassed me so that sometimes, at odd moments, I shut myself up audibly to rehearse—it was at once a fantastic relief and a renewed despair—the manner in which I might come to the point. I approached it from one side and the other while, in my room, I flung myself about, but I always broke down in the monstrous utterances of names. As they died away on my lips I said to myself that I should indeed help them to represent something infamous if by pro-nouncing them I should violate as rare a little case of instinctive delicacy as any schoolroom probably had ever known. When I said to myself: '*They* have the manners to be silent, and you, trusted as you are, the baseness to speak!' I felt myself crimson and covered my face with my hands. After these secret scenes I chattered more than ever, going on volubly enough till one of our prodigious, palpable hushes occurred — I can call them nothing else — the strange, dizzy lift or swim (I try for terms!) into a stillness, a pause of all life, that had nothing to do with the more or less noise we at the moment might be engaged in making and that I could hear

through any intensified mirth or quickened recita-
tion or louder strum of the piano. Then it was
that the others, the outsiders, were there. Though
they were not angels they 'passed,' as the French
say, causing me, while they stayed, to tremble with
the fear of their addressing to their younger victims
some yet more infernal message or more vivid image
than they had thought good enough for myself.

What it was least possible to get rid of was the
cruel idea that, whatever I had seen, Miles and
Flora saw *more*—things terrible and unguessable
and that sprang from dreadful passages of intercourse in the past. Such things naturally left on
the surface, for the time, a chill that we vociferously
denied we felt; and we had all three, with repetition,
got into such splendid training that we went, each
time, to mark the close of the incident, almost
automatically through the very same movements.
It was striking of the children at all events to kiss
me inveterately with a wild irrelevance and never
to fail—one or the other—of the precious question
that had helped us through many a peril. 'When
do you think he *will* come? Don't you think we
ought to write?'—there was nothing like that inquiry,
we found by experience, for carrying off an awkwardness. 'He,' of course, was their uncle in Harley Street;
and we lived in much profusion of theory that he
might at any moment arrive to mingle in our circle.
It was impossible to have given less encouragement
than he had administered to such a doctrine, but if
we had not had the doctrine to fall back upon we
should have deprived each other of some of our
finest exhibitions. He never wrote to them—that
may have been selfish, but it was a part of the

flattery of his trust of myself; for the way in which
a man pays his highest tribute to a woman is apt
to be put by the more festal celebration of one of
the sacred laws of his comfort. So I held that I
carried out the spirit of the pledge given not to
appeal to him when I let our young friends understand that their own letters were but charming
literary exercises. They were too beautiful to be
posted; I kept them myself; I have them all to
this hour. This was a rule, indeed, which only
added to the satiric effect of my being plied with
the supposition that he might at any moment be
among us. It was exactly as if our young friends
knew how almost more awkward than anything else
that might be for me. There appears to me, moreover, as I look back no note in all this more extraordinary than the mere fact that, in spite of my
tension and of their triumph, I never lost patience
with them. Adorable they must in truth have been,
I now feel, since I didn't in these days hate them!
Would exasperation, however, if relief had longer
been postponed, finally have betrayed me? It little
matters, for relief arrived. I call it relief though it
was only the relief that a snap brings to a strain or
the burst of a thunderstorm to a day of suffocation.
It was at least change, and it came with a rush.

XIV

WALKING to church a certain Sunday morning, I had little Miles at my side and his sister, in advance of us and at Mrs. Grose's, well in sight. It was a crisp, clear day, the first of its order for some time; the night had brought a touch of frost and the autumn air, bright and sharp, made the church bells almost gay. It was an odd accident of thought that I should have happened at such a moment to be particularly and very gratefully struck with the obedience of my little charges. Why did they never resent my inexorable, my perpetual society? Something or other had brought nearer home to me that I had all but pinned the boy to my shawl, and that in the way our companions were marshalled before me I might have appeared to provide against some danger of rebellion. I was like a jailer with an eye to possible surprises and escapes. But all this belonged—I mean their magnificent little surrender —just to the special array of the facts that were most abysmal. Turned out for Sunday by his uncle's tailor, who had had a free hand and a notion of pretty waistcoats and of his grand little air, Miles's whole title to independence, the rights of his sex and situation, were so stamped upon him that if he had suddenly struck for freedom I should have had nothing to say. I was by the strangest of chances wondering how I should meet him when the revolution unmistakably occurred. I call it a revolution because I now see how, with the word he spoke, the curtain rose on the last act of my dreadful drama and the catastrophe was precipitated. 'Look here, my dear, you know,' he charmingly said, 'when in the world, please, am I going back to school?'

Transcribed here the speech sounds harmless enough, particularly as uttered in the sweet, high, casual pipe with which, at all interlocutors, but above all at his eternal governess, he threw off intonations as if he were tossing roses. There was something in them that always made one 'catch,' and I caught at any rate now so effectually that I stopped as short as if one of the trees of the park had fallen across the road. There was something new, on the spot, between us, and he was perfectly aware I recognized it, though to enable me to do so he had no need to look a whit less candid and charming than usual. I could feel in him how he already, from my at first finding nothing to reply, perceived the advantage he had gained. I was so slow to find anything that he had plenty of time, after a minute, to continue with his suggestive but inconclusive smile: 'You know, my dear, that for a fellow to be with a lady *always*——!' His 'my dear' was constantly on his lips for me, and nothing could have expressed more the exact shade of the sentiment with which I desired to inspire my pupils than its fond familiarity. It was so respectfully easy.

But oh, how I felt that at present I must pick my own phrases! I remember that, to gain time, I tried to laugh, and I seemed to see in the beautiful face with which he watched me how ugly and queer I looked. 'And always with the same lady?' I returned.

He neither blenched nor winked. The whole thing was virtually out between us. 'Ah, of course she's a jolly "perfect" lady; but after all I'm a fellow, don't you see? who's—well, getting on.'

I lingered there with him an instant ever so kindly. 'Yes, you're getting on.' Oh, but I felt helpless!

I have kept to this day the heartbreaking little idea of how he seemed to know that and to play with it. 'And you can't say I've not been awfully good, can you?'

I laid my hand on his shoulder, for though I felt how much better it would have been to walk on, I was not yet quite able. 'No, I can't say that, Miles.'

'Except just that one night, you know——!'

'That one night?' I couldn't look as straight as he.

'Why, when I went down—went out of the house.'

'Oh, yes. But I forget what you did it for.'

'You forget?'—he spoke with the sweet extravagance of childish reproach. 'Why, it was just to show you I could!'

'Oh, yes—you could.'

'And I can again.'

I felt I might perhaps after all succeed in keeping my wits about me. 'Certainly. But you won't.'

'No, not *that* again. It was nothing.'

'It was nothing,' I said. 'But we must go on.'

He resumed our walk with me, passing his hand into my arm. 'Then when *am* I going back?'

I wore, in turning it over, my most responsible air. 'Were you very happy at school?'

He just considered. 'Oh, I'm happy enough anywhere!'

'Well, then,' I quavered, 'if you're just as happy here——!'

'Ah, but that isn't everything! Of course *you* know a lot——'

'But you hint that you know almost as much?' I risked as he paused.

'Not half I want to!' Miles honestly professed. 'But it isn't so much that.'

'What is it, then?'

'Well—I want to see more life.'

'I see; I see.' We had arrived within sight of the church and of various persons, including several of the household of Ely, on their way to it and clustered about the door to see us go in. I quickened our step; I wanted to get there before the question between us opened up much further; I reflected hungrily that he would have for more than an hour to be silent; and I thought with envy of the comparative dusk of the pew and of the almost spiritual help of the hassock on which I might bend my knees. I seemed literally to be running a race with some confusion to which he was about to reduce me, but I felt he had got in first when, before we had entered the churchyard, he threw out:

'I want my own sort!'

It literally made me bound forward. 'There aren't many of your own sort, Miles!' I laughed. 'Unless perhaps dear little Flora!'

'You really compare me to a baby girl?'

This found me singularly weak. 'Don't you then *love* our sweet Flora?'

'If I didn't—and you too; if I didn't——!' he

repeated as if retreating for a jump, yet leaving his thought so unfinished that, after we had come into the gate, another stop, which he imposed on me by the pressure of his arm, had become inevitable. Mrs. Grose and Flora had passed into the church, the other worshippers had followed and we were, for the minute, alone among the old, thick graves. We had paused, on the path from the gate, by a low, oblong, table-like tomb.

'Yes, if you didn't——?'

He looked, while I waited, about at the graves. 'Well, you know what!' But he didn't move, and he presently produced something that made me drop straight down on the stone slab as if suddenly to rest. 'Does my uncle think what *you* think?'

I markedly rested. 'How do you know what I think?'

'Ah, well, of course I don't; for it strikes me you never tell me. But I mean does *he* know?'

'Know what, Miles?'

'Why, the way I'm going on.'

I recognized quickly enough that I could make, to this inquiry, no answer that wouldn't involve something of a sacrifice of my employer. Yet it struck me that we were all, at Bly, sufficiently sacrificed to make that venial. 'I don't think your uncle much cares.'

Miles, on this, stood looking at me. 'Then don't you think he can be made to?'

'In what way?'

'Why, by his coming down.'

'But who'll get him to come down?'

'*I* will!' the boy said with extraordinary brightness and emphasis. He gave me another look charged with that expression and then marched off alone into church.

XV

THE business was practically settled from the moment I never followed him. It was a pitiful surrender to agitation, but my being aware of this had somehow no power to restore me. I only sat there on my tomb and read into what our young friend had said to me the fullness of its meaning; by the time I had grasped the whole of which I had also embraced, for absence, the pretext that I was ashamed to offer my pupils and the rest of the congregation such an example of delay. What I said to myself, above all, was that Miles had got something out of me and that the gauge of it for him would be just this awkward collapse. He had got out of me that there was something I was much afraid of, and that he should probably be able to make use of my fear to gain, for his own purpose, more freedom. My fear was of having to deal with the intolerable question of the grounds of his dismissal from school, since that was really but the question of the horrors gathered behind. That his uncle should arrive to treat with me of these things was a solution that, strictly speaking, I ought now to have desired to bring on; but I could so little face the ugliness and the pain of it that I simply procrastinated and lived from hand to mouth. The boy, to my deep discomposure, was immensely in the right, was in a position to say to me: 'Either you clear up with my guardian the mystery of this interruption of my studies, or you

cease to expect me to lead with you a life that 's so
unnatural for a boy.' What was so unnatural for
the particular boy I was concerned with was this
sudden revelation of a consciousness and a plan.

That was what really overcame me, what prevented my going in. I walked round the church,
hesitating, hovering; I reflected that I had already,
with him, hurt myself beyond repair. Therefore
I could patch up nothing and it was too extreme
an effort to squeeze beside him into the pew: he
would be so much more sure than ever to pass his
arm into mine and make me sit there for an hour
in close silent contact with his commentary on our
talk. For the first minute since his arrival I wanted
to get away from him. As I paused beneath the high
east window and listened to the sounds of worship
I was taken with an impulse that might master me,
I felt, and completely, should I give it the least
encouragement. I might easily put an end to my
ordeal by getting away altogether. Here was my
chance; there was no one to stop me; I could give the
whole thing up—turn my back and bolt. It was
only a question of hurrying again, for a few prepara-
tions, to the house which the attendance at church
of so many of the servants would practically have
left unoccupied. No one, in short, could blame me
if I should just drive desperately off. What was it
to get away if I should get away only till dinner?
That would be in a couple of hours, at the end of
which—I had the acute prevision—my little pupils
would play at innocent wonder about my non-
appearance in their train.

'What *did* you do, you naughty bad thing? Why
in the world, to worry us so—and take our thoughts

off too, don't you know?—did you desert us at
the very door?' I couldn't meet such questions
nor, as they asked them, their false little lovely
eyes; yet it was all so exactly what I should have to
meet that, as the prospect grew sharp to me, I at
last let myself go.

I got, so far as the immediate moment was concerned, away; I came straight out of the churchyard
and, thinking hard, retraced my steps through the
park. It seemed to me that by the time I reached
the house I had made up my mind to cynical flight.
The Sunday stillness both of the approaches and of
the interior, in which I met no one, fairly stirred
me with a sense of opportunity. Were I to get off
quickly this way I should get off without a scene,
without a word. My quickness would have to be
remarkable, however, and the question of a conveyance was the great one to settle. Tormented, in
the hall, with difficulties and obstacles, I remember
sinking down at the foot of the staircase—suddenly
collapsing there on the lowest step and then, with
a revulsion, recalling that it was exactly where, more
than a month before, in the darkness of night and
just so bowed with evil things, I had seen the spectre
of the most horrible of women. At this I was able
to straighten myself; I went the rest of the way
up; I made, in my turmoil, for the schoolroom, where
there were objects belonging to me that I should
have to take. But I opened the door to find again,
in a flash, my eyes unsealed. In the presence of
what I saw I reeled straight back upon resistance.

Seated at my own table in the clear noonday
light I saw a person whom, without my previous
experience, I should have taken at the first blush

for some housemaid who might have stayed at home to look after the place and who, availing herself of rare relief from observation and of the schoolroom table and my pens, ink, and paper, had applied herself to the considerable effort of a letter to her sweetheart. There was an effort in the way that, while her arms rested on the table, her hands, with evident weariness, supported her head; but at the moment I took this in I had already become aware that, in spite of my entrance, her attitude strangely persisted. Then it was—with the very act of its announcing itself—that her identity flared up in a change of posture. She rose, not as if she had heard me, but with an indescribable grand melancholy of indifference and detachment, and, within a dozen feet of me, stood there as my vile predecessor. Dishonoured and tragic, she was all before me; but even as I fixed and, for memory, secured it, the awful image passed away. Dark as midnight in her dark dress, her haggard beauty and her unutterable woe, she had looked at me long enough to appear to say that her right to sit at my table was as good as mine to sit at hers. While these instants lasted indeed I had the extraordinary chill of a feeling that it was I who was the intruder. It was as a wild protest against it that, actually addressing her— 'You terrible, miserable woman!'—I heard myself break into a sound that, by the open door, rang through the long passage and the empty house. She looked at me as if she heard me, but I had recovered myself and cleared the air. There was nothing in the room the next minute but the sunshine and the sense that I must stay.

XVI

I HAD so perfectly expected the return of the others
to be marked by a demonstration that I was freshly
upset at having to find them merely dumb and
discreet about my desertion. Instead of gaily de-
nouncing and caressing me they made no allusion
to my having failed them, and I was left, for the
time, on perceiving that she too said nothing, to study
Mrs. Grose's odd face. I did this to such purpose
that I made sure they had in some way bribed her
to silence; a silence that, however, I would engage
to break down on the first private opportunity.
This opportunity came before tea: I secured five
minutes with her in the housekeeper's room, where,
in the twilight, amid a smell of lately-baked bread,
but with the place all swept and garnished, I found
her sitting in pained placidity before the fire. So
I see her still, so I see her best: facing the flame
from her straight chair in the dusky, shining room,
a large, clean picture of the 'put away'—of drawers
closed and locked and rest without a remedy.

'Oh, yes, they asked me to say nothing; and to
please them—so long as they were there—of course
I promised. But what had happened to you?'

'I only went with you for the walk,' I said. 'I had
then to come back to meet a friend.'

She showed her surprise. 'A friend—*you*?'

'Oh, yes, I've a couple!' I laughed. 'But did
the children give you a reason?'

'For not alluding to your leaving us? Yes; they said you 'd like it better. *Do* you like it better?'

My face had made her rueful. 'No, I like it worse!' But after an instant I added: 'Did they say why I should like it better?'

'No; Master Miles only said, "We must do nothing but what she likes"!'

'I wish indeed he would! And what did Flora say?'

'Miss Flora was too sweet. She said, "Oh, of course, of course!"—and I said the same.'

I thought a moment. 'You were too sweet, too —I can hear you all. But none the less, between Miles and me, it 's now all out.'

'All out?' My companion stared. 'But what, miss?'

'Everything. It doesn't matter. I 've made up my mind. I came home, my dear,' I went on, 'for a talk with Miss Jessel.'

I had by this time formed the habit of having Mrs. Grose literally well in hand in advance of my sounding that note; so that even now, as she bravely blinked under the signal of my word, I could keep her comparatively firm. 'A talk! Do you mean she spoke?'

'It came to that. I found her, on my return, in the schoolroom.'

'And what did she say?' I can hear the good woman still, and the candour of her stupefaction. 'That she suffers the torments——!'

It was this, of a truth, that made her, as she filled out my picture, gape. 'Do you mean,' she faltered '—of the lost?'

'Of the lost. Of the damned. And that 's why,

to share them——' I faltered myself with the horror of it.

But my companion, with less imagination, kept me up. 'To share them——?'

'She wants Flora.' Mrs. Grose might, as I gave it to her, fairly have fallen away from me had I not been prepared. I still held her there, to show I was. 'As I 've told you, however, it doesn't matter.'

'Because you 've made up your mind? But to what?'

'To everything.'

'And what do you call "everything"?'

'Why, to sending for their uncle.'

'Oh, miss, in pity do,' my friend broke out.

'Ah, but I will, I *will*! I see it 's the only way. What 's "out," as I told you, with Miles is that if he thinks I 'm afraid to—and has ideas of what he gains by that—he shall see he 's mistaken. Yes, yes; his uncle shall have it here from me on the spot (and before the boy himself if necessary) that if I 'm to be reproached with having done nothing again about more school——'

'Yes, miss——' my companion pressed me.

'Well, there 's that awful reason.'

There were now clearly so many of these for my poor colleague that she was excusable for being vague. 'But—a—which?'

'Why, the letter from his old place.'

'You 'll show it to the master?'

'I ought to have done so on the instant.'

'Oh, no!' said Mrs. Grose with decision.

'I 'll put it before him,' I went on inexorably, 'that I can't undertake to work the question on behalf of a child who has been expelled——'

'For we 've never in the least known what!' Mrs. Grose declared.

'For wickedness. For what else—when he 's so clever and beautiful and perfect? Is he stupid? Is he untidy? Is he infirm? Is he ill-natured? He 's exquisite—so it can be only *that*; and that would open up the whole thing. After all,' I said, 'it 's their uncle's fault. If he left here such people——!'

'He didn't really in the least know them. The fault's mine.' She had turned quite pale.

'Well, you shan't suffer,' I answered.

'The children shan't!' she emphatically returned.

I was silent awhile; we looked at each other. 'Then what am I to tell him?'

'You needn't tell him anything. *I 'll* tell him.'

I measured this. 'Do you mean you 'll write——?' Remembering she couldn't, I caught myself up. 'How do you communicate?'

'I tell the bailiff. *He* writes.'

'And should you like him to write our story?'

My question had a sarcastic force that I had not fully intended, and it made her after a moment inconsequently break down. The tears were again in her eyes. 'Ah, miss, *you* write!'

'Well—to-night,' I at last returned; and on this we separated.

XVII

I WENT so far, in the evening, as to make a beginning.
The weather had changed back, a great wind was
abroad, and beneath the lamp, in my room, with
Flora at peace beside me, I sat for a long time
before a blank sheet of paper and listened to the
lash of the rain and the batter of the gusts.   Finally
I went out, taking a candle; I crossed the passage
and listened a minute at Miles's door.   What, under
my endless obsession, I had been impelled to listen
for was some betrayal of his not being at rest, and
I presently caught one, but not in the form I had
expected.   His voice tinkled out.   'I say, you there
—come in.'   It was gaiety in the gloom!

I went in with my light and found him in bed,
very wide awake but very much at his ease.   'Well,
what are *you* up to?' he asked with a grace of
sociability in which it occurred to me that Mrs.
Grose, had she been present, might have looked in
vain for proof that anything was 'out.'

I stood over him with my candle.   'How did you
know I was there?'

'Why, of course, I heard you.   Did you fancy
you made no noise?   You 're like a troop of cavalry!'
he beautifully laughed.

'Then you weren't asleep?'

'Not much!   I lie awake and think.'

I had put my candle, designedly, a short way
off, and then, as he held out his friendly old hand

to me, had sat down on the edge of his bed. 'What is it,' I asked, 'that you think of?'

'What in the world, my dear, but *you*?'

'Ah, the pride I take in your appreciation doesn't insist on that! I had so far rather you slept.'

'Well, I think also, you know, of this queer business of ours.'

I marked the coolness of his firm little hand. 'Of what queer business, Miles?'

'Why, the way you bring me up. And all the rest!'

I fairly held my breath a minute, and even from my glimmering taper there was light enough to show how he smiled up at me from his pillow. 'What do you mean by all the rest?'

'Oh, you know, you know!'

I could say nothing for a minute, though I felt as I held his hand and our eyes continued to meet that my silence had all the air of admitting his charge and that nothing in the whole world of reality was perhaps at that moment so fabulous as our actual relation. 'Certainly you shall go back to school,' I said, 'if it be that that troubles you. But not to the old place—we must find another, a better. How could I know it did trouble you, this question, when you never told me so, never spoke of it at all?' His clear listening face, framed in its smooth whiteness, made him for the minute as appealing as some wistful patient in a children's hospital; and I would have given, as the resemblance came to me, all I possessed on earth really to be the nurse or the sister of charity who might have helped to cure him. Well, even as it was I perhaps might help! 'Do you know you've never

said a word to me about your school—I mean the
old one; never mentioned it in any way?'

He seemed to wonder; he smiled with the same
loveliness. But he clearly gained time; he waited,
he called for guidance. 'Haven't I?' It wasn't
for *me* to help him—it was for the thing I had met!
Something in his tone and the expression of his
face, as I got this from him, set my heart aching
with such a pang as it had never yet known; so
unutterably touching was it to see his little brain
puzzled and his little resources taxed to play, under
the spell laid on him, a part of innocence and consistency. 'No, never—from the hour you came
back. You 've never mentioned to me one of your
masters, one of your comrades, nor the least little
thing that ever happened to you at school. Never,
little Miles — no, never — have you given me an
inkling of anything that *may* have happened there.
Therefore you can fancy how much I 'm in the dark.
Until you came out, that way, this morning, you
had since the first hour I saw you scarce even made
a reference to anything in your previous life. You
seemed so perfectly to accept the present.' It was
extraordinary how my absolute conviction of his
secret precocity—or whatever I might call the poison
of an influence that I dared but half-phrase—made
him, in spite of the faint breath of his inward trouble,
appear as accessible as an older person, forced me
to treat him as an intelligent equal. 'I thought you
wanted to go on as you are.'

It struck me that at this he just faintly coloured.
He gave, at any rate, like a convalescent slightly
fatigued, a languid shake of his head. 'I don't—
I don't. I want to get away.'

'You 're tired of Bly?'

'Oh, no, I like Bly.'

'Well, then——?'

'Oh, *you* know what a boy wants!'

I felt I didn't know so well as Miles, and I took temporary refuge. 'You want to go to your uncle?'

Again, at this, with his sweet ironic face, he made a movement on the pillow. 'Ah, you can't get off with that!'

I was silent a little, and it was I now, I think, who changed colour. 'My dear, I don't want to get off!'

'You can't even if you do. You can't, you can't!'—he lay beautifully staring. 'My uncle must come down and you must completely settle things.'

'If we do,' I returned with some spirit, 'you may be sure it will be to take you quite away.'

'Well, don't you understand that that 's exactly what I 'm working for? You 'll have to *tell* him— about the way you 've let it all drop: you 'll have to tell him a tremendous lot!'

The exultation with which he uttered this helped me somehow for the instant to meet him rather more. 'And how much will *you*, Miles, have to tell him? There are things he 'll ask you!'

He turned it over. 'Very likely. But what things?'

'The things you 've never told me. To make up his mind what to do with you. He can't send you back——'

'I don't want to go back!' he broke in. 'I want a new field.'

He said it with admirable serenity, with positive, unimpeachable gaiety; and doubtless it was that very note that most evoked for me the poignancy, the unnatural childish tragedy, of his probable reappearance at the end of three months with all this bravado and still more dishonour. It overwhelmed me now that I should never be able to bear that, and it made me let myself go. I threw myself upon him and in the tenderness of my pity I embraced him. 'Dear little Miles, dear little Miles——!'

My face was close to his, and he let me kiss him, simply taking it with indulgent good-humour. 'Well, old lady?'

'Is there nothing—nothing at all that you want to tell me?'

He turned off a little, facing round toward the wall and holding up his hand to look at as one had seen sick children look. 'I've told you—I told you this morning.'

Oh, I was sorry for him! 'That you just want me not to worry you?'

He looked round at me now as if in recognition of my understanding him; then ever so gently, 'To let me alone,' he replied.

There was even a strange little dignity in it, something that made me release him, yet, when I had slowly risen, linger beside him. God knows *I* never wished to harass him, but I felt that merely, at this, to turn my back on him was to abandon or, to put it more truly, to lose him. 'I've just begun a letter to your uncle,' I said.

'Well, then, finish it!'

I waited a minute. 'What happened before?'

He gazed up at me again. 'Before what?'

'Before you came back. And before you went away.'

For some time he was silent, but he continued to meet my eyes. 'What happened?'

It made me, the sound of the words, in which it seemed to me I caught for the very first time a small faint quaver of consenting consciousness —it made me drop to my knees beside the bed and seize once more the chance of possessing him. 'Dear little Miles, dear little Miles, if you *knew* how I want to help you! It 's only that, it 's nothing but that, and I 'd rather die than give you a pain or do you a wrong—I 'd rather die than hurt a hair of you. Dear little Miles'—oh I brought it out now even if I *should* go too far—'I just want you to help me to save you!' But I knew in a moment after this that I had gone too far. The answer to my appeal was instantaneous, but it came in the form of an extraordinary blast and chill, a gust of frozen air and a shake of the room as great as if, in the wild wind, the casement had crashed in. The boy gave a loud, high shriek which, lost in the rest of the shock of sound, might have seemed, indistinctly, though I was so close to him, a note either of jubilation or of terror. I jumped to my feet again and was conscious of darkness. So for a moment we remained, while I stared about me and saw the drawn curtains unstirred and the window tight. 'Why, the candle 's out!' I then cried.

'It was I who blew it, dear!' said Miles.

XVIII

THE next day, after lessons, Mrs. Grose found a moment to say to me quietly: 'Have you written, miss?'

'Yes—I 've written.' But I didn't add—for the hour—that my letter, sealed and directed, was still in my pocket. There would be time enough to send it before the messenger should go to the village. Meanwhile there had been on the part of my pupils no more brilliant, more exemplary morning. It was exactly as if they had both had at heart to gloss over any recent little friction. They performed the dizziest feats of arithmetic, soaring quite out of *my* feeble range, and perpetrated, in higher spirits than ever, geographical and historical jokes. It was conspicuous of course in Miles in particular that he appeared to wish to show how easily he could let me down. This child, to my memory, really lives in a setting of beauty and misery that no words can translate; there was a distinction all his own in every impulse he revealed; never was a small natural creature, to the uninformed eye all frankness and freedom, a more ingenious, a more extraordinary little gentleman. I had perpetually to guard against the wonder of contemplation into which my initiated view betrayed me; to check the irrelevant gaze and discouraged sigh in which I constantly both attacked and renounced the enigma of what such a little gentleman could have done that deserved a penalty. Say that, by the dark prodigy I knew, the imagination of all evil *had* been opened up to him: all the justice within me ached for the proof that it could ever have flowered into an act.

He had never at any rate been such a little gentleman as when, after our early dinner on this dreadful day, he came round to me and asked if I shouldn't like him for half an hour to play to me. David playing to Saul could never have shown a finer sense of the occasion. It was literally a charming exhibition of tact, of magnanimity, and quite tantamount to his saying outright: 'The true knights we love to read about never push an advantage too far. I know what you mean now: you mean that—to be let alone yourself and not followed up—you'll cease to worry and spy upon me, won't keep me so close to you, will let me go and come. Well, I "come," you see—but I don't go! There'll be plenty of time for that. I do really delight in your society and I only want to show you that I contended for a principle.' It may be imagined whether I resisted this appeal or failed to accompany him again, hand in hand, to the schoolroom. He sat down at the old piano and played as he had never played; and if there are those who think he had better have been kicking a football I can only say that I wholly agree with them. For at the end of a time that under his influence I had quite ceased to measure I started up with a strange sense of having literally slept at my post. It was after luncheon, and by the schoolroom fire, and yet I hadn't really in the least slept; I had only done something much worse—I had forgotten. Where all this time was Flora? When I put the question to Miles he played on a minute before answering, and then could only say: 'Why, my dear, how do *I* know?'—breaking moreover into a happy laugh which immediately after, as if it were a vocal accompaniment, he prolonged into incoherent, extravagant song.

I went straight to my room, but his sister was not there; then, before going downstairs, I looked into several others. As she was nowhere about she would surely be with Mrs. Grose, whom in the comfort of that theory I accordingly proceeded in quest of. I found her where I had found her the evening before, but she met my quick challenge with blank scared ignorance. She had only supposed that, after the repast, I had carried off both the children; as to which she was quite in her right, for it was the very first time I had allowed the little girl out of my sight without some special provision. Of course now indeed she might be with the maids, so that the immediate thing was to look for her without an air of alarm. This we promptly arranged between us; but when, ten minutes later and in pursuance of our arrangement, we met in the hall, it was only to report on either side that after guarded inquiries we had altogether failed to trace her. For a minute there, apart from observation, we exchanged mute alarms, and I could feel with what high interest my friend returned me all those I had from the first given her.

'She 'll be above,' she presently said—'in one of the rooms you haven't searched.'

'No; she 's at a distance.' I had made up my mind. 'She has gone out.'

Mrs. Grose stared. 'Without a hat!'

I naturally also looked volumes. 'Isn't that woman always without one?'

'She's with *her*?'

'She's with *her*!' I declared. 'We must find them.'

My hand was on my friend's arm, but she failed for the moment, confronted with such an account of the matter, to respond to my pressure. She communed on the contrary, where she stood, with her uneasiness. 'And where's Master Miles?'

'Oh, *he*'s with Quint. They'll be in the schoolroom.'

'Lord, miss!' My view, I was myself aware—and therefore I suppose my tone—had never yet reached so calm an assurance.

'The trick's played,' I went on; 'they've successfully worked their plan. He found the most divine little way to keep me quiet while she went off.'

'"Divine"?' Mrs. Grose bewilderedly echoed.

'Infernal, then!' I almost cheerfully rejoined. 'He has provided for himself as well. But come!'

She had helplessly gloomed at the upper regions. 'You leave him——?'

'So long with Quint? Yes—I don't mind that now.'

She always ended at these moments by getting possession of my hand, and in this manner she could at present still stay me. But after gasping an instant at my sudden resignation, 'Because of your letter?' she eagerly brought out.

I quickly, by way of answer, felt for my letter, drew it forth, held it up, and then, freeing myself, went and laid it on the great hall-table. 'Luke

will take it,' I said as I came back. I reached
the house-door and opened it; I was already on
the steps.

My companion still demurred: the storm of the
night and the early morning had dropped, but
the afternoon was damp and grey. I came down
to the drive while she stood in the doorway. 'You
go with nothing on?'

'What do I care when the child has nothing?
I can't wait to dress,' I cried, 'and if you must do
so I leave you. Try meanwhile yourself upstairs.'

'With *them*?' Oh, on this the poor woman
promptly joined me!

XIX

WE went straight to the lake, as it was called at
Bly, and I dare say rightly called, though it may
have been a sheet of water less remarkable than
my untravelled eyes supposed it. My acquaintance
with sheets of water was small, and the pool of
Bly, at all events on the few occasions of my consenting, under the protection of my pupils, to affront
its surface in the old flat-bottomed boat moored
there for our use, had impressed me both with its
extent and its agitation. The usual place of em-
barkation was half a mile from the house, but I
had an intimate conviction that, wherever Flora
might be, she was not near home. She had not
given me the slip for any small adventure, and,
since the day of the very great one that I had shared
with her by the pond, I had been aware, in our
walks, of the quarter to which she most inclined.
This was why I had now given to Mrs. Grose's
steps so marked a direction—a direction making
her, when she perceived it, oppose a resistance that
showed me she was freshly mystified. 'You 're
going to the water, miss?——you think she 's *in*——?'

'She may be, though the depth is, I believe,
nowhere very great. But what I judge most likely
is that she 's on the spot from which, the other
day, we saw together what I told you.'

'When she pretended not to see——?'

'With that astounding self-possession! I've always been sure she wanted to go back alone. And now her brother has managed it for her.'

Mrs. Grose still stood where she had stopped. 'You suppose they really *talk* of them?'

I could meet this with an assurance! 'They say things that, if we heard them, would simply appal us.'

'And if she *is* there——?'

'Yes?'

'Then Miss Jessel is?'

'Beyond a doubt. You shall see.'

'Oh, thank you!' my friend cried, planted so firm that, taking it in, I went straight on without her. By the time I reached the pool, however, she was close behind me, and I knew that, whatever, to her apprehension, might befall me, the exposure of sticking to me struck her as her least danger. She exhaled a moan of relief as we at last came in sight of the greater part of the water without a sight of the child. There was no trace of Flora on that nearer side of the bank where my observation of her had been most startling, and none on the opposite edge, where, save for a margin of some twenty yards, a thick copse came down to the water. This expanse, oblong in shape, was so narrow compared to its length that, with its ends out of view, it might have been taken for a scant river. We looked at the empty stretch, and then I felt the suggestion in my friend's eyes. I knew what she meant and I replied with a negative headshake.

'No, no; wait! She has taken the boat.'

My companion stared at the vacant mooring-place and then again across the lake. 'Then where is it?'

'Our not seeing it is the strongest of proofs. She has used it to go over, and then has managed to hide it.'

'All alone—that child?'

'She's not alone, and at such times she's not a child: she's an old, old woman.' I scanned all the visible shore while Mrs. Grose took again, into the queer element I offered her, one of her plunges of submission; then I pointed out that the boat might perfectly be in a small refuge formed by one of the recesses of the pool, an indentation masked, for the hither side, by a projection of the bank and by a clump of trees growing close to the water.

'But if the boat's there, where on earth's *she*?' my colleague anxiously asked.

'That's exactly what we must learn.' And I started to walk further.

'By going all the way round?'

'Certainly, far as it is. It will take us but ten minutes, yet it's far enough to have made the child prefer not to walk. She went straight over.'

'Laws!' cried my friend again; the chain of my logic was ever too strong for her. It dragged her at my heels even now, and when we had got half-way round—a devious tiresome process, on ground much broken and by a path choked with over-growth—I paused to give her breath. I sustained her with a grateful arm, assuring her that she might hugely help me; and this started us afresh, so that in the course of but few minutes more we reached a point from which we found the boat to be where

I had supposed it. It had been intentionally left as much as possible out of sight and was tied to one of the stakes of a fence that came, just there, down to the brink and that had been an assistance to disembarking. I recognized, as I looked at the pair of short, thick oars, quite safely drawn up, the prodigious character of the feat for a little girl; but I had by this time lived too long among wonders and had panted to too many livelier measures. There was a gate in the fence, through which we passed, and that brought us after a trifling interval more into the open. Then 'There she is!' we both exclaimed at once.

Flora, a short way off, stood before us on the grass and smiled as if her performance had now become complete. The next thing she did, however, was to stoop straight down and pluck—quite as if it were all she was there for—a big, ugly spray of withered fern. I at once felt sure she had just come out of the copse. She waited for us, not herself taking a step, and I was conscious of the rare solemnity with which we presently approached her. She smiled and smiled, and we met; but it was all done in a silence by this time flagrantly ominous. Mrs. Grose was the first to break the spell: she threw herself on her knees and, drawing the child to her breast, clasped in a long embrace the little, tender, yielding body. While this dumb convulsion lasted I could only watch it—which I did the more intently when I saw Flora's face peep at me over our companion's shoulder. It was serious now—the flicker had left it; but it strengthened the pang with which I at that moment envied Mrs. Grose the simplicity of *her* relation. Still, all this while, nothing more passed between us save that Flora had let her foolish fern again drop to the ground. What she and I had virtually said to each other was that pretexts were useless now. When Mrs. Grose finally got up she kept the child's hand, so that the two were still before me; and the singular reticence of our communion was even more marked in the frank look she addressed me. 'I 'll be hanged,' it said, 'if *I 'll* speak!'

It was Flora who, gazing all over me in candid wonder, was the first. She was struck with our bare-headed aspect. 'Why, where are your things?'

'Where yours are, my dear!' I promptly returned.

She had already got back her gaiety and appeared to take this as an answer quite sufficient. 'And where 's Miles?' she went on.

There was something in the small valour of it that quite finished me: these three words from her were in a flash like the glitter of a drawn blade, the jostle of the cup that my hand for weeks and weeks had held high and full to the brim and that now, even before speaking, I felt overflow in a deluge. 'I 'll tell you if you 'll tell *me*——' I heard myself say, then heard the tremor in which it broke.

'Well, what?'

Mrs. Grose's suspense blazed at me, but it was too late now, and I brought the thing out handsomely. 'Where, my pet, is Miss Jessel?'

XX

JUST as in the churchyard with Miles, the whole thing was upon us. Much as I had made of the fact that this name had never once, between us, been sounded, the quick smitten glare with which the child's face now received it fairly likened my breach of the silence to the smash of a pane of glass. It added to the interposing cry, as if to stay the blow, that Mrs. Grose at the same instant uttered over my violence—the shriek of a creature scared, or rather wounded, which, in turn, within a few seconds, was completed by a gasp of my own. I seized my colleague's arm. 'She 's there, she 's there!'

Miss Jessel stood before us on the opposite bank exactly as she had stood the other time, and I remember, strangely, as the first feeling now produced in me, my thrill of joy at having brought on a proof. She was there, so I was justified; she was there, so I was neither cruel nor mad. She was there for poor scared Mrs. Grose, but she was there most for Flora and no moment of my monstrous time was perhaps so extraordinary as that in which I consciously threw out to her—with the sense that, pale and ravenous demon as she was, she would catch and understand it—an inarticulate message of gratitude. She rose erect on the spot my friend and I had lately quitted, and there wasn't in all the long reach of her desire an inch of her evil that fell short. This first vividness of vision and emotion were things of a few seconds, during which Mrs. Grose's dazed blink across to where I pointed struck me as showing that she too at last saw, just as it carried my own eyes precipitately to the child. The revelation then of the manner in which Flora was affected startled me in truth far more than it would have done to find her also merely agitated, for direct dismay was of course not what I had expected. Prepared and on her guard as our pursuit had actually made her, she would repress every betrayal; and I was therefore at once shaken by my first glimpse of the particular one for which I had not allowed. To see her, without a convulsion of her small pink face, not even feign to glance in the direction of the prodigy I announced, but only, instead of that, turn at *me* an expression of hard, still gravity, an expression absolutely new and unprecedented and that appeared to read and accuse and judge me—this was a stroke that somehow converted the little girl herself into a figure portentous. I gaped at her coolness even though my certitude of her thoroughly seeing was never greater than at that instant, and then, in the immediate need to defend myself, I called her passionately to witness. 'She's there, you little unhappy thing—there, there, *there*, and you know it as well as you know me!' I had said shortly before to Mrs. Grose that she was not at these times a child, but an old, old woman, and my description of her couldn't have been more strikingly confirmed than in the way in which, for all notice of this, she simply showed me, without an expressional concession or admission, a countenance of deeper

and deeper, of indeed suddenly quite fixed reproba-
tion. I was by this time—if I can put the whole
thing at all together—more appalled at what I
may properly call her manner than at anything
else, though it was quite simultaneously that I
became aware of having Mrs. Grose also, and very
formidably, to reckon with. My elder companion,
the next moment, at any rate, blotted out everything but her own flushed face and her loud shocked
protest, a burst of high disapproval. 'What a
dreadful turn, to be sure, miss! Where on earth
do you see anything?'

I could only grasp her more quickly yet, for even
while she spoke the hideous plain presence stood
undimmed and undaunted. It had already lasted
a minute, and it lasted while I continued, seizing
my colleague, quite thrusting her at it and presenting her to it, to insist with my pointing hand.
'You don't see her exactly as *we* see?—you mean
to say you don't now—*now*? She's as big as a
blazing fire! Only look, dearest woman, *look*——!'
She looked, just as I did, and gave me, with her
deep groan of negation, repulsion, compassion—the
mixture with her pity of her relief at her exemption
—a sense, touching to me even then, that she would
have backed me up if she had been able. I might
well have needed that, for with this hard blow of
the proof that her eyes were hopelessly sealed I
felt my own situation horribly crumble, I felt—I
saw—my livid predecessor press, from her position,
on my defeat, and I took the measure, more than
all, of what I should have from this instant to deal
with in the astounding little attitude of Flora.
Into this attitude Mrs. Grose immediately and

violently entered, breaking, even while there pierced through my sense of ruin a prodigious private triumph, into breathless reassurance.

'She isn't there, little lady, and nobody's there —and you never see nothing, my sweet! How can poor Miss Jessel—when poor Miss Jessel's dead and buried? *We* know, don't we, love?'—and she appealed, blundering in, to the child. 'It's all a mere mistake and a worry and a joke—and we'll go home as fast as we can!'

Our companion, on this, had responded with a strange quick primness of propriety, and they were again, with Mrs. Grose on her feet, united, as it were, in shocked opposition to me. Flora continued to fix me with her small mask of disaffection, and even at that minute I prayed God to forgive me for seeming to see that, as she stood there holding tight to our friend's dress, her incomparable childish beauty had suddenly failed, had quite vanished. I've said it already—she was literally, she was hideously hard; she had turned common and almost ugly. 'I don't know what you mean. I see nobody. I see nothing. I never *have*. I think you're cruel. I don't like you!' Then, after this deliverance, which might have been that of a vulgarly pert little girl in the street, she hugged Mrs. Grose more closely and buried in her skirts the dreadful little face. In this position she launched an almost furious wail. 'Take me away, take me away—oh, take me away from *her*!'

'From *me*?' I panted.

'From you—from you!' she cried.

Even Mrs. Grose looked across at me dismayed, while I had nothing to do but communicate again with the figure that on the opposite bank, without a movement, as rigidly still as if catching, beyond the interval, our voices, was as vividly there for my disaster as it was not there for my service. The wretched child had spoken exactly as if she had got from some outside source each of her stabbing little words, and I could therefore, in the full despair of all I had to accept, but sadly shake my head at her. 'If I had ever doubted all my doubt would at present have gone. I 've been living with the miserable truth, and now it has only too much closed round me. Of course I 've lost you: I 've interfered, and you 've seen, under *her* dictation'—with which I faced, over the pool again, our infernal witness—'the easy and perfect way to meet it. I 've done my best, but I 've lost you. Good-bye.' For Mrs. Grose I had an imperative, an almost frantic 'Go, go!' before which, in infinite distress, but mutely possessed of the little girl and clearly convinced, in spite of her blindness, that something awful had occurred and some collapse engulfed us she retreated, by the way we had come, as fast as she could move.

Of what first happened when I was left alone I had no subsequent memory. I only knew that at the end of, I suppose, a quarter of an hour, an odorous dampness and roughness, chilling and piercing my trouble, had made me understand that I must have thrown myself, on my face, to the ground and given way to a wildness of grief. I must have lain there long and cried and wailed, for when I raised my head the day was almost done. I got up and looked a moment, through the twilight, at the grey pool and its blank haunted

edge, and then I took, back to the house, my dreary
and difficult course. When I reached the gate in
the fence the boat, to my surprise, was gone, so
that I had a fresh reflection to make on Flora's
extraordinary command of the situation. She passed
that night, by the most tacit and, I should add,
were not the word so grotesque a false note, the
happiest of arrangements, with Mrs. Grose. I saw
neither of them on my return, but on the other
hand I saw, as by an ambiguous compensation,
a great deal of Miles. I saw—I can use no other
phrase—so much of him that it fairly measured
more than it had ever measured. No evening I
had passed at Bly was to have had the portentous
quality of this one; in spite of which—and in spite
also of the deeper depths of consternation that
had opened beneath my feet—there was literally,
in the ebbing actual, an extraordinarily sweet sad-
ness. On reaching the house I had never so much
as looked for the boy; I had simply gone straight
to my room to change what I was wearing and
to take in, at a glance, much material testimony
to Flora's rupture. Her little belongings had all
been removed. When later, by the schoolroom fire,
I was served with tea by the usual maid, I indulged,
on the article of my other pupil, in no inquiry
whatever. He had his freedom now—he might
have it to the end! Well, he did have it; and it
consisted—in part at least—of his coming in at
about eight o'clock and sitting down with me in
silence. On the removal of the tea-things I had
blown out the candles and drawn my chair closer:
I was conscious of a mortal coldness and felt as
if I should never again be warm. So when he

appeared I was sitting in the glow with my thoughts.
He paused a moment by the door as if to look at
me; then—as if to share them—came to the other
side of the hearth and sank into a chair. We sat
there in absolute stillness; yet he wanted, I felt,
to be with me.

XXI

BEFORE a new day, in my room, had fully broken, my eyes opened to Mrs. Grose, who had come to my bedside with worse news. Flora was so markedly feverish that an illness was perhaps at hand; she had passed a night of extreme unrest, a night agitated above all by fears that had for their subject not in the least her former but wholly her present governess. It was not against the possible re-entrance of Miss Jessel on the scene that she protested—it was conspicuously and passionately against mine. I was at once on my feet, and with an immense deal to ask; the more that my friend had discernibly now girded her loins to meet me afresh. This I felt as soon as I had put to her the question of her sense of the child's sincerity as against my own. 'She persists in denying to you that she saw, or has ever seen, anything?'

My visitor's trouble truly was great. 'Ah, miss, it isn't a matter on which I can push her. Yet it isn't either, I must say, as if I much needed to. It has made her, every inch of her, quite old.'

'Oh, I see her perfectly from here. She resents, for all the world like some high little personage, the imputation on her truthfulness and, as it were, her respectability. "Miss Jessel indeed—*she*!" Ah, she's "respectable," the chit! The impression she gave me there yesterday was, I assure you, the very strangest of all; it was quite beyond any of the others. I *did* put my foot in it! She 'll never speak to me again.'

Hideous and obscure as it all was, it held Mrs. Grose briefly silent; then she granted my point with a frankness which, I made sure, had more behind it. 'I think indeed, miss, she never will. She do have a grand manner about it!'

'And that manner' — I summed it up — 'is practically what 's the matter with her now.'

Oh, that manner. I could see in my visitor's face, and not a little else besides! 'She asks me every three minutes if I think you 're coming in.'

'I see—I see.' I too, on my side, had so much more than worked it out. 'Has she said to you since yesterday—except to repudiate her familiarity with anything so dreadful—a single other word about Miss Jessel?'

'Not one, miss. And of course, you know,' my friend added, 'I took it from her by the lake that just then and there at least there *was* nobody.'

'Rather! And naturally you take it from her still.'

'I don't contradict her. What else can I do?'

'Nothing in the world! You 've the cleverest little person to deal with. They 've made them —their two friends, I mean—still cleverer even than nature did; for it was wondrous materia to play on! Flora has now her grievance, and she 'll work it to the end.'

'Yes, miss; but to *what* end?'

'Why, that of dealing with me to her uncle. She 'll make me out to him the lowest creature——!'

I winced at the fair show of the scene in Mrs. Grose's face; she looked for a minute as if she

sharply saw them together. 'And him who thinks
so well of you!'

'He has an odd way—it comes over me now,'
I laughed, '—of proving it! But that doesn't
matter. What Flora wants of course is to get rid
of me.'

My companion bravely concurred. 'Never again
to so much as look at you.'

'So that what you've come to me now for,' I
asked, 'is to speed me on my way?' Before she
had time to reply, however, I had her in check.
'I've a better idea—the result of my reflections.
My going *would* seem the right thing, and on Sunday
I was terribly near it. Yet that won't do. It's
you who must go. You must take Flora.'

My visitor, at this, did speculate. 'But where in
the world——?'

'Away from here. Away from *them*. Away, even
most of all, now, from me. Straight to her uncle.'

'Only to tell on you——?'

'No, not "only"! To leave me, in addition,
with my remedy.'

She was still vague. 'And what *is* your remedy?'

'Your loyalty, to begin with. And then Miles's.'

She looked at me hard. 'Do you think he——?'

'Won't, if he has the chance, turn on me? Yes,
I venture still to think it. At all events I want to
try. Get off with his sister as soon as possible
and leave me with him alone.' I was amazed,
myself, at the spirit I had still in reserve, and therefore perhaps a trifle the more disconcerted at the
way in which, in spite of this fine example of it,
she hesitated. 'There's one thing, of course,' I
went on: 'they mustn't, before she goes, see each

other for three seconds.' Then it came over me that, in spite of Flora's presumable sequestration from the instant of her return from the pool, it might already be too late. 'Do you mean,' I anxiously asked, 'that they *have* met?'

At this she quite flushed. 'Ah, miss, I'm not such a fool as that. If I've been obliged to leave her three or four times, it has been each time with one of the maids, and at present, though she's alone, she's locked in safe. And yet—and yet!' There were too many things.

'And yet what?'

'Well, are you so sure of the little gentleman?'

'I'm not sure of anything but *you*. But I have, since last evening, a new hope. I think he wants to give me an opening. I do believe that—poor little exquisite wretch!—he wants to speak. Last evening, in the firelight and the silence, he sat with me for two hours as if it were just coming.'

Mrs. Grose looked hard through the window at the grey gathering day. 'And did it come?'

'No, though I waited and waited I confess it didn't, and it was without a breach of the silence, or so much as a faint allusion to his sister's condition and absence, that we at last kissed for good night. All the same,' I continued, 'I can't, if her uncle sees her, consent to his seeing her brother without my having given the boy—and most of all because things have got so bad—a little more time.'

My friend appeared on this ground more reluctant than I could quite understand. 'What do you mean by more time?'

'Well, a day or two—really to bring it out. He'll then be on *my* side—of which you see the importance.

If nothing comes I shall only fail, and you at the worst have helped me by doing on your arrival in town whatever you may have found possible.' So I put it before her, but she continued for a little so lost in other reasons that I came again to her aid. 'Unless indeed,' I wound up, 'you really want *not* to go.'

I could see it, in her face, at last clear itself; she put out her hand to me as a pledge. 'I 'll go—I 'll go. I 'll go this morning.'

I wanted to be very just. 'If you *should* wish still to wait I 'd engage she shouldn't see me.'

'No, no: it 's the place itself. She must leave it.' She held me a moment with heavy eyes, then brought out the rest. 'Your idea 's the right one. I myself, miss——'

'Well?'

'I can't stay.'

The look she gave me with it made me jump at possibilities. 'You mean that, since yesterday you *have* seen——?'

She shook her head with dignity. 'I 've *heard*——!'

'Heard?'

'From that child—horrors! There!' she sighed with tragic relief. 'On my honour, miss, she says things——!' But at this evocation she broke down; she dropped with a sudden cry upon my sofa and, as I had seen her do before, gave way to all the anguish of it.

It was in quite another manner that I for my part let myself go. 'Oh, thank God!'

She sprang up again at this, drying her eyes with a groan. '"Thank God"?'

'It so justifies me!'

'It does that, miss!'

I couldn't have desired more emphasis, but I just waited. 'She 's so horrible?'

I saw my colleague scarce knew how to put it. 'Really shocking.'

'And about me?'

'About you, miss—since you must have it. It 's beyond everything, for a young lady; and I can't think wherever she must have picked up——'

'The appalling language she applies to me? I can, then!' I broke in with a laugh that was doubtless significant enough.

It only in truth left my friend still more grave. 'Well, perhaps I ought to also—since I 've heard some of it before! Yet I can't bear it,' the poor woman went on while with the same movement she glanced, on my dressing-table, at the face of my watch. 'But I must go back.'

I kept her, however. 'Ah, if you can't bear it——!'

'How can I stop with her, you mean? Why, just *for* that: to get her away. Far from this,' she pursued, 'far from *them*——'

'She may be different? she may be free?' I seized her almost with joy. 'Then in spite of yesterday you *believe*——'

'In such doings?' Her simple description of them required, in the light of her expression, to be carried no further, and she gave me the whole thing as she had never done. 'I believe.'

Yes, it was a joy, and we were still shoulder to shoulder: if I might continue sure of that I should care but little what else happened. My support in the presence of disaster would be the same as it had been in my early need of confidence, and if my friend would answer for my honesty I would answer for all the rest. On the point of taking leave of her, none the less, I was to some extent embarrassed. 'There's one thing of course—it occurs to me—to remember. My letter, giving the alarm, will have reached town before you.'

I now felt still more how she had been beating about the bush and how weary at last it had made her. 'Your letter won't have got there. Your letter never went.'

'What then became of it?'

'Goodness knows! Master Miles——'

'Do you mean *he* took it?' I gasped.

She hung fire, but she overcame her reluctance. 'I mean that I saw yesterday, when I came back with Miss Flora, that it wasn't where you had put it. Later in the evening I had the chance to question Luke, and he declared that he had neither noticed nor touched it.' We could only exchange, on this, one of our deeper mutual soundings, and it was Mrs. Grose who first brought up the plumb with an almost elate 'You see!'

'Yes, I see that if Miles took it instead he probably will have read it and destroyed it.'

'And don't you see anything else?'

I faced her a moment with a sad smile. 'It strikes me that by this time your eyes are open even wider than mine.'

They proved to be so indeed, but she could still almost blush to show it. 'I make out now what he must have done at school.' And she gave, in her simple sharpness, an almost droll disillusioned nod. 'He stole!'

I turned it over—I tried to be more judicial. 'Well—perhaps.'

She looked as if she found me unexpectedly calm. 'He stole *letters*!'

She couldn't know my reasons for a calmness after all pretty shallow; so I showed them off as I might. 'I hope then it was to more purpose than in this case! The note, at all events, that I put on the table yesterday,' I pursued, 'will have given him so scant an advantage—for it contained only the bare demand for an interview—that he's already much ashamed of having gone so far for so little, and that what he had on his mind last evening was precisely the need of confession.' I seemed to myself for the instant to have mastered it, to see it all. 'Leave us, leave us'—I was already, at the door, hurrying her off. 'I'll get it out of him. He'll meet me. He'll confess. If he confesses he's saved. And if he's saved——'

'Then *you* are?' The dear woman kissed me on this, and I took her farewell. 'I'll save you without him!' she cried as she went.

XXII

YET it was when she had got off—and I missed her on the spot—that the great pinch really came. If I had counted on what it would give me to find myself alone with Miles I quickly recognized that it would give me at least a measure. No hour of my stay in fact was so assailed with apprehensions as that of my coming down to learn that the carriage containing Mrs. Grose and my younger pupil had already rolled out of the gates. Now I *was*, I said to myself, face to face with the elements, and for much of the rest of the day, while I fought my weakness, I could consider that I had been supremely rash. It was a tighter place still than I had yet turned round in; all the more that, for the first time, I could see in the aspect of others a confused reflection of the crisis. What had happened naturally caused them all to stare; there was too little of the explained, throw out whatever we might, in the suddenness of my colleague's act. The maids and the men looked blank; the effect of which on my nerves was an aggravation until I saw the necessity of making it a positive aid. It was in short by just clutching the helm that I avoided total wreck; and I dare say that, to bear up at all, I became that morning very grand and very dry. I welcomed the consciousness that I was charged with much to do, and I caused it to be known as well that, left thus to myself, I was quite remarkably firm. I wandered with that manner, for the next hour or two, all over the place and looked, I have no doubt, as if I were ready for any onset. So, for the benefit of whom it might concern, I paraded with a sick heart.

The person it appeared least to concern proved to be, till dinner, little Miles himself. My perambulations had given me meanwhile no glimpse of him, but they had tended to make more public the change taking place in our relation as a consequence of his having at the piano, the day before, kept me, in Flora's interest, so beguiled and befooled. The stamp of publicity had of course been fully given by her confinement and departure, and the change itself was now ushered in by our nonobservance of the regular custom of the schoolroom. He had already disappeared when, on my way down, I pushed open his door, and I learned below that he had breakfasted—in the presence of a couple of the maids—with Mrs. Grose and his sister. He had then gone out, as he said, for a stroll; than which nothing, I reflected, could better have expressed his frank view of the abrupt transformation of my office. What he would now permit this office to consist of was yet to be settled: there was at least a queer relief—I mean for myself in especial—in the renouncement of one pretension. If so much had sprung to the surface I scarce put it too strongly in saying that what had perhaps sprung highest was the absurdity of our prolonging the fiction that I had anything more to teach him. It sufficiently stuck out that, by tacit little tricks in which even more than myself he carried out the care for my dignity, I had had to appeal to

him to let me off straining to meet him on the
ground of his true capacity. He had at any rate
his freedom now; I was never to touch it again;
as I had amply shown, moreover, when, on his
joining me in the schoolroom the previous night,
I uttered, in reference to the interval just concluded,
neither challenge nor hint. I had too much, from
this moment, my other ideas. Yet when he at
last arrived the difficulty of applying them, the
accumulations of my problem, were brought straight
home to me by the beautiful little presence on
which what had occurred had as yet, for the eye,
dropped neither stain nor shadow.

To mark, for the house, the high state I cultivated
I decreed that my meals with the boy should be
served, as we called it, downstairs; so that I had
been awaiting him in the ponderous pomp of the
room outside the window of which I had had from
Mrs. Grose, that first scared Sunday, my flash of
something it would scarce have done to call light.
Here at present I felt afresh—for I had felt it again
and again—how my equilibrium depended on the
success of my rigid will, the will to shut my eyes
as tight as possible to the truth that what I had
to deal with was, revoltingly, against nature. I
could only get on at all by taking 'nature' into
my confidence and my account, by treating my
monstrous ordeal as a push in a direction unusual,
of course, and unpleasant, but demanding after
all, for a fair front, only another turn of the screw
of ordinary human virtue. No attempt, none the
less, could well require more tact than just this
attempt to supply, oneself, *all* the nature. How
could I put even a little of that article into a sup-

pression of reference to what had occurred? How
on the other hand could I make a reference without
a new plunge into the hideous obscure? Well,
a sort of answer, after a time, had come to me,
and it was so far confirmed as that I was met, incontestably, by the quickened vision of what was
rare in my little companion. It was, indeed, as if
he had found even now—as he had so often found
at lessons—still some other delicate way to ease
me off. Wasn't there light in the fact which, as
we shared our solitude, broke out with a specious
glitter it had never yet quite worn?—the fact that
(opportunity aiding, precious opportunity which had
now come) it would be preposterous, with a child
so endowed, to forgo the help one might wrest
from absolute intelligence? What had his intelligence been given him for but to save him? Mightn't
one, to reach his mind, risk the stretch of a stiff arm
across his character? It was as if, when we were
face to face in the dining-room, he had literally
shown me the way. The roast mutton was on the
table, and I had dispensed with attendance. Miles,
before he sat down, stood a moment with his hands
in his pockets and looked at the joint, on which
he seemed on the point of passing some humorous
judgment. But what he presently produced was:
'I say, my dear, is she really very awfully ill?'

'Little Flora? Not so bad but that she'll
presently be better. London will set her up.
Bly had ceased to agree with her. Come here and
take your mutton.'

He alertly obeyed me, carried the plate carefully
to his seat and, when he was established, went on.
'Did Bly disagree with her so terribly all at once?'

'Not so suddenly as you might think. One had seen it coming on.'

'Then why didn't you get her off before?'

'Before what?'

'Before she became too ill to travel.'

I found myself prompt. 'She's *not* too ill to travel: she only might have become so if she had stayed. This was just the moment to seize. The journey will dissipate the influence'—oh, I was grand!—'and carry it off.'

'I see, I see'—Miles, for that matter, was grand too. He settled to his repast with the charming little 'table manner' that, from the day of his arrival, had relieved me of all grossness of admonition. Whatever he had been expelled from school for, it wasn't for ugly feeding. He was irreproachable, as always, to-day; but was unmistakably more conscious. He was discernibly trying to take for granted more things than he found, without assistance, quite easy; and he dropped into peaceful silence while he felt his situation. Our meal was of the briefest—mine a vain pretence, and I had the things immediately removed. While this was done Miles stood again with his hands in his little pockets and his back to me—stood and looked out of the wide window through which, that other day, I had seen what pulled me up. We continued silent while the maid was with us— as silent, it whimsically occurred to me, as some young couple who, on their wedding-journey, at the inn, feel shy in the presence of the waiter. He turned round only when the waiter had left us. 'Well—so we're alone!'

XXIII

'Oh, more or less.' I imagine my smile was pale. 'Not absolutely. We shouldn't like that!' I went on.

'No—I suppose we shouldn't. Of course, we 've the others.'

'We 've the others—we 've, indeed, the others,' I concurred.

'Yet even though we have them,' he returned, still with his hands in his pockets and planted there in front of me, 'they don't much count, do they?'

I made the best of it, but I felt wan. 'It depends on what you call "much"!'

'Yes'—with all accommodation—'everything depends!' On this, however, he faced to the window again and presently reached it with his vague, restless, cogitating step. He remained there awhile with his forehead against the glass, in contemplation of the stupid shrubs I knew and the dull things of November. I had always my hypocrisy of 'work,' behind which I now gained the sofa. Steadying myself with it there as I had repeatedly done at those moments of torment that I have described as the moments of my knowing the children to be given to something from which I was barred, I sufficiently obeyed my habit of being prepared for the worst. But an extraordinary impression dropped on me as I extracted a meaning from the boy's embarrassed back—none other than the impression that I was not barred now. This inference grew

in a few minutes to sharp intensity and seemed
bound up with the direct perception that it was
positively *he* who was. The frames and squares
of the great window were a kind of image, for him,
of a kind of failure. I felt that I saw him, in any
case, shut in or shut out. He was admirable but
not comfortable: I took it in with a throb of hope.
Wasn't he looking through the haunted pane for
something he couldn't see?—and wasn't it the first
time in the whole business that he had known such
a lapse? The first, the very first: I found it a
splendid portent. It made him anxious, though he
watched himself; he had been anxious all day and,
even while in his usual sweet little manner he sat
at table, had needed all his small strange genius
to give it a gloss. When he at last turned round
to meet me it was almost as if this genius had
succumbed. 'Well, I think I'm glad Bly agrees
with me!'

'You'd certainly seemed to have seen, these
twenty-four hours, a good deal more of it than
for some time before. I hope,' I went on bravely,
'that you've been enjoying yourself.'

'Oh, yes, I've been ever so far; all round about—
miles and miles away. I've never been so free.'

He had really a manner of his own, and I could
only try to keep up with him. 'Well, do you like it?'

He stood there smiling; then at last he put into
two words—'Do *you*?'—more discrimination than
I had ever heard two words contain. Before I had
time to deal with that, however, he continued as
if with the sense that this was an impertinence to
be softened. 'Nothing could be more charming
than the way you take it, for of course if we're

alone together now it's you that are alone most.
But I hope,' he threw in, 'you don't particularly
mind!'

'Having to do with you?' I asked. 'My dear
child, how can I help minding? Though I've renounced all claim to your company—you're so
beyond me—I at least greatly enjoy it. What else
should I stay on for?'

He looked at me more directly, and the expression
of his face, graver now, struck me as the most
beautiful I had ever found in it. 'You stay on
just for *that*?'

'Certainly. I stay on as your friend and from
the tremendous interest I take in you till something
can be done for you that may be more worth your
while. That needn't surprise you.' My voice trembled so that I felt it impossible to suppress the
shake. 'Don't you remember how I told you,
when I came and sat on your bed the night of the
storm, that there was nothing in the world I wouldn't
do for you?'

'Yes, yes!' He, on his side, more and more
visibly nervous, had a tone to master; but he was
so much more successful than I that, laughing out
through his gravity, he could pretend we were
pleasantly jesting. 'Only that, I think, was to get
me to do something for *you*!'

'It was partly to get you to do something,' I
conceded. 'But, you know, you didn't do it.'

'Oh, yes,' he said with the brightest superficial
eagerness, 'you wanted me to tell you something.'

'That's it. Out, straight out. What you have
on your mind, you know.'

'Ah, then is *that* what you've stayed over for?'

He spoke with a gaiety through which I could still catch the finest little quiver of resentful passion; but I can't begin to express the effect upon me of an implication of surrender even so faint. It was as if what I had yearned for had come at last only to astonish me. 'Well, yes—I may as well make a clean breast of it. It was precisely for that.'

He waited so long that I supposed it for the purpose of repudiating the assumption on which my action had been founded; but what he finally said was: 'Do you mean now—here?'

'There couldn't be a better place or time.' He looked round him uneasily, and I had the rare—oh, the queer!—impression of the very first symptom I had seen in him of the approach of immediate fear. It was as if he were suddenly afraid of me—which struck me, indeed, as perhaps the best thing to make him. Yet in the very pang of the effort I felt it vain to try sternness, and I heard myself the next instant so gentle as to be almost grotesque. 'You want so to go out again?'

'Awfully!' He smiled at me heroically, and the touching little bravery of it was enhanced by his actually flushing with pain. He had picked up his hat, which he had brought in, and stood twirling it in a way that gave me, even as I was just nearly reaching port, a perverse horror of what I was doing. To do it in *any* way was an act of violence, for what did it consist of but the obtrusion of the idea of grossness and guilt on a small, helpless creature who had been for me a revelation of the possibilities of beautiful intercourse? Wasn't it base to create for a being so exquisite a mere alien awkwardness? I suppose I now read into our situation a clearness

it couldn't have had at the time, for I seem to see
our poor eyes already lighted with some spark
of a prevision of the anguish that was to come.
So we circled about with terrors and scruples, fighters
not daring to close.   But it was for each other we
feared!   That kept us a little longer suspended
and unbruised.   'I'll tell you everything,' Miles
said—'I mean I'll tell you anything you like.
You'll stay on with me, and we shall both be all
right, and I *will* tell you—I *will*.   But not now.'

'Why not now?'

My resistance turned him from me and kept him
once more at his window in a silence during which,
between us, you might have heard a pin drop.
Then he was before me again with the air of a person
for whom, outside, someone who had frankly to be
reckoned with was waiting.   'I have to see Luke.'

I had not yet reduced him to quite so vulgar a
lie, and I felt proportionately ashamed.   But,
horrible as it was, his lies made up my truth.   I
achieved thoughtfully a few loops of my knitting.

'Well, then go to Luke, and I'll wait for what
you promise.   Only in return for that satisfy, before
you leave me, one very much smaller request.'

He looked as if he felt he had succeeded enough
to be able still a little to bargain.   'Very much
smaller——?'

'Yes, a mere fraction of the whole.   Tell me'
—oh, my work preoccupied me, and I was off-
hand!—'if, yesterday afternoon, from the table
in the hall, you took, you know, my letter.'

XXIV

My grasp of how he received this suffered for a
minute from something that I can describe only
as a fierce split of my attention—a stroke that at
first, as I sprang straight up, reduced me to the
mere blind movement of getting hold of him, drawing
him close and, while I just fell for support against
the nearest piece of furniture, instinctively keeping
him with his back to the window. The appearance
was full upon us that I had already had to deal
with here: Peter Quint had come into view like
a sentinel before a prison. The next thing I saw
was that, from outside, he had reached the window,
and then I knew that, close to the glass and glaring
in through it, he offered once more to the room
his white face of damnation. It represents but
grossly what took place within me at the sight
to say that on the second my decision was made;
yet I believe that no woman so overwhelmed ever
in so short a time recovered her command of the
act. It came to me in the very horror of the immediate presence that the act would be, seeing and
facing what I saw and faced, to keep the boy himself unaware. The inspiration—I can call it by
no other name—was that I felt how voluntarily,
how transcendently, I *might*. It was like fighting
with a demon for a human soul, and when I had
fairly so appraised it I saw how the human soul
—held out, in the tremor of my hands, at arms'

length—had a perfect dew of sweat on a lovely childish forehead. The face that was close to mine was as white as the face against the glass, and out of it presently came a sound, not low nor weak, but as if from much further away, that I drank like a waft of fragrance.

'Yes—I took it.'

At this, with a moan of joy, I enfolded, I drew him close; and while I held him to my breast, where I could feel in the sudden fever of his little body the tremendous pulse of his little heart, I kept my eyes on the thing at the window and saw it move and shift its posture. I have likened it to a sentinel, but its slow wheel, for a moment, was rather the prowl of a baffled beast. My present quickened courage, however, was such that, not too much to let it through, I had to shade, as it were, my flame. Meanwhile the glare of the face was again at the window, the scoundrel fixed as if to watch and wait. It was the very confidence that I might now defy him, as well as the positive certitude, by this time, of the child's unconsciousness, that made me go on. 'What did you take it for?'

'To see what you said about me.'

'You opened the letter?'

'I opened it.'

My eyes were now, as I held him off a little again, on Miles's own face, in which the collapse of mockery showed me how complete was the ravage of uneasiness. What was prodigious was that at last, by my success, his sense was sealed and his communication stopped: he knew that he was in presence, but knew not of what, and knew still less that I

also was and that I did know.   And what did this
strain of trouble matter when my eyes went back
to the window only to see that the air was clear
again and—by my personal triumph—the influence
quenched?   There was nothing there.   I felt that
the cause was mine and that I should surely get
all.   'And you found nothing!'—I let my elation
out.

He gave me the most mournful, thoughtful little
headshake.   'Nothing.'

'Nothing, nothing!' I almost shouted in my joy.

'Nothing, nothing,' he sadly repeated.

I kissed his forehead; it was drenched.   'So what
have you done with it?'

'I 've burnt it.'

'Burnt it?'   It was now or never.   'Is that what
you did at school?'

Oh, what this brought up!   'At school?'

'Did you take letters?—or other things?'

'Other things?'   He appeared now to be thinking
of something far off and that reached him only
through the pressure of his anxiety.   Yet it did
reach him.   'Did I *steal*?'

I felt myself redden to the roots of my hair as
well as wonder if it were more strange to put to
a gentleman such a question or to see him take
it with allowances that gave the very distance of
his fall in the world.   'Was it for that you mightn't
go back?'

The only thing he felt was rather a dreary little
surprise.   'Did you know I mightn't go back?'

'I know everything.'

He gave me at this the longest and strangest look.
'Everything?'

'Everything. Therefore *did* you——?' But I couldn't say it again.

Miles could, very simply. 'No. I didn't steal.'

My face must have shown him I believed him utterly; yet my hands—but it was for pure tenderness—shook him as if to ask him why, if it was all for nothing, he had condemned me to months of torment. 'What then did you do?'

He looked in vague pain all round the top of the room and drew his breath, two or three times over, as if with difficulty. He might have been standing at the bottom of the sea and raising his eyes to some faint green twilight. 'Well—I said things.'

'Only that?'

'They thought it was enough!'

'To turn you out for?'

Never, truly, had a person 'turned out' shown so little to explain it as this little person! He appeared to weigh my question, but in a manner quite detached and almost helpless. 'Well, I suppose I oughtn't.'

'But to whom did you say them?'

He evidently tried to remember, but it dropped—he had lost it. 'I don't know!'

He almost smiled at me in the desolation of his surrender, which was, indeed, practically, by this time, so complete that I ought to have left it there. But I was infatuated—I was blind with victory, though even then the very effect that was to have brought him so much nearer was already that of added separation. 'Was it to every one?' I asked.

'No; it was only to——' But he gave a sick little headshake 'I don't remember their names.'

'Were they then so many?'

'No—only a few. Those I liked.'

Those he liked? I seemed to float not into clearness, but into a darker obscure, and within a minute there had come to me out of my very pity the appalling alarm of his being perhaps innocent. It was for the instant confounding and bottomless, for if he *were* innocent what then on earth was *I*? Paralysed, while it lasted, by the mere brush of the question, I let him go a little, so that, with a deep-drawn sigh, he turned away from me again; which, as he faced toward the clear window, I suffered, feeling that I had nothing now there to keep him from. 'And did they repeat what you said?' I went on after a moment.

He was soon at some distance from me, still breathing hard and again with the air, though now without anger for it, of being confined against his will. Once more, as he had done before, he looked up at the dim day as if, of what had hitherto sustained him, nothing was left but an unspeakable anxiety. 'Oh, yes,' he nevertheless replied—'they must have repeated them. To those *they* liked,' he added.

There was somehow less of it than I had expected; but I turned it over. 'And these things came round——?'

'To the masters? Oh, yes!' he answered very simply. 'But I didn't know they'd tell.'

'The masters? They didn't—they've never told. That's why I ask you.'

He turned to me again his little beautiful fevered face. 'Yes, it was too bad.'

'Too bad?'

'What I suppose I sometimes said. To write home.'

I can't name the exquisite pathos of the contradiction given to such a speech by such a speaker; I only know that the next instant I heard myself throw off with homely force: 'Stuff and nonsense!' But the next after that I must have sounded stern enough. 'What *were* these things?'

My sternness was all for his judge, his executioner; yet it made him avert himself again, and that movement made *me*, with a single bound and an irrepressible cry, spring straight upon him. For there again, against the glass, as if to blight his confession and stay his answer, was the hideous author of our woe—the white face of damnation. I felt a sick swim at the drop of my victory and all the return of my battle, so that the wildness of my veritable leap only served as a great betrayal. I saw him, from the midst of my act, meet it with a divination, and on the perception that even now he only guessed, and that the window was still to his own eyes free, I let the impulse flame up to convert the climax of his dismay into the very proof of his liberation. 'No more, no more, no more!' I shrieked to my visitant as I tried to press him against me.

'Is she *here*?' Miles panted as he caught with his sealed eyes the direction of my words. Then as his strange 'she' staggered me and, with a gasp, I echoed it, 'Miss Jessel, Miss Jessel!' he with sudden fury gave me back.

I seized, stupefied, his supposition—some sequel to what we had done to Flora, but this made me only want to show him that it was better still than that. 'It 's not Miss Jessel! But it 's at the window —straight before us. It 's *there*—the coward horror, there for the last time!'

At this, after a second in which his head made the movement of a baffled dog's on a scent and then gave a frantic little shake for air and light, he was at me in a white rage, bewildered, glaring vainly over the place and missing wholly, though it now, to my sense, filled the room like the taste of poison, the wide overwhelming presence. 'It 's *he*?'

I was so determined to have all my proof that I dashed into ice to challenge him. 'Whom do you mean by "he"?'

'Peter Quint—you devil!' His face gave again, round the room, its convulsed supplication. '*Where?*'

They are in my ears still, his supreme surrender of the name and his tribute to my devotion. 'What does he matter now, my own?—what will he *ever* matter? *I* have you,' I launched at the beast, 'but he has lost you for ever!' Then, for the demonstration of my work, 'There, *there!*' I said to Miles.

But he had already jerked straight round, stared, glared again, and seen but the quiet day. With the stroke of the loss I was so proud of he uttered the cry of a creature hurled over an abyss, and the grasp with which I recovered him might have been that of catching him in his fall. I caught him, yes, I held him—it may be imagined with what a passion; but at the end of a minute I began to feel what it truly was that I held. We were alone with the quiet day, and his little heart, dispossessed, had stopped.

THE ASPERN PAPERS

I

I HAD taken Mrs. Prest into my confidence; without her in truth I should have made but little advance, for the fruitful idea in the whole business dropped from her friendly lips. It was she who found the short cut and loosed the Gordian knot. It is not supposed easy for women to rise to the large free view of anything, anything to be done; but they sometimes throw off a bold conception—such as a man wouldn't have risen to—with singular serenity. 'Simply make them take you in on the footing of a lodger'—I don't think that unaided I should have risen to that. I was beating about the bush, trying to be ingenious, wondering by what combination of arts I might become an acquaintance, when she offered this happy suggestion that the way to become an acquaintance was first to become an intimate. Her actual knowledge of the Misses Bordereau was scarcely larger than mine, and indeed, I had brought with me from England some definite facts that were new to her. Their name had been mixed up ages before with one of the greatest names of the century, and they now lived obscurely in Venice, lived on very small means, unvisited, unapproachable, in a sequestered and dilapidated old palace: this was the substance of my friend's impression of them. She herself had been established in Venice some fifteen years and had done a great deal of good there; but the circle of her benevolence had never embraced the two shy, mysterious and, as was somehow supposed, scarcely respectable Americans—they were believed to have lost in their long exile all national quality, besides being as their na ne implied of some remoter French affiliation—who asked no favours and desired no attention. In the early years of her residence she had made an attempt to see them, but this had been successful only as regards the little one, as Mrs. Prest called the niece; though in fact I afterwards found her the bigger of the two in inches. She had heard Miss Bordereau was ill and had a suspicion she was in want, and had gone to the house to offer aid, so that if there were suffering, American suffering in particular, she shouldn't have it on her conscience. The 'little one' had received her in the great cold tarnished Venetian *sala*, the central hall of the house, paved with marble and roofed with dim cross - beams, and hadn't even asked her to sit down. This was not encouraging for me, who wished to sit so fast, and I remarked as much to Mrs. Prest. She replied, however, with profundity: 'Ah, but there's all the difference: I went to confer a favour and you'll go to ask one. If they're proud you'll be on the right side.' And she offered to show me their house to begin with— to row me thither in her gondola. I let her know I had already been to look at it half a dozen times; but I accepted her invitation, for it charmed me to hover about the place. I had made my way to it the day after my arrival in Venice—it had been described to me in advance by the friend in England to whom I owed definite information as to their possession of the papers—laying siege to it with my eyes while I considered my plan of campaign. Jeffrey Aspern had never been in it that I knew of, but some note of his voice seemed to abide there by a roundabout implication and in a 'dying fall.'

Mrs. Prest knew nothing about the papers, but was interested in my curiosity, as always in the joys and sorrows of her friends. As we went, however, in her gondola, gliding there under the sociable hood with the bright Venetian picture framed on either side by the movable window, I saw how my eagerness amused her and that she found my interest in my possible spoil a fine case of monomania. 'One would think you expected from it the answer to the riddle of the universe,' she said; and I denied the impeachment only by replying that if I had to choose between that precious solution and a bundle of Jeffrey Aspern's letters I knew, indeed which would appear to me the greater boon. She pretended to make light of his genius and I took no pains to defend him. One doesn't defend one's god: one's god is in himself a defence. Besides, to-day, after his long comparative obscuration, he hangs high in the heaven of our literature for all the world to see; he's a part of the light by which we walk. The most I said was that he was no doubt not a woman's poet; to which she rejoined aptly enough that he had been at least Miss Bordereau's. The strange thing had been for me to discover in England that she was still alive: it was as if I had been told Mrs. Siddons was, or Queen Caroline, or the famous Lady Hamilton, for it seemed to me that she belonged to a generation as extinct. 'Why, she must be tremendously old—at least a hundred,' I had said;

but on coming to consider dates I saw it not strictly involved that she should have far exceeded the common span. None the less she was of venerable age and her relations with Jeffrey Aspern had occurred in her early womanhood. 'That's her excuse,' said Mrs. Prest half sententiously and yet also somewhat as if she were ashamed of making a speech so little in the real tone of Venice. As if a woman needed an excuse for having loved the divine poet! He had been not only one of the most brilliant minds of his day—and in those years, when the century was young, there were, as every one knows, many—but one of the most genial men and one of the handsomest.

The niece, according to Mrs. Prest, was of minor antiquity, and the conjecture was risked that she was only a grand-niece. This was possible; I had nothing but my share in the very limited knowledge of my English fellow-worshipper John Cumnor, who had never seen the couple. The world, as I say, had recognized Jeffrey Aspern, but Cumnor and I had recognized him most. The multitude to-day flocked to his temple, but of that temple he and I regarded ourselves as the appointed ministers. We held, justly, as I think, that we had done more for his memory than any one else, and had done it simply by opening lights into his life. He had nothing to fear from us because he had nothing to fear from the truth, which alone at such a distance of time we could be interested in establishing. His early death had been the only dark spot, as it were, on his fame, unless the papers in Miss Bordereau's hands should perversely bring out others. There had been an impression about 1825 that he had

'treated her badly just as there had been an impression that he had 'served,' as the London populace
says, several other ladies in the same masterful
way. Each of these cases Cumnor and I had been
able to investigate, and we had never failed to
acquit him conscientiously of any grossness. I
judged him perhaps more indulgently than my
friend; certainly, at any rate, it appeared to me
that no man could have walked straighter in the
given circumstances. These had been almost always
difficult and dangerous. Half the women of his
time, to speak literally, had flung themselves at
his head, and while the fury raged—the more that
it was very catching—accidents, some of them
grave, had not failed to occur. He was not a
woman's poet, as I had said to Mrs. Prest, in the
modern phase of his reputation; but the situation
had been different when the man's own voice was
mingled with his song. That voice, by every testimony, was one of the most charming ever heard.
'Orpheus and the Maenads!' had been of course
my foreseen judgment when first I turned over his
correspondence. Almost all the Maenads were un-
reasonable and many of them unbearable. It struck
me that he had been kinder and more considerate
than in his place—if I could imagine myself in
any such box—I should have found the trick of.
    It was certainly strange beyond all strangeness,
and I shall not take up space with attempting to
explain it, that whereas among all these other
relations and in these other directions of research
we had to deal with phantoms and dust, the mere
echoes, the one living source of information that
had lingered on into our time had been unheeded

by us. Every one of Aspern's contemporaries had, according to our belief, passed away; we had not been able to look into a single pair of eyes into which his had looked or to feel a transmitted contact in any aged hand that his hand had touched. Most dead of all did poor Miss Bordereau appear, and yet she alone had survived. We exhausted in the course of months our wonder that we had not found her out sooner, and the substance of our explanation was that she had kept so quiet. The poor lady on the whole had had reason for doing so. But it was a revelation to us that self-effacement on such a scale had been possible in the latter half of the nineteenth century—the age of newspapers and telegrams and photographs and interviewers. She had taken no great trouble for it either—hadn't hidden herself away in an undiscovered hole, had boldly settled down in a city of exhibition. The one apparent secret of her safety had been that Venice contained so many much greater curiosities. And then accident had somehow favoured her, as was shown for example in the fact that Mrs. Prest had never happened to name her to me, though I had spent three weeks in Venice—under her nose as it were—five years before. My friend, indeed, had not named her much to any one; she appeared almost to have forgotten the fact of her continuance. Of course Mrs. Prest hadn't the nerves of an editor. It was meanwhile no explanation of the old woman's having eluded us to say that she lived abroad, for our researches had again and again taken us —not only by correspondence but by personal inquiry—to France, to Germany, to Italy, in which countries, not counting his important stay in England,

so many of the too few years of Aspern's career
had been spent. We were glad to think at least
that in all our promulgations—some people now
consider I believe that we have overdone them—
we had only touched in passing and in the most
discreet manner on Miss Bordereau's connection.
Oddly enough, even if we had had the material
—and we had often wondered what could have
become of it—this would have been the most difficult
episode to handle.

The gondola stopped, the old palace was there; it
was a house of the class which in Venice carries even
in extreme dilapidation the dignified name. 'How
charming! It's grey and pink!' my companions
exclaimed; and that is the most comprehensive
description of it. It was not particularly old, only
two or three centuries; and it had an air not so
much of decay as of quiet discouragement, as if it
had rather missed its career. But its wide front,
with a stone balcony from end to end of the *piano
nobile* or most important floor, was architectural
enough, with the aid of various pilasters and arches;
and the stucco with which in the intervals it had
long ago been endued was rosy in the April afternoon. It overlooked a clean, melancholy, rather
lonely canal, which had a narrow *riva* or convenient
footway on either side. 'I don't know why—there
are no brick gables,' said Mrs. Prest, 'but this corner
has seemed to me before more Dutch than Italian,
more like Amsterdam than like Venice. It's ec-
centrically neat for reasons of its own; and though
you may pass on foot scarcely any one ever thinks
of doing so. It's as negative—considering *where*
it is—as a Protestant Sunday. Perhaps the people

are afraid of the Misses Bordereau. I dare say they have the reputation of witches.'

I forget what answer I made to this—I was given up to two other reflections. The first of these was that if the old lady lived in such a big and imposing house she couldn't be in any sort of misery and, therefore, wouldn't be tempted by a chance to let a couple of rooms. I expressed this fear to Mrs. Prest, who gave me a very straight answer. 'If she didn't live in a big house how could it be a question of her having rooms to spare? If she were not amply lodged you 'd lack ground to approach her. Besides, a big house here, and especially in this *quartier perdu*, proves nothing at all: it 's perfectly consistent with a state of penury. Dilapidated old *palazzi*, if you 'll go out of the way for them, are to be had for five shillings a year. And as for the people who live in them—no, until you 've explored Venice socially as much as I have, you can form no idea of their domestic desolation. They live on nothing, for they 've nothing to live on.' The other idea that had come into my head was connected with a high blank wall which appeared to confine an expanse of ground on one side of the house. Blank I call it, but it was figured over with the patches that please a painter, repaired breaches, crumblings of plaster, extrusions of brick that had turned pink with time; while a few thin trees, with the poles of certain rickety trellises, were visible over the top. The place was a garden and apparently attached to the house. I suddenly felt that so attached it gave me my pretext.

I sat looking out on all this with Mrs. Prest (it was covered with the golden glow of Venice) from

the shade of our *felze*, and she asked me if I would
go in then, while she waited for me, or come back
another time. At first I couldn't decide—it was
doubtless very weak of me. I wanted still to think
I *might* get a footing, and was afraid to meet failure,
for it would leave me, as I remarked to my companion, without another arrow for my bow. 'Why
not another?' she inquired as I sat there hesitating
and thinking it over; and she wished to know why
even now and before taking the trouble of becoming
an inmate—which might be wretchedly uncomfortable after all, even if it succeeded—I hadn't the
resource of simply offering them a sum of money
down. In that way I might get what I wanted
without bad nights.

'Dearest lady,' I exclaimed, 'excuse the impatience
of my tone when I suggest that you must have
forgotten the very fact—surely I communicated it
to you—which threw me on your ingenuity. The
old woman won't have her relics and tokens so
much as spoken of; they're personal, delicate,
intimate, and she hasn't the feelings of the day,
God bless her! If I should sound that note first
I should certainly spoil the game. I can arrive
at my spoils only by putting her off her guard,
and I can put her off her guard only by ingratiating
diplomatic arts. Hypocrisy, duplicity are my only
chance. I'm sorry for it, but there's no baseness
I wouldn't commit for Jeffrey Aspern's sake. First
I must take tea with her—then tackle the main
job.' And I told over what had happened to John
Cumnor on his respectfully writing to her. No
notice whatever had been taken of his first letter,
and the second had been answered very sharply,

in six lines, by the niece. 'Miss Bordereau requested her to say that she couldn't imagine what he meant by troubling them. They had none of Mr. Aspern's "literary remains," and if they *had* had wouldn't have dreamed of showing them to any one on any account whatever. She couldn't imagine what he was talking about and begged he would let her alone.' I certainly didn't want to be met that way.

'Well,' said Mrs. Prest after a moment and all provokingly, 'perhaps they really haven't anything. If they deny it flat how are you sure?'

'John Cumnor 's sure, and it would take me long to tell you how his conviction, or his very strong presumption—strong enough to stand against the old lady's not unnatural fib—has built itself up. Besides, he makes much of the internal evidence of the niece's letter.'

'The internal evidence?'

'Her calling him "Mr. Aspern."'

'I don't see what that proves.'

'It proves familiarity, and familiarity implies the possession of mementoes, of tangible objects. I can't tell you how that "Mr." affects me—how it bridges over the gulf of time and brings our hero near to me—nor what an edge it gives to my desire to see Juliana. You don't say "Mr." Shakespeare.'

'Would I, any more, if I had a box full of his letters?'

'Yes, if he had been your lover and someone wanted them!' And I added that John Cumnor was so convinced, and so all the more convinced by Miss Bordereau's tone, that he would have come himself to Venice on the undertaking were it not for the obstacle of his having, for any confidence,

to disprove his identity with the person who had
written to them, which the old ladies would be
sure to suspect in spite of dissimulation and a
change of name. If they were to ask him point-
blank if he were not their snubbed correspondent
it would be too awkward for him to lie; whereas
I was fortunately not tied in that way. I was a
fresh hand—I could protest without lying.

'But you 'll have to take a false name,' said
Mrs. Prest. 'Juliana lives out of the world as
much as it is possible to live, but she has none the
less probably heard of Mr. Aspern's editors. She
perhaps possesses what you 've published.'

'I 've thought of that,' I returned; and I drew
out of my pocket-book a visiting card neatly engraved
with a well-chosen *nom de guerre*.

'You 're very extravagant — it adds to your
immorality. You might have done it in pencil
or ink,' said my companion.

'This looks more genuine.'

'Certainly you 've the courage of your curiosity.
But it will be awkward about your letters; they
won't come to you in that mask.'

'My banker will take them in and I shall go
every day to get them. It will give me a little
walk.'

'Shall you depend all on that?' asked Mrs. Prest.
'Aren't you coming to see me?'

'Oh, you 'll have left Venice for the hot months
long before there are any results. I 'm prepared
to roast all summer—as well as through the long
hereafter perhaps you 'll say! Meanwhile John
Cumnor will bombard me with letters addressed, in
my feigned name, to the care of the *padrona*.'

'She 'll recognize his hand,' my companion suggested.

'On the envelope he can disguise it.'

'Well, you 're a precious pair! Doesn't it occur to you that even if you 're able to say you 're not Mr. Cumnor in person they may still suspect you of being his emissary?'

'Certainly, and I see only one way to parry that.'

'And what may that be?'

I hesitated for a moment. 'To make love to the niece.'

'Ah,' cried my friend, 'wait till you see her!'

II

'I MUST work the garden—I must work the garden,'
I said to myself five minutes later and while I
waited, upstairs, in the long, dusky *sala*, where
the bare scaglicla floor gleamed vaguely in a chink
of the closed shutters. The place was impressive,
yet looked somehow cold and cautious. Mrs. Prest
had floated away, giving me a rendezvous at the
end of half an hour by some neighbouring water-
steps; and I had been let into the house, after
pulling the rusty bell-wire, by a small red-headed
and white-faced maid-servant, who was very young
and not ugly and wore clicking pattens and a shawl
in the fashion of a hood. She had not contented
herself with opening the door from above by the
usual arrangement of a creaking pulley, though
she had looked down at me first from an upper
window, dropping the cautious challenge which in
Italy precedes the act of admission. I was so
irritated as a general thing by this survival of
medieval manners, though as so fond, if yet so
special, an antiquarian I suppose I ought to have
liked it; but, with my resolve to be genial from
the threshold at any price, I took my false card
out of my pocket and held it up to her smiling as
if it were a magic token. It had the effect of one
indeed, for it brought her, as I say, all the way down.
I begged her to hand it to her mistress, having
first written on it in Italian the words: 'Could

you very kindly see a gentleman, a travelling American, for a moment?' The little maid wasn't hostile—even that was perhaps something gained. She coloured, she smiled, and looked both frightened and pleased. I could see that my arrival was a great affair, that visits in such a house were rare, and that she was a person who would have liked a bustling place. When she pushed forward the heavy door behind me I felt my foot in the citadel and promised myself ever so firmly to keep it there. She pattered across the damp, stony lower hall and I followed her up the high staircase—stonier still, as it seemed—without an invitation. I think she had meant I should wait for her below, but such was not my idea, and I took up my station in the *sala*. She flitted, at the far end of it, into impenetrable regions, and I looked at the place with my heart beating as I had known it to do in dentists' parlours. It had a gloomy grandeur, but owed its character almost all to its noble shape and to the fine architectural doors, as high as those of grand frontages, which, leading into the various rooms, repeated themselves on either side at intervals. They were surmounted with old, faded, painted escutcheons, and here and there in the spaces between them hung brown pictures, which I noted as speciously bad, in battered and tarnished frames that were yet more desirable than the canvases themselves. With the exception of several straw-bottomed chairs that kept their backs to the wall the grand obscure vista contained little else to minister to effect. It was evidently never used save as a passage, and scantly even as that. I may add that by the time the door through which the maid-servant had escaped opened again my eyes had grown used to the want of light

I hadn't meanwhile meant by my private ejaculation that I must myself cultivate the soil of the tangled enclosure which lay beneath the windows, but the lady who came toward me from the distance over the hard, shining floor might have supposed as much from the way in which, as I went rapidly to meet her, I exclaimed, taking care to speak Italian: 'The garden, the garden—do me the pleasure to tell me if it 's yours!'

She stopped short, looking at me with wonder; and then, 'Nothing here is mine,' she answered in English, coldly and sadly.

'Oh, you 're English; how delightful!' I ingenuously cried. 'But surely the garden belongs to the house.'

'Yes, but the house doesn't belong to me.' She was a long, lean, pale person, habited apparently in a dull-coloured dressing-gown, and she spoke very simply and mildly. She didn't ask me to sit down, any more than years before—if she were the niece —she had asked Mrs. Prest, and we stood face to face in the empty, pompous hall.

'Well, then, would you kindly tell me to whom I must address myself? I 'm afraid you will think me horribly intrusive, but you know I *must* have a garden—upon my honour I must!'

Her face was not young, but it was candid; it was not fresh, but it was clear. She had large eyes which were not bright, and a great deal of hair which was not dressed,' and long fine hands which were—possibly—not clean. She clasped these members almost convulsively as, with a confused, alarmed look, she broke out: 'Oh, don't take it away from us; we like it ourselves!'

'You have the use of it then?'

'Oh, yes. If it wasn't for that——!' And she gave a wan, vague smile.

'Isn't it a luxury, precisely? That's why, intending to be in Vence some weeks, possibly all summer, and having some literary work, some reading and writing to do, so that I must be quiet and yet if possible a great deal in the open air— that's why I've felt a garden to be really indispensable. I appeal to your own experience,' I went on with as sociable a smile as I could risk. 'Now can't I look at yours?'

'I don't know, I don't understand,' the poor woman murmured, planted there and letting her weak wonder deal—helplessly enough, as I felt— with my strangeness.

'I mean only from one of those windows—such grand ones as you have here—if you'll let me open the shutters.' And I walked toward the back of the house. When I had advanced half-way I stopped and waited as in the belief she would accompany me. I had been of necessity quite abrupt, but I strove at the same time to give her the impression of extreme courtesy. 'I've looked at furnished rooms all over the place, and it seems impossible to find any with a garden attached. Naturally in a place like Venice gardens are rare. It's absurd if you like, for a man, but I can't live without flowers.'

'There are none to speak of down there.' She came nearer, as if, though she mistrusted me, I had drawn her by an invisible thread. I went on again, and she continued as she followed me:

'We 've a few, but they 're very common. It costs too much to cultivate them; one has to have a man.'

'Why shouldn't I be the man?' I asked. 'I 'll work without wages; or rather I 'll put in a gardener. You shall have the sweetest flowers in Venice.'

She protested against this with a small quaver of sound that might have been at the same time a gush of rapture for my free sketch. Then she gasped: 'We don't know you—we don't know you.'

'You know me as much as I know you; or rather much more, because you know my name. And if you 're English I 'm almost a countryman.'

'We 're not English,' said my companion watching me in practical submission while I threw open the shutters of one of the divisions of the wide high window.

'You speak the language so beautifully: might I ask what you are?' Seen from above the garden was in truth shabby, yet I felt at a glance that it had great capabilities. She made no rejoinder, she was so lost in her blankness and gentleness, and I exclaimed: 'You don't mean to say you 're also by chance American?'

'I don't know. We used to be.'

'Used to be? Surely you haven't changed?'

'It 's so many years ago. We don't seem to be anything now.'

'So many years that you 've been living here? Well, I don't wonder at that; it 's a grand old house. I suppose you all use the garden,' I went on, 'but I assure you I shouldn't be in your way. I 'd be very quiet and stay quite in one corner.'

'We all use it?' she repeated after me vaguely,

not coming close to the window but looking at
my shoes. She appeared to think me capable of
throwing her out.

'I mean all your family—as many as you are.'

'There's only one other than me. She's very
old. She never goes down.'

I feel again my thrill at this close identification
of Juliana; in spite of which, however, I kept my
head. 'Only one other in all this great house!'
I feigned to be not only amazed but almost scandalized.
'Dear lady, you must have space then to spare!'

'To spare?' she repeated—almost as for the rich
unwonted joy of her spoken words.

'Why you surely don't live (two quiet women—I
see *you* are quiet, at any rate) in fifty rooms!' Then
with a burst of hope and cheer I put the question
straight: 'Couldn't you for a good rent *let* me two
or three? That would set me up!'

I had now struck the note that translated my
purpose, and I needn't reproduce the whole of
the tune I played. I ended by making my enter-
tainer believe me an undesigning person, though
of course, I didn't even attempt to persuade her
I was not an eccentric one. I repeated that I
had studies to pursue; that I wanted quiet; that
I delighted in a garden and had vainly sought one
up and down the city; that I would undertake
that before another month was over the dear old
house should be smothered in flowers. I think
it was the flowers that won my suit, for I afterwards
found that Miss Tina—for such the name of this
high tremulous spinster proved somewhat incon-
gruously to be—had an insatiable appetite for
them. When I speak of my suit as won I mean

that before I left her she had promised me she
would refer the question to her aunt. I invited
information as to who her aunt might be and she
answered 'Why, Miss Bordereau!' with an air of
surprise, as if I might have been expected to know.
There were contradictions like this in Miss Tina
which, as I observed later, contributed to make
her rather pleasingly incalculable and interesting.
It was the study of the two ladies to live so that
the world shouldn't talk of them or touch them,
and yet they had never altogether accepted the
idea that it didn't hear of them. In Miss Tina at
any rate a grateful susceptibility to human contact
had not died out, and contact of a limited order
there would be if I should come to live in the house.

'We 've never done anything of the sort; we 've
never had a lodger or any kind of inmate.' So
much as this she made a point of saying to me.
'We 're very poor, we live very badly—almost on
nothing. The rooms are very bare—those you
might take; they 've nothing at all in them. I
don't know how you 'd sleep, how you 'd eat.'

'With your permission I could easily put in a
bed and a few tables and chairs. *C'est la moindre
des choses* and the affair of an hour or two. I know
a little man from whom I can hire for a trifle what
I should so briefly want, what I should use; my
gondolier can bring the things round in his boat.
Of course, in this great house you must have a
second kitchen, and my servant who 's a wonderfully handy fellow'—this personage was an evocation
of the moment—'can easily cook me a chop there.
My tastes and habits are of the simplest; I live on
flowers!' And then I ventured to add that if they

were very poor it was all the more reason they should let their rooms. They were bad economists— I had never heard of such a waste of material.

I saw in a moment my good lady had never before been spoken to in any such fashion—with a humorous firmness that didn't exclude sympathy, that was quite founded on it. She might easily have told me that my sympathy was impertinent, but this by good fortune didn't occur to her. I left her with the understanding that she would submit the question to her aunt and that I might come back the next day for their decision.

'The aunt will refuse; she'll think the whole proceeding very *louche*!' Mrs. Prest declared shortly after this, when I had resumed my place in her gondola. She had put the idea into my head and now—so little are women to be counted on—she appeared to take a despondent view of it. Her pessimism provoked me and I pretended to have the best hopes; I went so far as to boast of a distinct prevision of success. Upon this Mrs. Prest broke out: 'Oh, I see what's in your head! You fancy you've made such an impression in five minutes that she's dying for you to come and can be depended on to bring the old one round. If you do get in you'll count it as a triumph.'

I did count it as a triumph, but only for the commentator — in the last analysis — not for the man, who had not the tradition of personal conquest. When I went back on the morrow the little maid-servant conducted me straight through the long *sala*—it opened there as before in large perspective and was lighter now, which I thought a good omen— into the apartment from which the recipient of my

former visit had emerged on that occasion. It
was a spacious, shabby parlour with a fine old painted
ceiling under which a strange figure sat alone at one
of the windows. They come back to me now almost
with the palpitation they caused, the successive
states marking my consciousness that as the door
of the room closed behind me I was really face
to face with the Juliana of some of Aspern's most
exquisite and most renowned lyrics. I grew used
to her afterwards, though never completely; but
as she sat there before me my heart beat as fast
as if the miracle of resurrection had taken place
for my benefit. Her presence seemed somehow to
contain and express his own, and I felt nearer to
him at that first moment of seeing her than I ever
had been before or ever have been since. Yes, I
remember my emotions in their order, even including
a curious little tremor that took me when I saw the
niece not to be there. With her, the day before,
I had become sufficiently familiar, but it almost
exceeded my courage—much as I had longed for
the event—to be left alone with so terrible a relic
as the aunt. She was too strange, too literally
resurgent. Then came a check from the perception
that we weren't really face to face, inasmuch as
she had over her eyes a horrible green shade which
served for her almost as a mask. I believed for
the instant that she had put it on expressly, so that
from underneath it she might take me all in without
my getting at herself. At the same time it created
a presumption of some ghastly death's-head lurking
behind it. The divine Juliana as a grinning skull
—the vision hung there until it passed. Then it
came to me that she *was* tremendously old—so

old that death might take her at any moment, before I should have time to compass my end. The next thought was a correction to that; it lighted up the situation. She would die next week, she would die to-morrow—then I could pounce on her possessions and ransack her drawers. Meanwhile she sat there neither moving nor speaking. She was very small and shrunken, bent forward with her hands in her lap. She was dressed in black and her head was wrapped in a piece of old black lace which showed no hair.

My emotion keeping me silent she spoke first, and the remark she made was exactly the most unexpected.

III

'Our house is very far from the centre, but the little canal is very *comme il faut*.'

'It's the sweetest corner of Venice and I can imagine nothing more charming,' I hastened to reply. The old lady's voice was very thin and weak, but it had an agreeable, cultivated murmur and there was wonder in the thought that that individual note had been in Jeffrey Aspern's ear.

'Please do sit down there. I hear very well,' she said quietly, as if perhaps I had been shouting; and the chair she pointed to was at a certain distance. I took possession of it, assuring her I was perfectly aware of my intrusion and of my not having been properly introduced, and that I could but throw myself on her indulgence. Perhaps the other lady, the one I had had the honour of seeing the day before, would have explained to her about the garden. That was literally what had given me courage to take a step so unconventional. I had fallen in love at sight with the whole place—she herself was probably so used to it that she didn't know the impression it was capable of making on a stranger—and I had felt it really a case to risk something. Was her own kindness in receiving me a sign that I was not wholly out in my calculation? It would make me extremely happy to think so. I could give her my word of honour that I was a most respectable, inoffensive person and that as a co-tenant of the palace, so to speak, they would be barely conscious of my existence. I would conform to any regulations, any restrictions, if they would only let me enjoy the garden. Moreover I should be delighted to give her references, guarantees; they would be of the very best, both in Venice and in England, as well as in America.

She listened to me in perfect stillness, and I felt her look at me with great penetration, though I could see only the lower part of her bleached and shrivelled face. Independently of the refining process of old age it had a delicacy which once must have been great. She had been very fair, she had had a wonderful complexion. She was silent a little after I had ceased speaking; then she began: 'If you 're so fond of a garden why don't you go to *terra firma*, where there are so many far better than this?'

'Oh, it 's the combination!' I answered, smiling; and then with rather a flight of fancy: 'It 's the idea of a garden in the middle of the sea.'

'This isn't the middle of the sea; you can't so much as see the water.'

I stared a moment, wondering if she wished to convict me of fraud. 'Can't see the water? Why, dear madam, I can come up to the very gate in my boat.'

She appeared inconsequent, for she said vaguely in reply to this: 'Yes, if you 've got a boat. I haven't any; it 's many years since I have been in one of the *gondole*.' She uttered these words as if they designed a curious far-away craft known to her only by hearsay.

'Let me assure you of the pleasure with which

I would put mine at your service!' I returned.
I had scarcely said this, however, before I became
aware that the speech was in questionable taste
and might also do me the injury of making me
appear too eager, too possessed of a hidden motive.
But the old woman remained impenetrable and
her attitude worried me by suggesting that she
had a fuller vision of me than I had of her. She
gave me no thanks for my somewhat extravagant
offer, but remarked that the lady I had seen the
day before was her niece; she would presently come
in. She had asked her to stay away a little on
purpose—had had her reasons for seeing me first
alone. She relapsed into silence and I turned
over the fact of these unmentioned reasons and
the question of what might come yet; also that
of whether I might venture on some judicious remark
in praise of her companion. I went so far as to
say I should be delighted to see our absent friend
again: she had been so very patient with me, considering how odd she must have thought me—a
declaration which drew from Miss Bordereau another
of her whimsical speeches.

'She has very good manners; I bred her up myself!'
I was on the point of saying that that accounted
for the easy grace of the niece, but I arrested myself
in time, and the next moment the old woman went
on: 'I don't care who you may be—I don't want
to know; it signifies very little to-day.' This had
all the air of being a formula of dismissal, as if
her next words would be that I might take myself
off now that she had had the amusement of looking
on the face of such a monster of indiscretion. Therefore I was all the more surprised when she added

in her soft, venerable quaver: 'You may have as many rooms as you like—if you 'll pay me a good deal of money.'

I hesitated but an instant, long enough to measure what she meant in particular by this condition. First it struck me that she must have really a large sum in her mind; then I reasoned quickly that her idea of a large sum would probably not correspond to my own. My deliberation, I think, was not so visible as to diminish the promptitude with which I replied: 'I will pay with pleasure and of course in advance whatever you may think it proper to ask me.'

'Well, then, a thousand francs a month,' she said instantly, while her baffling green shade continued to cover her attitude.

The figure, as they say, was startling and my logic had been at fault. The sum she had mentioned was, by the Venetian measure of such matters, exceedingly large; there was many an old palace in an out-of-the-way corner that I might on such terms have enjoyed the whole of by the year. But so far as my resources allowed I was prepared to spend money, and my decision was quickly taken. I would pay her with a smiling face what she asked, but in that case I would make it up by getting hold of my 'spoils' for nothing. Moreover, if she had asked five times as much I should have risen to the occasion, so odious would it have seemed to me to stand chaffering with Aspern's Juliana. It was queer enough to have a question of money with her at all. I assured her that her views perfectly met my own and that on the morrow I should have the pleasure of putting three months' rent into her

hand.   She received this announcement with apparent
complacency and with no discoverable sense that
after all it would become her to say that I ought
to see the rooms first.   This didn't occur to her,
and indeed, her serenity was mainly what I wanted.
Our little agreement was just concluded when the
door opened and the younger lady appeared on
the threshold.   As soon as Miss Bordereau saw her
niece she cried out almost gaily: 'He'll give three
thousand—three thousand to-morrow!'

Miss Tina stood still, her patient eyes turning
from one of us to the other; then she brought out
scarcely above her breath: 'Do you mean francs?'

'Did you mean francs or dollars?' the old woman
asked of me at this.

'I think francs were what you said,' I sturdily
smiled.

'That's very good,' said Miss Tina, as if she
had felt how overreaching her own question might
have looked.

'What do *you* know?   You're ignorant,' Miss
Bordereau remarked; not with acerbity but with
a strange soft coldness.

'Yes, of money—certainly of money!' Miss Tina
hastened to concede.

'I'm sure you've your own fine branches of
knowledge,' I took the liberty of saying genially.
There was something painful to me, somehow, in
the turn the conversation had taken, in the discussion of dollars and francs.

'She had a very good education when she was
young.   I looked into that myself,' said Miss Bordereau.   Then she added: 'But she has learned
nothing since.'

'I have always been with *you*,' Miss Tina rejoined very mildly, and of a certainty with no intention of an epigram.

'Yes, but for that——!' her aunt declared with more satirical force. She evidently meant that but for this her niece would never have got on at all; the point of the observation, however, being lost on Miss Tina, though she blushed at hearing her history revealed to a stranger. Miss Bordereau went on, addressing herself to me: 'And what time will you come to-morrow with the money?'

'The sooner the better. If it suits you I 'll come at noon.'

'I am always here, but I have my hours,' said the old woman as if her convenience were not to be taken for granted.

'You mean the times when you receive?'

'I never receive. But I 'll see you at noon, when you come with the money.'

'Very good, I shall be punctual.' To which I I added: 'May I shake hands with you on our contract?' I thought there ought to be some little form; it would make me really feel easier, for I was sure there would be no other. Besides, though Miss Bordereau couldn't to-day be called personally attractive and there was something even in her wasted antiquity that bade one stand at one's distance, I felt an irresistible desire to hold in my own for a moment the hand Jeffrey Aspern had pressed.

For a minute she made no answer, and I saw that my proposal failed to meet with her appro-bation. She indulged in no movement of with-drawal which I half expected; she only said coldly:

'I belong to a time when that was not the custom.'

I felt rather snubbed. I exclaimed good-humouredly to Miss Tina: 'Oh, you'll do as well!' I shook hands with her while she assented with a small flutter. 'Yes, yes, to show it's all arranged!'

'Shall you bring the money in gold?' Miss Bordereau demanded as I was turning to the door.

I looked at her a moment. 'Aren't you a little afraid, after all, of keeping such a sum as that in the house?' It was not that I was annoyed at her avidity, but was truly struck with the disparity between such a treasure and such scanty means of guarding it.

'Whom should I be afraid of if I'm not afraid of you?' she asked with her shrunken grimness.

'Ah, well,' I laughed, 'I shall be in point of fact a protector and I'll bring gold if you prefer.'

'Thank you,' the old woman returned with dignity and with an inclination of her head which evidently signified my dismissal. I passed out of the room, thinking how hard it would be to circumvent her. As I stood in the *sala* again I saw that Miss Tina had followed me, and I supposed that as her aunt had neglected to suggest I should take a look at my quarters it was her purpose to repair the omission. But she made no such overture; she only stood there with a dim, though not a languid smile, and with an effect of irresponsible, incompetent youth almost comically at variance with the faded facts of her person. She was not infirm, like her aunt, but struck me as more deeply futile, because her inefficiency was inward, which was not the case with Miss Bordereau's. I waited to see if she would offer to show me the rest of the house, but I didn't precipitate the question, inasmuch as my plan was from the moment to spend as much of my time as possible in her society. A minute, indeed, elapsed before I committed myself.

'I've had better fortune than I hoped. It was very kind of her to see me. Perhaps you said a good word for me.'

'It was the idea of the money,' said Miss Tina.

'And did you suggest that?'

'I told her you'd perhaps pay largely.'

'What made you think that?'

'I told her I thought you were rich.'

'And what put that into your head?'

'I don't know; the way you talked.'

'Dear me, I must talk differently now,' I returned. 'I'm sorry to say it's not the case.'

'Well,' said Miss Tina, 'I think that in Venice the *forestieri* in general often give a great deal for something that after all isn't much.' She appeared to make this remark with a comforting intention, to wish to remind me that if I had been extravagant I wasn't foolishly singular. We walked together along the *sala,* and as I took its magnificent measure I said that I was afraid it wouldn't form part of my *quartiere.* Were my rooms by chance to be among those that opened into it? 'Not if you go above—to the second floor,' she answered as if she had rather taken for granted I would know my proper place.

'And I infer that that's where your aunt would like me to be.'

'She said your apartments ought to be very distinct.'

'That certainly would be best.' And I listened

with respect while she told me that above I should
be free to take whatever I might like; that there
was another staircase, but only from the floor on
which we stood, and that to pass from it to the
garden-level or to come up to my lodging I should
have to cross the great hall. This was an immense
point gained; I foresaw that it would constitute my
whole leverage in my relations with the two ladies.
When I asked Miss Tina how I was to manage at
present to find my way up she replied with an access
of that sociable shyness which constantly marked
her manner:

'Perhaps you can't. I don't see—unless I should
go with you.' She evidently hadn't thought of
this before.

We ascended to the upper floor and visited a
long succession of empty rooms. The best of them
looked over the garden; some of the others had
above the opposite rough-tiled house-tops a view
of the blue lagoon. They were all dusty and even
a little disfigured with long neglect, but I saw that
by spending a few hundred francs I should be able
to make three or four of them habitable enough.
My experiment was turning out costly, yet now
that I had all but taken possession I ceased to allow
this to trouble me. I mentioned to my companion
a few of the things I should put in, but she replied
rather more precipitately than usual that I might
do exactly what I liked: she seemed to wish to
notify me that the Misses Bordereau would take
none but the most veiled interest in my proceedings.
I guessed that her aunt had instructed her to adopt
this tone, and I may as well say now that I came
afterwards to distinguish perfectly (as I believed)

between the speeches she made on her own responsibility and those the old woman imposed upon her. She took no notice of the unswept condition of the rooms and indulged neither in explanations nor in apologies. I said to myself that this was a sign Juliana and her niece—disenchanting idea!—were untidy persons with a low Italian standard; but I afterwards recognized that a lodger who had forced an entrance had no *locus standi* as a critic. We looked out of a good many windows, for there was nothing within the rooms to look at, and still I wanted to linger. I asked her what several different objects in the prospect might be, but in no case did she appear to know. She was evidently not familiar with the view—it was as if she had not looked at it for years—and I presently saw that she was too preoccupied with something else to pretend to care for it. Suddenly she said—the remark was not suggested:

'I don't know whether it will make any difference to you, but the money is for me.'

'The money——?'

'The money you 're going to bring.'

'Why, you 'll make me wish to stay here two or three years!' I spoke as benevolently as possible, though it had begun to act on my nerves that these women so associated with Aspern should so constantly bring the pecuniary question back.

'That would be very good for me,' she answered almost gaily.

'You put me on my honour!'

She looked as if she failed to understand this, but went on: 'She wants me to have more. She thinks she 's going to die.'

'Ah, not soon I hope!' I cried with genuine feeling. I had perfectly considered the possibility of her destroying her documents on the day she should feel her end at hand. I believed that she would cling to them till then, and I was as convinced of her reading Aspern's letters over every night or at least pressing them to her withered lips. I would have given a good deal for some view of these solemnities. I asked Miss Tina if her venerable relative were seriously ill, and she replied that she was only very tired—she had lived so extraordinarily long. That was what she said herself —she wanted to die for a change. Besides, all her friends had been dead for ages; either they ought to have remained or she ought to have gone. That was another thing her aunt often said: she was not at all resigned—resigned, that is, to life.

'But people don't die when they like, do they?' Miss Tina inquired. I took the liberty of asking why, if there was actually enough money to maintain both of them, there would not be more than enough in case of her being left alone. She considered this difficult problem a moment and then said: 'Oh, well, you know, she takes care of me. She thinks that when I'm alone I shall be a great fool and shan't know how to manage.'

'I should have supposed rather that you took care of *her*. I'm afraid she's very proud.'

'Why, have you discovered that already?' Miss Tina cried with a dimness of glad surprise.

'I was shut up with her there for a considerable time and she struck me, she interested me extremely. It didn't take me long to make my discovery. She won't have much to say to me while I'm here.'

'No, I don't think she will,' my companion averred.

'Do you suppose she has some suspicion of me?'

Miss Tina's honest eyes gave me no sign I had touched a mark. 'I shouldn't think so—letting you in after all so easily.'

'You call it easily? She has covered her risk,' I said. 'But where is it one could take an advantage of her?'

'I oughtn't to tell you if I knew, ought I?' And Miss Tina added, before I had time to reply to this, smiling dolefully: 'Do you think we've any weak points?'

'That's exactly what I'm asking. You'd only have to mention them for me to respect them religiously.'

She looked at me hereupon with that air of timid but candid and even gratified curiosity with which she had confronted me from the first; after which she said: 'There's nothing to tell. We're terribly quiet. I don't know how the days pass. We've no life.'

'I wish I might think I should bring you a little.'

'Oh, we know what we want,' she went on. 'It's all right.'

There were twenty things I desired to ask her: how in the world did they live; whether they had any friends or visitors, any relations in America or in other countries. But I judged such probings premature; I must leave it to a later chance. 'Well, don't *you* be proud,' I contented myself with saying. 'Don't hide from me altogether.'

'Oh, I must stay with my aunt,' she returned without looking at me. And at the same moment, abruptly, without any ceremony of parting, she

quitted me and disappeared, leaving me to make
my own way downstairs. I stayed awhile longer,
wandering about the bright desert—the sun was
pouring in—of the old house, thinking the situation
over on the spot. Not even the pattering little
serva came to look after me, and I reflected that
after all this treatment showed confidence.

IV

PERHAPS it did, but all the same, six weeks later, towards the middle of June, the moment when Mrs. Prest undertook her annual migration, I had made no measurable advance. I was obliged to confess to her that I had no results to speak of. My first step had been unexpectedly rapid, but there was no appearance it would be followed by a second. I was a thousand miles from taking tea with my hostesses—that privilege of which, as I reminded my good friend, we both had had a vision. She reproached me with lacking boldness and I answered that even to be bold you must have an opportunity: you may push on through a breach, but you can't batter down a dead wall. She returned that the breach I had already made was big enough to admit an army and accused me of wasting precious hours in whimpering in her *salon* when I ought to have been carrying on the struggle in the field. It is true that I went to see her very often—all on the theory that it would console me (I freely expressed my discouragement) for my want of success on my own premises. But I began to feel that it didn't console me to be perpetually chaffed for my scruples, especially since I was really so vigilant; and I was rather glad when my ironic friend closed her house for the summer. She had expected to gather amusement from the drama of my intercourse with the Misses Bordereau, and was disappointed that the intercourse, and consequently the drama, had not come off. 'They 'll lead you on to your ruin,' she said before she left Venice. 'They 'll get all your money without showing you a scrap.' I think I settled down to my business with more concentration after her departure.

It was a fact that up to that time I had not, save on a single brief occasion, had even a moment's contact with my queer hostesses. The exception had occurred when I carried them according to my promise the terrible three thousand francs. Then I found Miss Tina awaiting me in the hall, and she took the money from my hand with a promptitude that prevented my seeing her aunt. The old lady had promised to receive me, yet apparently thought nothing of breaking that vow. The money was contained in a bag of chamois leather, of respectable dimensions, which my banker had given me, and Miss Tina had to make a big fist to receive it. This she did with extreme solemnity, though I tried to treat the affair a little as a joke. It was in no jocular strain, yet it was with a clearness akin to a brightness that she inquired, weighing the money in her two palms: 'Don't you think it 's too much?' To which I replied that this would depend on the amount of pleasure I should get for it. Hereupon she turned away from me quickly, as she had done the day before, murmuring in a tone different from any she had used hitherto: 'Oh, pleasure, pleasure—there 's no pleasure in this house!'

After that, for a long time, I never saw her, and I wondered the common chances of the day shouldn't have helped us to meet. It could only be evident that she was immensely on her guard against them; and in addition to this the house was so big that for each other we were lost in it. I used to look out for her hopefully as I crossed the *sala* in my comings and goings, but I was not rewarded with a glimpse of the tail of her dress. It was as if she never peeped out of her aunt's apartment. I used to wonder what she did there week after week and year after year. I had never met so stiff a policy of seclusion; it was more than keeping quiet—it was like hunted creatures feigning death. The two ladies appeared to have no visitors whatever and no sort of contact with the world. I judged at least that people couldn't have come to the house and that Miss Tina couldn't have gone out without my catching some view of it. I did what I disliked myself for doing—considering it but as once in a way: I questioned my servant about their habits and let him infer that I should be interested in any information he might glean. But he gleaned amazingly little for a knowing Venetian: it must be added that where there is a perpetual fast there are very few crumbs on the floor. His ability in other ways was sufficient, if not quite all I had attributed to him on the occasion of my first interview with Miss Tina. He had helped my gondolier to bring me round a boat-load of furniture; and when these articles had been carried to the top of the palace and distributed according to our associated wisdom he organized my household with such dignity as answered to its being composed exclusively of himself. He made me in short as comfortable as I could be with my indifferent prospects. I should have been glad if he had fallen in love with Miss Bordereau's maid or, failing this, had taken her in aversion; either event might have brought about some catastrophe, and a catastrophe might have led to some parley. It was my idea that she would have been sociable, and I myself on various occasions saw her flit to and fro on domestic errands, so that I was sure she was accessible. But I tasted of no gossip from that fountain, and I afterwards learned that Pasquale's affections were fixed upon an object that made him heedless of other women. This was a young lady with a powdered face, a yellow cotton gown and much leisure, who used often to come to see him. She practised, at her convenience, the art of a stringer of beads—these ornaments are made in Venice to profusion; she had her pocket full of them and I used to find them on the floor of my apartment—and kept an eye on the possible rival in the house. It was not for me, of course, to make the domestics tattle, and I never said a word to Miss Bordereau's cook.

It struck me as a proof of the old woman's resolve to have nothing to do with me that she should never have sent me a receipt for my three months' rent. For some days I looked out for it and then, when I had given it up, wasted a good deal of time in wondering what her reason had been for neglecting so indispensable and familiar a form. At first I was tempted to send her a reminder; after which I put by the idea—against my judgment as to what was right in the particular case—on the general ground of wishing to keep quiet. If Miss Bordereau suspected me of ulterior aims she would suspect me less if I should be businesslike, and yet I consented not to be. It was possible she intended her omission as an impertinence, a visible irony, to show how she could overreach people who attempted to overreach her. On that hypothesis it was well to let her see that one didn't notice her little tricks. The real reading of the matter, I afterwards gathered, was simply the poor lady's desire to emphasize the fact that I was in the enjoyment of a favour as rigidly limited as it had been liberally bestowed. She had given me part of her house, but she wouldn't add to that so much as a morsel of paper with her name on it. Let me say that even at first this didn't make me too miserable, for the whole situation had the charm of its oddity. I foresaw that I should have a summer after my own literary heart, and the sense of playing with my opportunity was much greater after all than any sense of being played with. There could be no Venetian business without patience, and since I adored the place I was much more in the spirit of it for having laid in a large provision. That spirit kept me perpetual company and seemed to look out at me from the revived immortal face —in which all his genius shone—of the great poet who was my prompter. I had invoked him and he had come; he hovered before me half the time; it was as if his bright ghost had returned to earth to assure me he regarded the affair as his own no less than as mine and that we should see it fraternally and fondly to a conclusion. It was as if he had said: 'Poor dear, be easy with her; she had some natural prejudices; only give her time. Strange as it may appear to you she was very attractive in 1820. Meanwhile aren't we in Venice together, and what better place is there for the meeting of dear friends? See how it glows with the advancing summer; how the sky and the sea and the rosy air and the marble of the palaces all shimmer and melt together.' My eccentric private errand became a part of the general romance and the general glory —I felt even a mystic companionship, a moral fraternity with all those who in the past had been in the service of art. They had worked for beauty, for a devotion; and what else was I doing? That element was in everything that Jeffrey Aspern had written, and I was only bringing it to light.

I lingered in the *sala* when I went to and fro; I used to watch—as long as I thought decent— the door that led to Miss Bordereau's part of the house. A person observing me might have supposed I was trying to cast a spell on it or attempting some odd experiment in hypnotism. But I was only praying it might open or thinking what treasure probably lurked behind it. I hold it singular, as I look back, that I should never have doubted for a moment that the sacred relics were there; never have failed to know the joy of being beneath the same roof with them. After all they were under my hand—they had not escaped me yet; and they made my life continuous, in a fashion, with the illustrious life they had touched at the other end. I lost myself in this satisfaction to the point of assuming—in my quiet extravagance—that poor Miss Tina also went back, and still went back, as I used to phrase it. She did indeed, the gentle spinster, but not quite so far as Jeffrey Aspern, who was simple hearsay to her quite as he was to me. Only she had lived for years with Juliana, she had seen and handled all mementoes and—

even though she was stupid—some esoteric knowledge had rubbed off on her. That was what the
old woman represented—esoteric knowledge; and
this was the idea with which my critical heart
used to thrill. It literally beat faster often, of
an evening when I had been out, as I stopped with
my candle in the re-echoing hall on my way up to
bed. It was as if at such a moment as that, in the
stillness and after the long contradiction of the
day, Miss Bordereau's secrets were in the air, the
wonder of her survival more vivid. These were
the acute impressions. I had them in another
form, with more of a certain shade of reciprocity,
during the hours I sat in the garden looking up over
the top of my book at the closed windows of my
hostess. In these windows no sign of life ever
appeared; it was as if, for fear of my catching a
glimpse of them, the two ladies passed their days
in the dark. But this only emphasized their having
matters to conceal; which I had wished to prove.
Their motionless shutters became as expressive as
eyes consciously closed, and I took comfort in the
probability that, though invisible themselves, they
kept me in view between the lashes.

I made a point of spending as much time as
possible in the garden, to justify the picture I had
originally given of my horticultural passion. And
I not only spent time, but (hang it! as I said) spent
precious money. As soon as I had got my rooms
arranged and could give the question proper thought
I surveyed the place with a clever expert and made
terms for having it put in order. I was sorry to
do this, for personally, I liked it better as it was,
with its weeds and its wild rich tangle, its sweet

characteristic Venetian shabbiness. I had to be consistent, to keep my promise that I would smother the house in flowers Moreover I clung to the fond fancy that by flowers I should make my way—I should succeed by big nosegays. I would batter the old women with lilies—I would bombard their citadel with roses. Their door would have to yield to the pressure when a mound of fragrance should be heaped against it. The place in truth had been brutally neglected. The Venetian capacity for dawdling is of the largest, and for a good many days unlimited litter was all my gardener had to show for his ministrations. There was a great digging of holes and carting about of earth, and after a while I grew so impatient that I had thoughts of sending for my 'results' to the nearest stand. But I felt sure my friends would see through the chinks of their shutters where such tribute *couldn't* have been gathered, and might so make up their minds against my veracity. I possessed my soul and finally, though the delay was long, perceived some appearances of bloom. This encouraged me and I waited serenely enough till they multiplied. Meanwhile the real summer days arrived and began to pass, and as I look back upon them they seem to me almost the happiest of my life. I took more and more care to be in the garden, whenever it was not too hot. I had an arbour arranged and a low table and an arm-chair put into it; and I carried out books and portfolios—I had always some business of writing in hand—and worked and waited and mused and hoped, while the golden hours elapsed and the plants drank in the light and the inscrutable old palace turned pale and then, as the day waned, began to recover and flush and my papers rustled in the wandering breeze of the Adriatic.

Considering how little satisfaction I got from it at first it is wonderful I shouldn't have grown more tired of trying to guess what mystic rites of ennui the Misses Bordereau celebrated in their darkened rooms; whether this had always been the tenor of their life and how in previous years they had escaped elbowing their neighbours. It was supposable they had then had other habits, forms, and resources; that they must once have been young or at least middle-aged. There was no end to the questions it was possible to ask about them and no end to the answers it was not possible to frame. I had known many of my country-people in Europe and was familiar with the strange ways they were liable to take up there; but the Misses Bordereau formed altogether a new type of the American absentee. Indeed, it was clear the American name had ceased to have any application to them—I had seen this in the ten minutes spent in the old woman's room. You could never have said whence they came from the appearance of either of them; wherever it was they had long ago shed and unlearned all native marks and notes. There was nothing in them one recognized or fitted, and, putting the question of speech aside, they might have been Norwegians or Spaniards. Miss Bordereau, after all, had been in Europe nearly three-quarters of a century; it appeared by some verses addressed to her by Aspern on the occasion of his own second absence from America—verses of which Cumnor and I had after infinite conjecture established solidly enough the date—that she was even then, as a girl of twenty, on the foreign side of the sea. There was a profession in the poem —I hope not just for the phrase—that he had come back for her sake. We had no real light on her circumstances at that moment, any more than we had upon her origin, which we believed to be of the sort usually spoken of as modest. Cumnor had a theory that she had been a governess in some family in which the poet visited and that, in consequence of her position, there was from the first something unavowed, or rather something quite clandestine, in their relations. I on the other hand had hatched a little romance according to which she was the daughter of an artist, a painter or a sculptor, who had left the Western world, when the century was fresh, to study in the ancient schools. It was essential to my hypothesis that this amiable man should have lost his wife, should have been poor and unsuccessful, and should have had a second daughter of a disposition quite different from Juliana's. It was also indispensable that he should have been accompanied to Europe by these young ladies and should have established himself there for the remainder of a struggling, saddened life. There was a further implication that Miss Bordereau had had in her youth a perverse and reckless, albeit a generous and fascinating character, and that she had braved some wondrous chances. By what passions had she been ravaged, by what adventures and sufferings had she been blanched, what store of memories had she laid away for the monotonous future?

I asked myself these things as I sat spinning

theories about her in my arbour and the bees droned
in the flowers. It was incontestable that, whether
for right or for wrong, most readers of certain of
Aspern's poems (poems not as ambiguous as the
sonnets—scarcely more divine, I think—of Shakespeare) had taken for granted that Juliana had not
always adhered to the steep footway of renunciation.
There hovered about her name a perfume of im-
penitent passion, an intimation that she had not
been exactly as the respectable young person in
general. Was this a sign that her singer had betrayed
her, had given her away, as we say nowadays, to
posterity? Certain it is that it would have been
difficult to put one's finger on the passage in which
her fair name suffered injury. Moreover, was not
any fame fair enough that was so sure of duration
and was associated with works immortal through
their beauty? It was a part of my idea that the
young lady had had a foreign lover—and say an
unedifying tragical rupture — before her meeting
with Jeffrey Aspern. She had lived with her father
and sister in a queer, old-fashioned, expatriated,
artistic Bohemia of the days when the aesthetic
was only the academic and the painters who knew
the best models of *contadina* and *pifferaro* wore
peaked hats and long hair. It was a society less
awake than the coteries of to-day—in its ignorance
of the wonderful chances, the opportunities of the
early bird, with which its path was strewn—to
tatters of old stuff and fragments of old crockery;
so that Miss Bordereau appeared not to have picked
up or have inherited many objects of importance.
There was no enviable *bric-à-brac*, with its provoking
legend of cheapness, in the room in which I had

seen her. Such a fact as that suggested bareness, but none the less it worked happily into the sentimental interest I had always taken in the early movement of my countrymen as visitors to Europe. When Americans went abroad in 1820 there was something romantic, almost heroic in it, as compared with the perpetual ferryings of the present hour, the hour at which photography and other conveniences have annihilated surprise. Miss Bordereau had sailed with her family on a tossing brig in the days of long voyages and sharp differences; she had had her emotions on the top of yellow diligences, passed the night at inns where she dreamed of travellers' tales, and was most struck, on reaching the Eternal City, with the elegance of Roman pearls and scarfs and mosaic brooches. There was something touching to me in all that, and my imagination frequently went back to the period. If Miss Bordereau carried it there, of course Jeffrey Aspern had at other times done so with greater force. It was a much more important fact, if one was looking at his genius critically, that he had lived in the days before the general transfusion. It had happened to me to regret that he had known Europe at all; I should have liked to see what he would have written without that experience, by which he had incontestably been enriched. But as his fate had ruled otherwise I went with him—I tried to judge how the general old order would have struck him. It was not only there, however, I watched him; the relations he had entertained with the special new had even a livelier interest. His own country after all had had most of his life, and his muse, as they said at that time, was essentially American. That was originally what I had prized him for; that at a period when our native land was nude and crude and provincial, when the famous 'atmosphere' it is supposed to lack was not even missed, when literature was lonely there and art and form almost impossible, he had found means to live and write like one of the first; to be free and general and not at all afraid; to feel, understand, and express everything.

V

I WAS seldom at home in the evening, for when I attempted to occupy myself in my apartments the lamplight brought in a swarm of noxious insects, and it was too hot for closed windows. Accordingly I spent the late hours either on the water—the moonlights of Venice are famous—or in the splendid square which serves as a vast forecourt to the strange old church of Saint Mark. I sat in front of Florian's café eating ices, listening to music, talking with acquaintances: the traveller will remember how the immense cluster of tables and little chairs stretches like a promontory into the smooth lake of the Piazza. The whole place, of a summer's evening, under the stars and with all the lamps, all the voices and light footsteps on marble—the only sounds of the immense arcade that encloses it—is an open-air saloon dedicated to cooling drinks and to a still finer degustation, that of the splendid impressions received during the day. When I didn't prefer to keep mine to myself there was always a stray tourist, disencumbered of his Baedeker, to discuss them with, or some domesticated painter rejoicing in the return of the season of strong effects. The great basilica, with its low domes and bristling embroideries, the mystery of its mosaic and sculpture, looked ghostly in the tempered gloom, and the sea-breeze passed between the twin columns of the Piazzetta, the lintels of a door no longer guarded, as gently as if a rich curtain swayed there. I used

211

sometimes on these occasions to think of the Misses Bordereau and of the pity of their being shut up in apartments which in the Venetian July even Venetian vastness couldn't relieve of some stuffiness. Their life seemed miles away from the life of the Piazza, and no doubt it was really too late to make the austere Juliana change her habits. But poor Miss Tina would have enjoyed one of Florian's ices, I was sure; sometimes I even had thoughts of carrying one home to her. Fortunately my patience bore fruit and I was not obliged to do anything so ridiculous.

One evening about the middle of July I came in earlier than usual—I forget what chance had led to this—and instead of going up to my quarters made my way into the garden. The temperature was very high; it was such a night as one would gladly have spent in the open air, and I was in no hurry to go to bed. I had floated home in my gondola, listening to the slow splash of the oar in the dark, narrow canals, and now the only thought that occupied me was that it would be good to recline at one's length in the fragrant darkness on a garden bench. The odour of the canal was doubtless at the bottom of that aspiration, and the breath of the garden, as I entered it, gave consistency to my purpose. It was delicious—just such an air as must have trembled with Romeo's vows when he stood among the thick flowers and raised his arms to his mistress's balcony. I looked at the windows of the palace to see if by chance the example of Verona—Verona being not far off—had been followed; but everything was dim, as usual, and everything was still. Juliana might on the summer nights of her youth have murmured down from open windows at Jeffrey Aspern, but Miss Tina was not a poet's mistress any more than I was a poet. This, however, didn't prevent my gratification from being great as I became aware on reaching the end of the garden that my younger *padrona* was seated in one of the bowers. At first I made out but an indistinct figure, not in the least counting on such an overture from one of my hostesses; it even occurred to me that some enamoured maidservant had stolen in to keep a tryst with her sweetheart. I was going to turn away, not to frighten her, when the figure rose to its height and I recognized Miss Bordereau's niece. I must do myself the justice that I didn't wish to frighten her either, and much as I had longed for some such accident I should have been capable of retreating. It was as if I had laid a trap for her by coming home earlier than usual and by adding to that oddity my invasion of the garden. As she rose she spoke to me, and then I guessed that perhaps, secure in my almost inveterate absence, it was her nightly practice to take a lonely airing. There was no trap in truth, because I had had no suspicion. At first I took the words she uttered for an impatience of my arrival; but as she repeated them—I hadn't caught them clearly—I had the surprise of hearing her say: 'Oh, dear, I 'm so glad you 've come!' She and her aunt had in common the property of unexpected speeches. She came out of the arbour almost as if to throw herself in my arms.

I hasten to add that I escaped this ordeal and that she didn't even then shake hands with me. It was an ease to her to see me and presently she told me why—because she was nervous when out of doors at night alone. The plants and shrubs looked so strange in the dark, and there were all sorts of queer sounds—she couldn't tell what they were—like the noises of animals. She stood close to me, looking about her with an air of greater security but without any demonstration of interest in me as an individual. Then I felt how little nocturnal prowlings could have been her habit, and I was also reminded—I had been afflicted by the same in talking with her before I took possession —that it was impossible to allow too much for her simplicity.

'You speak as if you were lost in the back-woods,' I cheeringly laughed. 'How you manage to keep out of this charming place when you 've only three steps to take to get into it is more than I 've yet been able to discover. You hide away amazingly so long as I 'm on the premises, I know; but I had a hope you peeped out a little at other times. You and your poor aunt are worse off than Carmelite nuns in their cells. Should you mind telling me how you exist without air, without exercise, without any sort of human contact? I don't see how you carry on the common business of life.'

She looked at me as if I had spoken a strange tongue, and her answer was so little of one that I felt it made for irritation. 'We go to bed very early—earlier than you 'd believe.' I was on the point of saying that this only deepened the mystery, but she gave me some relief by adding:

'Before you came we weren't so private. But I 've never been out at night.'

'Never in these fragrant alleys, blooming here under your nose?'

'Ah,' said Miss Tina, 'they were never nice till now!' There was a finer sense in this and a flattering comparison, so that it seemed to me I had gained some advantage. As I might follow that further by establishing a good grievance I asked her why, since she thought my garden nice, she had never thanked me in any way for the flowers I had been sending up in such quantities for the previous three weeks. I had not been discouraged—there had been, as she would have observed, a daily armful; but I had been brought up in the common forms and a word of recognition now and then would have touched me in the right place.

'Why, I didn't know they were for me!'

'They were for both of you. Why should I make a difference?'

Miss Tina reflected as if she might be thinking of a reason for that, but she failed to produce one. Instead of this she asked abruptly: 'Why in the world do you want so much to know us?'

'I ought, after all, to name a difference,' I replied. 'That question's your aunt's; it isn't yours. You wouldn't ask it if you hadn't been put up to it.'

'She didn't tell me to ask you,' Miss Tina replied without confusion. She was, indeed, the oddest mixture of shyness and straightness.

'Well, she has often wondered about it herself and expressed her wonder to you. She has insisted on it, so that she had put the idea into your head that I'm insufferably pushing. Upon my word, I think I've been very discreet. And how completely your aunt must have lost every tradition of sociability, to see anything out of the way in the idea that respectable, intelligent people, living as we do under the same roof, should occasionally exchange a remark! What could be more natural? We are of the same country and have at least some of the same tastes, since, like you, I 'm intensely fond of Venice.'

My friend seemed incapable of grasping more than one clause in any proposition, and she now spoke quickly, eagerly, as if she were answering my whole speech: 'I 'm not in the least fond of Venice. I should like to go far away!'

'Has she always kept you back so?' I went on, to show her I could be as irrelevant as herself.

'She told me to come out to-night; she has told me very often,' said Miss Tina. 'It is I who wouldn't come. I don't like to leave her.'

'Is she too weak, is she really failing?' I demanded, with more emotion, I think, than I meant to betray. I measured this by the way her eyes rested on me in the darkness. It embarrassed me a little, and to turn the matter off I continued genially: 'Do let us sit down together comfortably somewhere—while you tell me all about her.'

Miss Tina made no resistance to this. We found a bench less secluded, less confidential, as it were, than the one in the arbour; and we were still sitting there when I heard midnight ring out from those clear bells of Venice which vibrate with a solemnity of their own over the lagoon and hold the air so much more than the chimes of other places. We were together more than an hour and our interview gave, as it struck me, a great lift to my undertaking. Miss Tina accepted the situation without a protest; she had avoided me for three months, yet now she

treated me almost as if these three months had made
me an old friend. If I had chosen I might have
gathered from this that though she had avoided
me she had given a good deal of consideration to
doing so. She paid no attention to the flight of
time—never worried at my keeping her so long away
from her aunt. She talked freely, answering questions
and asking them and not even taking advantage of
certain longish pauses by which they were naturally
broken to say she thought she had better go in.
It was almost as if she were waiting for something
—something I might say to her—and intended to
give me my opportunity. I was the more struck
by this as she told me how much less well her aunt
had been for a good many days, and in a way that
was rather new. She was markedly weaker; at
moments she showed no strength at all; yet more
than ever before she wished to be left alone. That
was why she had told her to come out—not even to
remain in her own room, which was alongside; she
pronounced poor Miss Tina 'a worry, a bore, and a
source of aggravation.' She sat still for hours
together, as if for long sleep; she had always done
that, musing and dozing; but at such times formerly
she gave, in breaks, some small sign of life, of interest,
liking her companion to be near her with her work.
This sad personage confided to me that at present
her aunt was so motionless as to create the fear
she was dead; moreover, she scarce ate or drank—
one couldn't see what she lived on. The great thing
was that she still on most days got up; the serious
job was to dress her, to wheel her out of her bedroom.
She clung to as many of her old habits as possible
and had always, little company as they had received

for years, made a point of sitting in the great parlour.

I scarce knew what to think of all this—of Miss Tina's sudden conversion to sociability and of the strange fact that the more the old woman appeared to decline to her end the less she should desire to be looked after. The story hung indifferently together, and I even asked myself if it mightn't be a trap laid for me, the result of a design to make me show my hand. I couldn't have told why my companions (as they could only by courtesy be called) should have this purpose—why they should try to trip up so lucrative a lodger. But at any hazard I kept on my guard, so that Miss Tina shouldn't have occasion again to ask what I might really be 'up to.' Poor woman, before we parted for the night my mind was at rest as to what *she* might be. She was up to nothing at all.

She told me more about their affairs than I had hoped; there was no need to be prying, for it evidently drew her out simply to feel me listen and care. She ceased wondering why I *should*, and at last, while describing the brilliant life they had led years before, she almost chattered. It was Miss Tina who judged it brilliant; she said that when they first came to live in Venice, years and years back—I found her essentially vague about dates and the order in which events had occurred—there was never a week they hadn't some visitor or didn't make some pleasant *passeggio* in the town. They had seen all the curiosities; they had even been to the Lido in a boat—she spoke as if I might think there was a way on foot; they had had a collation there, brought in three baskets and spread out on the grass. I asked her what people she had known and she said, Oh, very nice ones—the Cavaliere Bombicci and the Contessa Altemura, with whom they had had a great friendship! Also English people—the Churtons and the Goldies and Mrs. Stock-Stock, whom they had loved dearly; she was dead and gone, poor dear. That was the case with most of their kind circle—this expression was Miss Tina's own; though a few were left, which was a wonder, considering how they had neglected them. She mentioned the names of two or three Venetian old women; of a certain doctor, very clever, who was so attentive—he came as a friend, he had really given up practice; of the *avvocato* Pochintesta, who wrote beautiful poems and had addressed one to her aunt. These people came to see them without fail every year, usually at the *capo d'anno*, and of old her aunt used to make them some little present—her aunt and she together: small things that she, Miss Tina turned out with her own hand, paper lamp-shades, or mats for the decanters of wine at dinner, or those woollen things that in cold weather are worn on the wrists. The last few years there hadn't been many presents; she couldn't think what to make and her aunt had lost interest and never suggested. But the people came all the same; if the good Venetians liked you once they liked you for ever.

There was affecting matter enough in the good faith of this sketch of former social glories; the picnic at the Lido had remained vivid through the ages and poor Miss Tina evidently was of the impression that she had had a dashing youth. She had in fact had a glimpse of the Venetian world in its gossiping, home-keeping, parsimonious professional walks; for I noted for the first time how nearly she had acquired by contact the trick of the familiar soft-sounding, almost infantile prattle of the place. I judged her to have imbibed this invertebrate dialect from the natural way the names of things and people—most purely local—rose to her lips. If she knew little of what they represented she knew still less of anything else. Her aunt had drawn in —the failure of interest in the table-mats and lamp-shades was a sign of that—and she hadn't been able to mingle in society or to entertain it alone; so that her range of reminiscence struck one as an old world altogether. Her tone, hadn't it been so decent, would have seemed to carry one back to the queer rococo Venice of Goldoni and Casanova. I found myself mistakenly thinking of her, too, as one of Jeffrey Aspern's contemporaries; this came from her having so little in common with my own. It was possible, I indeed reasoned, that she hadn't even heard of him; it might very well be that Juliana had forborne to lift for innocent eyes the veil that covered the temple of her glory. In this case she perhaps wouldn't know of the existence of the papers, and I welcomed that presumption—it made me feel more safe with her—till I remembered we had believed the letter of disavowal received by Cumnor to be in the handwriting of the niece. If it had been dictated to her she had of course to know what it was about; though the effect of it withal was to repudiate the idea of any connection with the poet. I held it probable, at all events, that Miss Tina hadn't read a word of his poetry. Moreover if, with her companion, she had always escaped invasion and research, there was little occasion for her having got it into her head that people were 'after' the letters. People had not been after them, for people hadn't heard of them. Cumnor's fruitless feeler would have been a solitary accident.

When midnight sounded Miss Tina got up; but she stopped at the door of the house only after she had wandered two or three times with me round the garden. 'When shall I see you again?' I asked before she went in; to which she replied with promptness that she should like to come out the next night. She added, however, that she shouldn't come—she was so far from doing everything she liked.

'You might do a few things *I* like,' I quite sincerely sighed.

'Oh, you—I don't believe you!' she murmured at this, facing me with her simple solemnity.

'Why don't you believe me?'

'Because I don't understand you.'

'That's just the sort of occasion to have faith.' I couldn't say more, though I should have liked to, as I saw I only mystified her; for I had no wish to have it on my conscience that I might pass for having made love to her. Nothing less should I have seemed to do had I continued to beg a lady to 'believe in me' in an Italian garden on a midsummer night. There was some merit in my scruples, for Miss Tina lingered and lingered: I made out in her the conviction that she shouldn't really soon come down again and the wish, therefore, to protract the present. She insisted, too, on making the talk between us personal to ourselves; and altogether her behaviour was such as would have been possible only to a perfectly artless and a considerably witless woman.

'I shall like the flowers better now that I know them also meant for me.'

'How could you have doubted it? If you'll tell me the kind you like best I'll send a double lot.'

'Oh, I like them all best!' Then she went on familiarly: 'Shall you study—shall you read and write—when you go up to your rooms?'

'I don't do that at night—at this season. The lamplight brings in the animals.'

'You might have known that when you came.'

'I did know it!'

'And in winter do you work at night?'

'I read a good deal, but I don't often write.' She listened as if these details had a rare interest, and suddenly a temptation quite at odds with all the prudence I had been teaching myself glimmered at me in her plain, mild face. Ah, yes, she was safe and I could make her safer! It seemed to me from one moment to another that I couldn't wait longer—that I really must take a sounding. So I went on: 'In general before I go to sleep (very often in bed; it's a bad habit, but I confess to it) I read some great poet. In nine cases out of ten it's a volume of Jeffrey Aspern.'

I watched her well as I pronounced that name, but I saw nothing wonderful. Why should I, indeed? Wasn't Jeffrey Aspern the property of the human race?

'Oh, *we* read him—we *have* read him,' she quietly replied.

'He's my poet of poets—I know him almost by heart.'

For an instant Miss Tina hesitated; then her sociability was too much for her. 'Oh, by heart —that 's nothing'; and, though dimly, she quite lighted. 'My aunt used to know him—to know him' — she paused an instant and I wondered what she was going to say—'to know him as a visitor.'

'As a visitor?' I guarded my tone.

'He used to call on her and take her out.'

I continued to stare. 'My dear lady, he died a hundred years ago!'

'Well,' she said amusingly, 'my aunt 's a hundred and fifty.'

'Mercy on us!' I cried; 'why didn't you tell me before? I should like so to ask her about him.'

'She wouldn't care for that—she wouldn't tell you,' Miss Tina returned.

'I don't care what she cares for! She *must* tell me—it 's not a chance to be lost.'

'Oh, you should have come twenty years ago. Then she still talked about him.'

'And what did she say?' I eagerly asked.

'I don't know—that he liked her immensely.'

'And she—didn't she like *him*?'

'She said he was a god.' Miss Tina gave me this information flatly, without expression; her tone might have made it a piece of trivial gossip. But it stirred me deeply as she dropped the words into the summer night; their sound might have been the light rustle of an old unfolded love-letter.

'Fancy, fancy!' I murmured. And then: 'Tell me this, please—has she got a portrait of him? They 're distressingly rare.'

'A portrait? I don't know,' said Miss Tina;

and now there was discomfiture in her face. 'Well, good night!' she added; and she turned into the house.

I accompanied her into the wide, dusky, stone-paved passage that corresponded on the ground floor with our grand *sala*. It opened at one end into the garden, at the other upon the canal, and was lighted now only by the small lamp always left for me to take up as I went to bed. An extinguished candle which Miss Tina apparently had brought down with her stood on the same table with it. 'Good night, good night!' I replied, keeping beside her as she went to get her light. 'Surely you 'd know, shouldn't you, if she had one?'

'If she had what?' the poor lady asked, looking at me queerly over the flame of her candle.

'A portrait of the god. I don't know what I wouldn't give to see it.'

'I don't know what she has got. She keeps her things locked up.' And Miss Tina went away toward the staircase with the sense evidently of having said too much.

I let her go—I wished not to frighten her—and I contented myself with remarking that Miss Bordereau wouldn't have locked up such a glorious possession as that: a thing a person would be proud of and hang up in a prominent place on the parlour-wall. Therefore of course she hadn't any portrait. Miss Tina made no direct answer to this and, candle in hand, with her back to me mounted two or three degrees. Then she stopped short and turned round, looking at me across the dusky space.

'Do you write—do you write?' There was a shake in her voice—she could scarcely bring it out.

'Do I write? Oh don't speak of my writing on the same day with Aspern's!'

'Do you write about *him*—do you pry into his life?'

'Ah, that's your aunt's question; it can't be yours!' I said in a tone of slightly wounded sensibility.

'All the more reason, then, that you should answer it. Do you, please?'

I thought I had allowed for the falsehoods I should have to tell, but I found that in fact when it came to the point I hadn't. Besides, now that I had an opening there was a kind of relief in being frank. Lastly—it was perhaps fanciful, even fatuous —I guessed that Miss Tina personally wouldn't in the last resort be less my friend. So after a moment's hesitation I answered: 'Yes, I've written about him and I'm looking for more material. In heaven's name have you got any?'

'*Santo Dio!*' she exclaimed, without heeding my question; and she hurried upstairs and out of sight. I might count upon her in the last resort, but for the present she was visibly alarmed. The proof of it was that she began to hide again, so that for a fortnight I kept missing her. I found my patience ebbing, and after four or five days of this I told the gardener to stop the 'floral tributes.'

VI

ONE afternoon, at last however, as I came down from my quarters to go out, I found her in the *sala*; it was our first encounter on that ground since I had come into the house. She put on no air of being there by accident; there was an ignorance of such arts in her honest, angular diffidence. That I might be quite sure she was waiting for me she mentioned it at once, but telling me with it that Miss Bordereau wished to see me: she would take me into the room at that moment if I had time. If I had been late for a love-tryst I would have stayed for this, and I quickly signified that I should be delighted to wait on my benefactress. 'She wants to talk with you—to know you,' Miss Tina said, smiling as if she herself appreciated that idea; and she led me to the door of her aunt's apartment. I stopped her a moment before she had opened it, looking at her with some curiosity. I told her that this was a great satisfaction to me and a great honour; but all the same I should like to ask what had made Miss Bordereau so markedly and suddenly change. It had been only the other day that she wouldn't suffer me near her. Miss Tina was not embarrassed by my question; she had as many little unexpected serenities, plausibilities, almost, as if she told fibs, but the odd part of them was that they had on the contrary their source in her truthfulness. 'Oh, my aunt varies,' she answered; 'it's so terribly dull— I suppose she's tired.'

'But you told me she wanted more and more to be alone.'

Poor Miss Tina coloured as if she found me too pushing. 'Well, if you don't believe she wants to see you, I haven't invented it! I think people often are capricious when they 're very old.'

'That 's perfectly true. I only wanted to be clear as to whether you 've repeated to her what I told you the other night.'

'What you told me!'

'About Jeffrey Aspern—that I 'm looking for materials.'

'If I had told her, do you think she 'd have sent for you?'

'That 's exactly what I want to know. If she wants to keep him to herself she might have sent for me to tell me so.'

'She won't speak of him,' said Miss Tina. Then as she opened the door she added in a lower tone: 'I told her nothing.'

The old woman was sitting in the same place in which I had seen her last, in the same position, with the same mystifying bandage over her eyes. Her welcome was to turn her almost invisible face to me and show me that while she sat silent she saw me clearly. I made no motion to shake hands with her; I now felt too well that this was out of place for ever. It had been sufficiently enjoined —too venerable to touch. There was something so grim in her aspect—it was partly the accident of her green shade—as I stood there to be measured, that I ceased on the spot to doubt her suspecting me, though I didn't in the least myself suspect that Miss Tina hadn't betrayed me, but the old woman's brooding instinct had served her; she had turned me over and over in the long, still hours and had guessed. The worst of it was that she looked terribly like an old woman who at a pinch would, even like Sardanapalus, burn her treasure. Miss Tina pushed a chair forward, saying to me: 'This will be a good place for you to sit.' As I took possession of it I asked after Miss Bordereau's health; expressed the hope that in spite of the very hot weather it was satisfactory. She answered that it was good enough —good enough; that it was a great thing to be alive.

'Oh, as to that, it depends upon what you compare it with!' I returned with a laugh.

'I don't compare—I don't compare. If I did that I should have given everything up long ago.'

I liked to take this for a subtle allusion to the rapture she had known in the society of Jeffrey Aspern—though it was true that such an allusion would have accorded ill with the wish I imputed to her to keep him buried in her soul. What it accorded with was my constant conviction that no human being had ever had a happier social gift than his, and what it seemed to convey was that nothing in the world was worth speaking of if one pretended to speak of that. But one didn't pretend! Miss Tina sat down beside her aunt, looking as if she had reason to believe some wonderful talk would come off between us.

'It 's about the beautiful flowers,' said the old lady; 'you sent us so many—I ought to have thanked you for them before. But I don't write letters and I receive company but at long intervals.'

She hadn't thanked me while the flowers continued to come, but she departed from her custom so far as to send for me as soon as she began to fear they wouldn't come any more. I noted this; I remembered what an acquisitive propensity she had shown me when when it was a question of extracting gold from me, and I privately rejoiced at the happy thought I had had in suspending my tribute. She had missed it and was willing to make a concession to bring it back. At the first sign of this concession I could only go to meet her. 'I 'm afraid you haven't had many, of late, but they shall begin again immediately—to-morrow, to-night.'

'Oh, do send us some to-night!' Miss Tina cried as if it were a great affair.

'What else should you do with them? It isn't a manly taste to make a bower of your room,' the old woman remarked.

'I don't make a bower of my room, but I 'm exceedingly fond of growing flowers, of watching their ways. There 's nothing unmanly in that: it has been the amusement of philosophers, of statesmen in retirement; even, I think, of great captains.'

'I suppose you know you can sell them—those you don't use,' Miss Bordereau went on. 'I dare say they wouldn't give you much for them; still, you could make a bargain.'

'Oh, I 've never in my life made a bargain, as you ought pretty well to have gathered. My gardener disposes of them and I ask no questions.'

'I 'd ask a few, I can promise you!' said Miss Bordereau; and it was so I first heard the strange sound of her laugh, which was as if the faint 'walking' ghost of her old-time tone had suddenly cut a caper. I couldn't get used to the idea that this vision of pecuniary profit was most what drew out the divine Juliana.

'Come into the garden yourself and pick them; come as often as you like; come every day. The flowers are all for you,' I pursued, addressing Miss Tina and carrying off this veracious statement by treating it as an innocent joke. 'I can't imagine why she doesn't come down,' I added for Miss Bordereau's benefit.

'You must make her come; you must come up and fetch her,' the old woman said to my satisfaction. 'That odd thing you 've made in the corner will do very well for her to sit in.'

The allusion to the most elaborate of my shady coverts, a sketchy 'summer-house,' was irreverent; it confirmed the impression I had already received that there was a flicker of impertinence in Miss Bordereau's talk, a vague echo of the boldness or the archness of her adventurous youth and which had somehow automatically outlived passions and faculties. None the less, I asked: 'Wouldn't it be possible for you to come down there yourself? Wouldn't it do you good to sit there in the shade and the sweet air?'

'Oh, sir, when I move out of this it won't be to sit in the air, and I 'm afraid that any that may be stirring around me won't be particularly sweet! It will be a very dark shade indeed. But that won't be just yet,' Miss Bordereau continued cannily, as if to correct any hopes this free glance at the last receptacle of her mortality might lead me to entertain. 'I 've sat here many a day and have had enough of arbours in my time. But I 'm not afraid to wait till I 'm called.'

Miss Tina had expected, as I felt, rare conversation, but perhaps she found it less gracious on her aunt's side—considering I had been sent for with a civil intention—than she had hoped. As to give the position a turn that would put our companion in a light more favourable she said to me: 'Didn't I tell you the other night that she had sent me out? You see I can do what I like!'

'Do you pity her—do you teach her to pity herself?' Miss Bordereau demanded, before I had time to answer this appeal. 'She has a much easier life than I had at her age.'

'You must remember it has been quite open to me,' I said, 'to think you rather inhuman.'

'Inhuman? That's what the poets used to call the women a hundred years ago. Don't try that; you won't do as well as they!' Juliana went on. 'There's no more poetry in the world—that *I* know of, at least. But I won't bandy words with you,' she said, and I well remember the old-fashioned, artificial sound she gave the speech. 'You make me talk, talk, talk! It isn't good for me at all.' I got up at this and told her I would take no more of her time; but she detained me to put a question: 'Do you remember, the day I saw you about the rooms, that you offered us the use of your gondola?' And when I assented, promptly struck again with her disposition to make a 'good thing' of my being there and wondering what she now had in her eye, she produced: 'Why don't you take that girl out in it and show her the place?'

'Oh, dear aunt, what do you want to do with me?' cried the 'girl,' with a piteous quaver. 'I know all about the place!'

'Well, then, go with him and explain!' said Miss
Bordereau, who gave an effect of cruelty to her
implacable power of retort. This showed her as a
sarcastic, profane, cynical old woman. 'Haven't
we heard that there have been all sorts of changes
in all these years? You ought to see them, and at
your age—I don't mean because you're so young
—you ought to take the chances that come. You're
old enough, my dear, and this gentleman won't
hurt you. He'll show you the famous sunsets, if
they still go on—*do* they go on? The sun set for
me so long ago. But that's not a reason. Besides,
I shall never miss you; you think you're too important. Take her to the Piazza; it used to be very
pretty,' Miss Bordereau continued, addressing herself to me. 'What have they done with the funny
old church? I hope it hasn't tumbled down. Let
her look at the shops; she may take some money,
she may buy what she likes.'

Poor Miss Tina had got up, discountenanced and
helpless, and as we stood there before her aunt it
would certainly have struck a spectator of the scene
that our venerable friend was making rare sport of
us. Miss Tina protested in a confusion of exclama-
tions and murmurs; but I lost no time in saying that
if she would do me the honour to accept the hospi-
tality of my boat I would engage she really shouldn't
be bored. Or if she didn't want so much of my
company, the boat itself, with the gondolier, was at
her service; he was a capital oar and she might
have every confidence. Miss Tina, without definitely
answering this speech, looked away from me and
out of the window quite as if about to weep, and
I remarked that once we had Miss Bordereau's

approval we could easily come to an understanding. We would take an hour, whichever she liked, one of the very next days. As I made my obeisance to the old lady I asked her if she would kindly permit me to see her again.

For a moment she kept me; then she said: 'Is it very necessary to your happiness?'

'It diverts me more than I can say.'

'You 're wonderfully civil. Don't you know it almost kills *me*?'

'How can I believe that when I see you more animated, more brilliant than when I came in?'

'That 's very true, aunt,' said Miss Tina. 'I think it does you good.'

'Isn't it touching, the solicitude we each have that the other shall enjoy himself?' sneered Miss Bordereau. 'If you think me brilliant to-day you don't know what you are talking about; you 've never seen an agreeable woman. What do you people know about good society?' she cried; but before I could tell her, 'Don't try to pay me a compliment; I 've been spoiled,' she went on. 'My door 's shut, but you may sometimes knock.'

With this she dismissed me and I left the room. The latch closed behind me, but Miss Tina, contrary to my hope, had remained within. I passed slowly across the hall and, before taking my way downstairs, waited a little. My hope was answered; after a minute my conductress followed me. 'That 's a delightful idea about the Piazza,' I said. 'When will you go—to-night, to-morrow?'

She had been disconcerted, as I have mentioned, but I had already perceived, and I was to observe again, that when Miss Tina was embarrassed she

didn't—as most women would have in like case—
turn away, floundering and hedging, but came
closer, as it were, with a deprecating, a clinging
appeal to be spared, to be protected. Her attitude
was a constant prayer for aid and explanation, and
yet no woman in the world could have been less of
a comedian. From the moment you were kind to
her she depended on you absolutely; her self-con-
sciousness dropped and she took the greatest intimacy,
the innocent intimacy that was all she could con-
ceive, for granted. She didn't know, she now
declared, what possessed her aunt, who had changed
so quickly, who had got some idea. I replied that
she must catch the idea and let me have it: we
would go and take an ice together at Florian's
and she should report while we listened to the
band.

'Oh, it will take me a long time to be able to
"report"!' she said rather ruefully; and she could
promise me this satisfaction neither for that night
nor for the next. I was patient now, however, for
I felt I had only to wait; and in fact at the end of
the week, one lovely evening after dinner, she stepped
into my gondola, to which in honour of the occasion
I had attached a second oar.

We swept in the course of five minutes into the
Grand Canal; whereupon she uttered a murmur
of ecstasy as fresh as if she had been a tourist just
arrived. She had forgotten the splendour of the
great water-way on a clear summer evening, and
how the sense of floating between marble palaces
and reflected lights disposed the mind to freedom
and ease. We floated long and far, and though my
friend gave no high-pitched voice to her glee I was

sure of her full surrender. She was more than pleased, she was transported; the whole thing was an immense liberation. The gondola moved with slow strokes, to give her time to enjoy it, and she listened to the plash of the oars, which grew louder and more musically liquid as we passed into narrow canals, as if it were a revelation of Venice. When I asked her how long it was since she had thus floated, she answered: 'Oh, I don't know; a long time—not since my aunt began to be ill.' This was not the only show of her extreme vagueness about the previous years and the line marking off the period of Miss Bordereau's eminence. I was not at liberty to keep her out long, but we took a considerable *giro* before going to the Piazza. I asked her no questions, holding off by design from her life at home and the things I wanted to know; I poured, rather, treasures of information about the objects before and around us into her ears, describing also Florence and Rome, discoursing on the charms and advantages of travel. She reclined, receptive, on the deep leather cushion, turned her eyes conscientiously to everything I noted and never mentioned to me till some time afterwards that she might be supposed to know Florence better than I, as she had lived there for years with her kinswoman. At last she said with the shy impatience of a child: 'Are we not really going to the Piazza? That 's what I want to see!' I immediately gave the order that we should go straight, after which we sat silent with the expectation of arrival. As some time still passed, however, she broke out of her own movement: 'I 've found out what 's the matter with my aunt: she 's afraid you 'll go!'

I quite gasped. 'What has put that into her head?'

'She has had an idea you've not been happy. That's why she is different now.'

'You mean, she wants to make me happier?'

'Well, she wants you not to go. She wants you to stay.'

'I suppose you mean on account of the rent,' I remarked candidly.

Miss Tina's candour but profited. 'Yes, you know; so that I shall have more.'

'How much does she want you to have?' I asked with all the gaiety I now felt. 'She ought to fix the sum, so that I may stay till it's made up.'

'Oh, that wouldn't please me,' said Miss Tina. 'It would be unheard of, your taking that trouble.'

'But suppose I should have my own reasons for staying in Venice?'

'Then it would be better for you to stay in some other house.'

'And what would your aunt say to that?'

'She wouldn't like it at all. But I should think you'd do well to give up your reasons and go away altogether.'

'Dear Miss Tina,' I said, 'it's not so easy to give up my reasons!'

She made no immediate answer to this, but after a moment broke out afresh: 'I think I know what your reasons are!'

'I dare say, because the other night I almost told you how I wished you'd help me to make them good.'

'I can't do that without being false to my aunt.'

'What do you mean by being false to her?'

'Why, she would never consent to what you want. She has been asked, she has been written to. It makes her fearfully angry.'

'Then she *has* papers of value?' I precipitately cried.

'Oh, she has everything!' sighed Miss Tina, with a curious weariness, a sudden lapse into gloom.

These words caused all my pulses to throb, for I regarded them as precious evidence. I felt them too deeply to speak and in the interval the gondola approached the Piazzetta. After we had disembarked I asked my companion if she would rather walk round the square or go and sit before the great café; to which she replied that she would do whichever I liked best—I must only remember again how little time she had. I assured her there was plenty to do both, and we made the circuit of the long arcades. Her spirits revived at the sight of the bright shop-windows, and she lingered and stopped admiring or disapproving of their contents, asking me what I thought of things, theorizing about prices. My attention wandered from her; her words of a while before, 'Oh, she has everything!' echoed so in my consciousness We sat down at last in the crowded circle at Florian's, finding an unoccupied table among those that were ranged in the square. It was a splendid night and all the world out of doors; Miss Tina couldn't have wished the elements more auspicious for her return to society. I saw she felt it all even more than she told, but her impressions were wellnigh too many for her. She had forgotten the attraction of the world and was learning that she had for the best years of her life been rather mercilessly cheated of it. This didn't make her

angry; but as she took in the charming scene her
face had, in spite of its smile of appreciation, the
flush of a wounded surprise. She didn't speak, sunk
in the sense of opportunities, for ever lost, that
ought to have been easy; and this gave me a chance
to say to her: 'Did you mean a while ago, that your
aunt has a plan of keeping me on by admitting
me occasionally to her presence?'

'She thinks it will make a difference with you
if you sometimes see her. She wants you so much
to stay that she's willing to make that concession.'

'And what good does she consider I think it will
do me to see her?'

'I don't know; it must be interesting,' said Miss
Tina simply. 'You told her you found it so.'

'So I did; but every one doesn't think that.'

'No, of course not, or more people would
try.'

'Well, if she's capable of making that reflection
she's capable also of making this further one,' I
went on: 'that I must have a particular reason for
not doing as others do, in spite of the interest she
offers—for not leaving her alone.' Miss Tina looked
as if she failed to grasp this rather complicated
proposition; so I continued: 'If you've not told
her what I said to you the other night may she not
at least have guessed it?'

'I don't know—she's very suspicious.'

'But she hasn't been made so by indiscreet
curiosity, by persecution?'

'No, no; it isn't that,' said Miss Tina, turning
on me a troubled face. 'I don't know how to say
it; it's on account of something—ages ago, before
I was born—in her life.'

'Something? What sort of thing?'—I asked it as if I could have no idea.

'Oh, she has never told me.' And I was sure my friend spoke the truth.

Her extreme limpidity was almost provoking, and I felt for the moment that she would have been more satisfactory if she had been less ingenuous. 'Do you suppose it's something to which Jeffrey Aspern's letters and papers—I mean the things in her possession—have reference?'

'I dare say it is' my companion exclaimed as if this were a very happy suggestion. 'I've never looked at any of those things.'

'None of them? Then how do you know what they are?'

'I don't,' said Miss Tina placidly. 'I've never had them in my hands. But I've seen them when she has had them out.'

'Does she have them out often?'

'Not now, but she used to. She's very fond of them.'

'In spite of their being compromising?'

'Compromising?' Miss Tina repeated as if vague to what that meant. I felt almost as one who corrupts the innocence of youth.

'I allude to their containing painful memories.'

'Oh, I don't think anything's painful.'

'You mean there's nothing to affect her reputation?'

An odder look even than usual came at this into the face of Miss Bordereau's niece—a confession, it seemed, of helplessness, an appeal to me to deal fairly, generously with her. I had brought her to the Piazza, placed her among charming influences, paid her an attention she appreciated, and now I appeared to show it all as a bribe—a bribe to make her turn in some way against her aunt. She was of a yielding nature and capable of doing almost anything to please a person markedly kind to her; but the greatest kindness of all would be not to presume too much on this. It was strange enough, as I afterwards thought, that she had not the least air of resenting my want of consideration for her aunt's character, which would have been in the worst possible taste if anything less vital—from my point of view—had been at stake. I don't think she really measured it. 'Do you mean she ever did something bad?' she asked in a moment.

'Heaven forbid I should say so, and it's none of my business. Besides, if she did,' I agreeably put it, 'that was in other ages, in another world. But why shouldn't she destroy her papers?'

'Oh, she loves them too much.'

'Even now, when she may be near her end?'

'Perhaps when she's sure of that she will.'

'Well, Miss Tina,' I said, 'that's just what I should like you to prevent.'

'How can I prevent it?'

'Couldn't you get them away from her?'

'And give them to you?'

This put the case, superficially, with sharp irony, but I was sure of her not intending that. 'Oh, I mean that you might let me see them and look them over. It isn't for myself, or that I should want them at any cost to any one else. It's simply that they would be of such immense interest to the public, such immeasurable importance as a contribution to Jeffrey Aspern's history.'

She listened to me in her usual way, as if I abounded

in matters she had never heard of, and I felt almost as base as the reporter of a newspaper who forces his way into a house of mourning. This was marked when she presently said: 'There was a gentleman who some time ago wrote to her in very much those words. He also wanted her papers.'

'And did she answer him?' I asked, rather ashamed of not having my friend's rectitude.

'Only when he had written two or three times. He made her very angry.'

'And what did she say?'

'She said he was a devil,' Miss Tina replied categorically.

'She used that expression in her letter?'

'Oh, no; she said it to me. She made me write to him.'

'And what did you say?'

'I told him there were no papers at all.'

'Ah, poor gentleman!' I groaned.

'I knew there were, but I wrote what she bade me.'

'Of course, you had to do that. But I hope I shan't pass for a devil.'

'It will depend upon what you ask me to do for you,' my companion smiled.

'Oh, if there's a chance of *your* thinking so my affair's in a bad way! I shan't ask you to steal for me, nor even to fib—for you *can't* fib, unless on paper. But the principal thing is this—to prevent her destroying the papers.'

'Why, I've no control of her,' said Miss Tina. 'It's she who controls me.'

'But she doesn't control her own arms and legs, does she? The way she would naturally destroy her letters would be to burn them. Now she can't burn them without fire, and she can't get fire unless you give it to her.'

'I've always done everything she has asked,' my poor friend pleaded. 'Besides, there's Olimpia.'

I was on the point of saying that Olimpia was probably corruptible, but I thought it best not to sound that note. So I simply put it that this frail creature might perhaps be managed.

'Every one can be managed by my aunt,' said Miss Tina. And then she remembered that her holiday was over; she must go home.

I laid my hand on her arm, across the table, to stay her a moment. 'What I want of you is a general promise to help me.'

'Oh, how *can* I, how *can* I?' she asked, wondering and troubled. She was half-surprised, half-frightened at my attaching that importance to her, at my calling on her for action.

'This is the main thing: to watch our friend carefully and warn me in time, before she commits that dreadful sacrilege.'

'I can't watch her when she makes me go out.'

'That's very true.'

'And when you do too.'

'Mercy on us—do you think she'll have done anything to-night?'

'I don't know. She's very cunning.'

'Are you trying to frighten me?' I asked.

I felt this question sufficiently answered when my companion murmured in a musing, almost envious way: 'Oh, but she loves them—she loves them!'

This reflection, repeated with such emphasis, gave me great comfort; but to obtain more of that balm

I said: 'If she shouldn't intend to destroy the objects
we speak of before her death she 'll probably have
made some disposition by will.'

'By will?'

'Hasn't she made a will for your benefit?'

'Ah, she has so little to leave. That 's why she
likes money,' said Miss Tina.

'Might I ask, since we 're really talking things
over, what you and she live on?'

'On some money that comes from America, from
a gentleman—I think a lawyer—in New York. He
sends it every quarter. It isn't much!'

'And won't she have disposed of that?'

My companion hesitated—I saw she was blushing.
'I believe it 's mine,' she said; and the look and
tone which accompanied these words betrayed so
the absence of the habit of thinking of herself that
I almost thought her charming. The next instant
she added: 'But she had in an *avvocato* here once,
ever so long ago. And some people came and signed
something.'

'They were probably witnesses. And you weren't
asked to sign? Well then,' I argued, rapidly and
hopefully, 'it 's because you 're the legatee. She
must have left all her documents to you!'

'If she has it 's with very strict conditions,' Miss
Tina responded, rising quickly, while the movement
gave the words a small character of decision. They
seemed to imply that the bequest would be accompanied with a proviso that the articles bequeathed
should remain concealed from every inquisitive eye,
and that I was very much mistaken if I thought
her the person to depart from an injunction so
absolute.

'Oh, of course, you 'll have to abide by the terms,' I said; and she uttered nothing to mitigate the rigour of this conclusion. None the less, later on, just before we disembarked at her own door after a return which had taken place almost in silence, she said to me abruptly: 'I 'll do what I can to help you.' I was grateful for this—it was very well so far as it went; but it didn't keep me from remembering that night in a worried waking hour that I now had her word for it to re-enforce my own impression that the old woman was full of craft.

VII

THE fear of what this side of her character might have led her to do made me nervous for days afterwards. I waited for an intimation from Miss Tina; I almost read it as her duty to keep me informed, to let me know definitely whether or no Miss Bordereau had sacrificed her treasures. But as she gave no sign I lost patience and determined to put the case to the very touch of my own senses. I sent late one afternoon to ask if I might pay the ladies a visit, and my servant came back with surprising news. Miss Bordereau could be approached without the least difficulty; she had been moved out into the *sala* and was sitting by the window that overlooked the garden. I descended and found this picture correct; the old lady had been wheeled forth into the world and had a certain air, which came mainly perhaps from some brighter element in her dress, of being prepared again to have converse with it. It had not yet, however, begun to flock about her; she was perfectly alone and, though the door stood open, I had at first no glimpse of Miss Tina. The window at which she sat had the afternoon shade and, one of the shutters having been pushed back, she could see the pleasant garden, where the summer sun had by this time dried up too many of the plants—she could see the yellow light and the long shadows.

'Have you come to tell me you 'll take the rooms for six months more?' she asked as I approached her, startling me by something coarse in her cupidity almost as much as if she hadn't already given me a specimen of it. Juliana's desire to make our acquaintance lucrative had been, as I have sufficiently indicated, a false note in my image of the woman who had inspired a great poet with immortal lines; but I may say here definitely that I after all recognized large allowance to be made for her. It was I who had kindled the unholy flame; it was I who had put into her head that she had the means of making money. She appeared never to have thought of that; she had been living wastefully for years, in a house five times too big for her, on a footing that I could explain only by the presumption that, excessive as it was, the space she enjoyed cost her next to nothing and that, small as were her revenues, they left her, for Venice, an appreciable margin. I had descended on her one day and taught her to calculate, and my almost extravagant comedy on the subject of the garden had presented me irresistibly in the light of a victim. Like all persons who achieve the miracle of changing their point of view late in life, she had been intensely converted; she had seized my hint with a desperate, tremulous clutch.

I invited myself to go and get one of the chairs that stood, at a distance, against the wall—she had given herself no concern as to whether I should sit or stand; and while I placed it near her I began gaily: 'Oh, dear madam, what an imagination you have, what an intellectual sweep! I'm a poor devil of a man of letters who lives from day to day. How can I take palaces by the year? My existence is precarious. I don't know whether six months hence I shall have bread to put in my mouth. I've treated myself for once; it has been an immense luxury. But when it comes to going on——!'

'Are your rooms too dear? If they are you can have more for the same money,' Juliana responded. 'We can arrange, we can *combinare*, as they say here.'

'Well, yes, since you ask me, they're too dear, much too dear,' I said. 'Evidently you suppose me richer than I am.'

She looked at me as from the mouth of her cave. 'If you write books don't you sell them?'

'Do you mean don't people buy them? A little, a very little—not so much as I could wish. Writing books, unless one be a great genius—and even then! —is the last road to fortune. I think there's no more money to be made by good letters.'

'Perhaps you don't choose nice subjects. What do you write about?' Miss Bordereau implacably pursued.

'About the books of other people. I'm a critic, a commentator, an historian, in a small way.' I wondered what she was coming to.

'And what other people now?'

'Oh, better ones than myself: the great writers mainly—the great philosophers and poets of the past; those who are dead and gone and can't, poor darlings, speak for themselves.'

'And what do you say about them?'

'I say they sometimes attached themselves to very clever women!' I replied as for pleasantness. I had measured, as I thought, my risk, but as my words fell upon the air they were to strike me as imprudent. However, I had launched them and I wasn't sorry, for perhaps after all the old woman would be willing to treat. It seemed tolerably obvious that she knew my secret; why, therefore, drag the process out? But she didn't take what I had said as a confession; she only asked:

'Do you think it's right to rake up the past?'

'I don't feel that I know what you mean by raking it up. How can we get at it unless we dig a little? The present has such a rough way of treading it down.'

'Oh, I like the past, but I don't like critics,' my hostess declared with her hard complacency.

'Neither do I, but I like their discoveries.'

'Aren't they mostly lies?'

'The lies are what they sometimes discover,' I said, smiling at the quiet impertinence of this. 'They often lay bare the truth.'

'The truth is God's, it isn't man's; we had better leave it alone. Who can judge of it?—who can say?'

'We're terribly in the dark, I know,' I admitted; 'but if we give up trying what becomes of all the fine things? What becomes of the work I just mentioned, that of the great philosophers and poets? It's all vain words if there's nothing to measure it by.'

'You talk as if you were a tailor,' said Miss Bordereau whimsically; and then she added quickly and in a different manner: 'This house is very fine; the proportions are magnificent. To-day I wanted to look at this part again. I made them bring me out here. When your man came just now to learn if I would see you I was on the point of sending for you to ask if you didn't mean to go on. I wanted to judge what I'm letting you have. This *sala* is very grand,' she pursued like an auctioneer, moving a little, as I guessed, her invisible eyes. 'I don't believe you often have lived in such a house, eh?'

'I can't afford to!' I said.

'Well, then, how much will you give me for six months?'

I was on the point of exclaiming—and the air of excruciation in my face would have denoted a moral fact—'Don't, Juliana; for *his* sake, don't!' But I controlled myself and asked less passionately: 'Why should I remain so long as that?'

'I thought you liked it,' said Miss Bordereau, with her shrivelled dignity.

'So I thought I should.'

For a moment she said nothing more, and I left my own words to suggest to her what they might. I half expected her to say, coldly enough, that if I had been disappointed we needn't continue the discussion, and this in spite of the fact that I believed her now to have in her mind—however it had come there—what would have told her that my disappointment was natural. But to my extreme surprise she ended by observing: 'If you don't think we 've treated you well enough perhaps we can discover some way of treating you better.' This speech was somehow so incongruous that it made me laugh again, and I excused myself by saying that she talked as if I were a sulky boy pouting in the corner and having to be 'brought round.' I hadn't a grain of complaint to make; and could anything have exceeded Miss Tina's graciousness in accompanying me a few nights before to the Piazza? At this the old woman went on: 'Well, you brought it on yourself!' And then in a different tone: 'She's a very fine girl.' I assented cordially to this proposition, and she expressed the hope that I did so not merely to be obliging, but that I really liked her. Meanwhile I wondered still more what Miss Bordereau was coming to. 'Except for me, to-day,' she said, 'she hasn't a relation in the world.' Did she, by describing her niece as amiable and unencumbered, wish to represent her as a *parti*?

It was perfectly true that I couldn't afford to go on with my rooms at a fancy price and that I had already devoted to my undertaking almost all the hard cash I had set apart for it. My patience and my time were by no means exhausted, but I should be able to draw upon them only on a more usual Venetian basis. I was willing to pay the precious personage with whom my pecuniary dealings were such a discord twice as much as any other *padrona di casa* would have asked, but I wasn't willing to pay her twenty times as much. I told her so plainly, and my plainness appeared to have some success, for she exclaimed: 'Very good; you've done what I asked you—you've made an offer!'

'Yes, but not for half a year. Only by the month.'

'Oh, I must think of that, then.' She seemed disappointed that I wouldn't tie myself to a period, and I guessed that she wished both to secure me and to discourage me; to say severely: 'Do you dream that you can get off with less than six months? Do you dream that even by the end of that time you'll be appreciably nearer your victory?' What was most in my mind was that she had a fancy to play me the trick of making me engage myself when in fact she had sacrificed her treasure. There was a moment when my suspense on the point was so acute that I all but broke out with the question, and what kept it back was but an instinctive recoil—lest it should be a mistake—from the last violence of self-exposure. She was such a subtle old witch that one could never tell where one stood with her. You may imagine whether it cleared up the puzzle when, just after she had said she would think of my proposal and without any formal transition, she drew out of her pocket with an embarrassed hand a small object wrapped in a crumpled white paper. She held it there a moment and then resumed: 'Do you know much about curiosities?'

'About curiosities?'

'About antiquities, the old gimcracks that people pay so much for to-day. Do you know the kind of price they bring?'

I thought I saw what was coming, but I said ingenuously: 'Do you want to buy something?'

'No, I want to sell. What would an amateur give me for that?' She unfolded the white paper and made a motion for me to take from her a small oval portrait. I possessed myself of it with fingers of which I could only hope that they didn't betray the intensity of their clutch, and she added: 'I would part with it only for a good price.'

At the first glance I recognized Jeffrey Aspern, and was well aware that I flushed with the act. As she was watching me, however, I had the consistency to exclaim: 'What a striking face! Do tell me who it is.'

'He's an old friend of mine, a very distinguished man in his day. He gave it me himself, but I'm afraid to mention his name, lest you never should have heard of him, critic and historian as you are. I know the world goes fast and one generation forgets another. He was all the fashion when I was young.'

She was perhaps amazed at my assurance, but I was surprised at hers; at her having the energy, in her state of health and at her time of life, to wish to sport with me to that tune simply for her private entertainment—the humour to test me and practise on me and befool me. This at least was the interpretation that I put upon her production of the relic, for I couldn't believe she really desired to sell it or cared for any information I might give her. What she wished was to dangle it before my eyes and put a prohibitive price on it. 'The face comes back to me, it torments me,' I said, turning the object this way and that and looking at it very critically. It was a careful but not a supreme work of art, larger than the ordinary miniature and representing a young man with a remarkably handsome face, in a high-collared green coat and a buff waistcoat. I felt in the little work a virtue of likeness and judged it to have been painted when the model was about twenty-five. There are, as all the world knows, three other portraits of the poet in existence, but none of so early a date as this elegant image. 'I've never seen the original, clearly a man of a past age, but I've seen other reproductions of this face,' I went on. 'You expressed doubt of this generation's having heard of the gentleman, but he strikes me for all the world as a celebrity. Now who is he? I can't put my finger on him—I can't give him a label. Wasn't he a writer? Surely, he's a poet.' I was determined that it should be she, not I, who should first pronounce Jeffrey Aspern's name.

My resolution was taken in ignorance of Miss Bordereau's extremely resolute character, and her lips never formed in my hearing the syllables that meant so much for her. She neglected to answer my question, but raised her hand to take back the picture, using a gesture which though impotent was in a high degree peremptory. 'It's only a person who should know for himself that would give me my price,' she said with a certain dryness.

'Oh, then you have a price?' I didn't restore the charming thing; not from any vindictive purpose, but because I instinctively clung to it. We looked at each other hard while I retained it.

'I know the least I would take. What it occurred to me to ask you about is the most I shall be able to get.'

She made a movement, drawing herself together as if, in a spasm of dread at having lost her prize, she had been impelled to the immense effort of rising to snatch it from me. I instantly placed it in her hand again, saying as I did so: 'I should like to have it myself, but with your ideas it would be quite beyond my mark.'

She turned the small oval plate over in her lap, with its face down, and I heard her catch her breath as after a strain or an escape. This, however, did not prevent her saying in a moment: 'You'd buy a likeness of a person you don't know by an artist who has no reputation?'

'The artist may have no reputation, but that thing's wonderfully well painted,' I replied, to give myself a reason.

'It's lucky you thought of saying that, because the painter was my father.'

'That makes the picture indeed precious!' I returned with gaiety; and I may add that a part of my cheer came from this proof I had been right in my theory of Miss Bordereau's origin. Aspern had, of course, met the young lady on his going to her father's studio as a sitter. I observed to Miss Bordereau that if she would entrust me with her property for twenty-four hours I should be happy to take advice on it; but she made no other reply than to slip it in silence into her pocket. This convinced me still more that she had no sincere intention of selling it during her lifetime, though she may have desired to satisfy herself as to the sum her niece, should she leave it to her, might expect eventually to obtain for it. 'Well, at any rate, I hope you won't offer it without giving me notice,' I said as she remained irresponsive. 'Remember me as a possible purchaser.'

'I should want your money first!' she returned with unexpected rudeness; and then, as if she bethought herself that I might well complain of such a tone and wished to turn the matter off, asked abruptly what I talked about with her niece when I went out with her that way of an evening.

'You speak as if we had set up the habit,' I replied. 'Certainly I should be very glad if it were to become our pleasant custom. But in that case I should feel a still greater scruple at betraying a lady's confidence.'

'Her confidence? Has my niece confidence?'

'Here she is—she can tell you herself,' I said; for Miss Tina now appeared on the threshold of the old woman's parlour. 'Have you confidence, Miss Tina? Your aunt wants very much to know.'

'Not in her, not in her!' the younger lady declared, shaking her head with a dolefulness that was neither jocular nor affected. 'I don't know what to do with her; she has fits of horrid imprudence. She's so easily tired—and yet she has begun to roam, to drag herself about the house.' And she looked down at her yoke-fellow of long years with a vacancy of wonder, as if all their contact and custom hadn't made her perversities, on occasion, any more easy to follow.

'I know what I'm about. I'm not losing my mind. I dare say you'd like to think so,' said Miss Bordereau with a crudity of cynicism.

'I don't suppose you came out here yourself. Miss Tina must have had to lend you a hand,' I interposed for conciliation.

'Oh, she insisted we should push her; and when she insists!' said Miss Tina, in the same tone of apprehension; as if there were no knowing what service she disapproved of her aunt might force her next to render.

'I've always got most things done I wanted, thank God! The people I've lived with have humoured me,' the old woman continued, speaking out of the white ashes of her vanity.

I took it pleasantly up. 'I suppose you mean they've obeyed you.'

'Well, whatever it is—when they like one.'

'It's just because I like you that I want to resist,' said Miss Tina with a nervous laugh.

'Oh, I expect you'll bring Miss Bordereau upstairs next to pay me a visit,' I went on; to which the old lady replied:

*I 912

'Oh, no; I can keep an eye on you from here!'

'You 're very tired; you 'll certainly be ill to-night!' cried Miss Tina.

'Nonsense, dear; I feel better at this moment than I 've done for a month. To-morrow I shall come out again. I want to be where I can see this clever gentleman.'

'Shouldn't you perhaps see me better in your sitting-room?' I asked.

'Don't you mean shouldn't you have a better chance at *me*?' she returned, fixing me a moment with her green shade.

'Ah, I haven't that anywhere! I look at you but don't see you.'

'You agitate her dreadfully—and that 's not good,' said Miss Tina, giving me a reproachful, deterrent headshake.

'I want to watch you—I want to watch you!' Miss Bordereau went on.

'Well, then, let us spend as much of our time together as possible—I don't care where. That will give you every facility.'

'Oh, I 've seen you enough for to-day. I 'm satisfied. Now I 'll go home,' Juliana said. Miss Tina laid her hands on the back of the wheeled chair and began to push, but I begged her to let me take her place. 'Oh, yes, you may move me this way—you shan't in any other!' the old woman cried as she felt herself propelled firmly and easily over the smooth, hard floor. Before we reached the door of her own apartment she bade me stop, and she took a long last look up and down the noble *sala*. 'Oh, it 's a prodigious house!' she murmured; after which I pushed her forward. When we had

entered the parlour Miss Tina let me know she
should now be able to manage, and at the same
moment the little red-haired *donna* came to meet
her mistress. Miss Tina's idea was evidently to get
her aunt immediately back to bed. I confess that
in spite of this urgency I was guilty of the indiscretion of lingering; it held me there to feel myself
so close to the objects I coveted—which would be
probably put away somewhere in the faded un-
sociable room. The place had indeed a bareness
that suggested no hidden values; there were neither
dusky nooks nor curtained corners, neither massive
cabinets nor chests with iron bands. Moreover it
was possible, it was perhaps even likely, that the
old lady had consigned her relics to her bedroom, to
some battered box that was shoved under the bed,
to the drawer of some lame dressing-table, where
they would be in the range of vision by the dim
night-lamp. None the less I turned an eye on every
article of furniture, on every conceivable cover for
a hoard, and noticed that there were half a dozen
things with drawers, and in particular a tall old
secretary with brass ornaments of the style of the
Empire—a receptacle somewhat infirm but still
capable of keeping rare secrets. I don't know why
this article so engaged me, small purpose as I had
of breaking into it; but I stared at it so hard that
Miss Tina noticed me and changed colour. Her
doing this made me think I was right and that,
wherever they might have been before, the Aspern
papers at that moment languished behind the peevish
little lock of the secretary. It was hard to turn
my attention from the dull mahogany front when
I reflected that a plain panel divided me from the

goal of my hopes; but I gathered up my slightly scattered prudence and with an effort took leave of my hostess. To make the effort graceful I said to her that I should certainly bring her an opinion about the little picture.

'The little picture?' Miss Tina asked in surprise.

'What do *you* know about it, my dear?' the old woman demanded. 'You needn't mind. I've fixed my price.'

'And what may that be?'

'A thousand pounds.'

'Oh, Lord!' cried poor Miss Tina irrepressibly.

'Is that what she talks to you about?' said Miss Bordereau.

'Imagine your aunt's wanting to know!' I had to separate from my younger friend with only those words, though I should have liked immensely to add: 'For heaven's sake meet me to-night in the garden!'

VIII

As it turned out, the precaution had not been needed, for three hours later, just as I had finished my dinner, Miss Tina appeared, unannounced, in the open doorway of the room in which my simple repasts were served. I remember well that I felt no surprise at seeing her; which is not a proof of my not believing in her timidity. It was immense, but in a case in which there was a particular reason for boldness it never would have prevented her from running up to my floor. I saw that she was now quite full of a particular reason; it threw her forward—made her seize me, as I rose to meet her, by the arm.

'My aunt's very ill; I think she's dying!'

'Never in the world,' I answered bitterly. 'Don't you be afraid!'

'Do go for a doctor—do, do! Olimpia's gone for the one we always have, but she doesn't come back; I don't know what has happened to her. I told her that if he wasn't at home she was to follow him where he had gone; but apparently she's following him all over Venice. I don't know what to do—she looks as if she were sinking.'

'May I see her, may I judge?' I asked. 'Of course I shall be delighted to bring someone; but hadn't we better send my man instead, so that I may stay with you?'

Miss Tina assented to this and I dispatched my servant for the best doctor in the neighbourhood. I hurried downstairs with her, and on the way she told me than an hour after I quitted them in the afternoon Miss Bordereau had had an attack of 'oppression,' a terrible difficulty in breathing. This had subsided, but had left her so exhausted that she didn't come up: she seemed all spent and gone. I repeated that she wasn't gone, that she wouldn't go yet; whereupon Miss Tina gave me a sharper sidelong glance than she had ever favoured me withal and said: 'Really, what do you mean? I suppose you don't accuse her of making-believe!' I forget what reply I made to this, but I fear that in my heart I thought the old woman capable of any weird manœuvre. Miss Tina wanted to know what I had done to her; her aunt had told her I had made her so angry. I declared I had done nothing whatever—I had been exceedingly careful; to which my companion rejoined that our friend had assured her she had had a scene with me—a scene that had upset her. I answered with some resentment that the scene had been of *her* making—that I couldn't think what she was angry with me for unless for not seeing my way to give a thousand pounds for the portrait of Jeffrey Aspern. 'And did she show you that? Oh, gracious—oh, deary me!' groaned Miss Tina, who seemed to feel the situation pass out of her control and the elements of her fate thicken round her. I answered her I'd give anything to possess it, yet that I had no thousand pounds; but I stopped when we came to the door of Miss Bordereau's room. I had an immense curiosity to pass it, but I thought it my duty to represent to Miss

Tina that if I made the invalid angry she ought perhaps to be spared the sight of me. 'The sight of you? Do you think she can *see*?' my companion demanded, almost with indignation. I did think so but forbore to say it, and I softly followed my conductress.

I remember that what I said to her as I stood for a moment beside the old woman's bed was: 'Does she never show you her eyes, then? Have you never seen them?' Miss Bordereau had been divested of her green shade, but—it was not my fortune to behold Juliana in her nightcap—the upper half of her face was covered by the fall of a piece of dingy lacelike muslin, a sort of extemporized hood which, wound round her head, descended to the end of her nose, leaving nothing visible but her white, withered cheeks and puckered mouth, closed tightly and, as it were, consciously. Miss Tina gave me a glance of surprise, evidently not seeing a reason for my impatience. 'You mean she always wears something? She does it to preserve them.'

'Because they're so fine?'

'Oh, to-day, to-day!' And Miss Tina shook her head, speaking very low. 'But they used to be magnificent!'

'Yes, indeed—we've Aspern's word for that.' And as I looked again at the old woman's wrappings I could imagine her not having wished to allow any supposition that the great poet had overdone it. But I didn't waste my time in considering Juliana, in whom the appearance of respiration was so slight as to suggest that no human attention could ever help her more. I turned my eyes once more all over the room, rummaging with them the closets, the chests of drawers, the tables. Miss Tina at once noted their direction and read, I think, what was in them; but she didn't answer it, turning away restlessly, anxiously, so that I felt rebuked, with reason, for an appetite wellnigh indecent in the presence of our dying companion. All the same, I took another view, endeavouring to pick out mentally the receptacle to try first, for a person who should wish to put his hand on Miss Bordereau's papers directly after her death. The place was a dire confusion; it looked like the dressing-room of an old actress. There were clothes hanging over chairs, odd-looking shabby bundles here and there, and various paste-board boxes piled together battered, bulging, and discoloured, which might have been fifty years old. Miss Tina after a moment noticed the direction of my eyes again, and, as if she guessed how I judged such appearances—forgetting I had no business to judge them at all—said, perhaps to defend herself from the imputation of complicity in the disorder:

'She likes it this way; we can't move things. There are old bandboxes she has had most of her life.' Then she added, half-taking pity on my real thought: 'Those things were *there*.' And she pointed to a small, low trunk which stood under a sofa that just allowed room for it. It struck me as a queer, superannuated coffer, of painted wood, with elaborate handles and shrivelled straps and with the colour— it had last been endued with a coat of light green —much rubbed off. It evidently had travelled with Juliana in the olden time—in the days of her adventures, which it had shared. It would have made a strange figure arriving at a modern hotel.

'*Were* there—they aren't now?' I asked, startled by Miss Tina's implication.

She was going to answer, but at that moment the doctor came in—the doctor whom the little maid had been sent to fetch and whom she had at last overtaken. My servant, going on his own errand, had met her with her companion in tow, and in the sociable Venetian spirit, retracing his steps with them, had also come up to the threshold of the *padrona's* room, where I saw him peep over the doctor's shoulder. I motioned him away the more instantly that the sight of his prying face reminded me how little I myself had to do there—an admonition confirmed by the sharp way the little doctor eyed me, his air of taking me for a rival who had the field before him. He was a short, fat, brisk gentleman who wore the tall hat of his profession and seemed to look at everything but his patient. He kept me still in range, as if it struck him I too should be better for a dose, so that I bowed to him and left him with the women, going down to smoke a cigar in the garden. I was nervous; I couldn't go further; I couldn't leave the place. I don't know exactly what I thought might happen, but I felt it important to be there. I wandered about the alleys —the warm night had come on—smoking cigar after cigar and studying the light in Miss Bordereau's windows. They were open now, I could see; the situation was different. Sometimes the light moved, but not quickly; it didn't suggest the hurry of a crisis. Was the old woman dying or was she already dead? Had the doctor said that there was nothing to be done at her tremendous age but to let her quietly pass away? or had he simply announced with

a look a little more conventional that the end of
the end had come? Were the other two women
just going and coming over the offices that follow
in such a case? It made me uneasy not to be nearer,
as if I thought the doctor himself might carry away
the papers with him. I bit my cigar hard while
it assailed me again that perhaps there were now
no papers to carry!

I wandered about an hour and more. I looked
out for Miss Tina at one of the windows, having a
vague idea that she might come there to give me
some sign. Wouldn't she see the red tip of my cigar
in the dark and feel sure I was hanging on to know
what the doctor had said? I'm afraid it's a proof
of the grossness of my anxieties that I should have
taken in some degree for granted at such an hour,
in the midst of the greatest change that could fall
on her, poor Miss Tina's having also a free mind for
them. My servant came down and spoke to me;
he knew nothing save that the doctor had gone
after a visit of half an hour. If he had stayed half
an hour then Miss Bordereau was still alive: it
couldn't have taken so long to attest her decease.
I sent the man out of the house; there were moments
when the sense of his curiosity annoyed me, and
this was one of them. *He* had been watching my
cigar-tip from an upper window, if Miss Tina hadn't;
he couldn't know what I was after and I couldn't
tell him, though I suspected in him fantastic private
theories about me which he thought fine and which,
had I more exactly known them, I should have
thought offensive.

I went upstairs at last, but I mounted no higher
than the *sala*. The door of Miss Bordereau's apart-

ment was open, showing from the parlour the dimness of a poor candle. I went towards it with a light tread, and at the same moment Miss Tina appeared and stood looking at me as I approached. 'She's better, she's better,' she said even before I had asked. 'The doctor has given her something; she woke up, came back to life while he was there. He says there's no immediate danger.'

'No immediate danger? Surely he thinks her condition serious!'

'Yes, because she had been excited. That affects her dreadfully.'

'It will do so again then, because she works herself up. She did so this afternoon.'

'Yes, she mustn't come out any more,' said Miss Tina with one of her lapses into a deeper detachment.

'What's the use of making such a remark as that,' I permitted myself to ask, 'if you begin to rattle her about again the first time she bids you?'

'I won't—I won't do it any more.'

'You must learn to resist her,' I went on.

'Oh, yes, I shall; I shall do so better if you tell me it's right.'

'You mustn't do it for me—you must do it for yourself. It all comes back to you, if you're scared and upset.'

'Well, I'm not upset now,' said Miss Tina placidly enough. 'She's very quiet.'

'Is she conscious again—does she speak?'

'No, she doesn't speak, but she takes my hand. She holds it fast.'

'Yes,' I returned, 'I can see what force she still has by the way she grabbed that picture this afternoon. But if she holds you fast how comes it that you 're here?'

Miss Tina waited a little; though her face was in deep shadow—she had her back to the light in the parlour and I had put down my own candle far off, near the door of the *sala*—I thought I saw her smile ingenuously. 'I came on purpose—I had heard your step.'

'Why, I came on tiptoe, as soundlessly as possible.'

'Well, I had heard you,' said Miss Tina.

'And is your aunt alone now?'

'Oh, no—Olimpia sits there.'

On my side I debated. 'Shall we then pass in there?' And I nodded at the parlour; I wanted more and more to be on the spot.

'We can't talk there—she 'll hear us.'

I was on the point of replying that in that case we 'd sit silent, but I felt too much this wouldn't do, there was something I desired so immensely to ask her. Thus I hinted we might walk a little in the *sala*, keeping more at the other end, where we shouldn't disturb our friend. Miss Tina assented unconditionally; the doctor was coming again, she said, and she would be there to meet him at the door. We strolled through the fine superfluous hall, where on the marble floor—particularly as at first we said nothing—our footsteps were more audible than I had expected. When we reached the other end—the wide window, inveterately closed, connecting with the balcony that overhung the canal—I submitted that we had best remain there, as she would see the doctor arrive the sooner. I opened the window and we passed out on the balcony. The air of the canal seemed even heavier, hotter than that of the *sala*.

The place was hushed and void; the quiet neighbourhood had gone to sleep. A lamp, here and there,
over the narrow black water glimmered in double;
the voice of a man going homeward singing, his
jacket on his shoulder and his hat on his ear, came
to us from a distance. This didn't prevent the
scene from being very *comme il faut*, as Miss Bordereau
had called it the first time I saw her.   Presently a gondola passed along the canal with its slow, rhythmical
splash, and as we listened we watched it in silence.
It didn't stop, it didn't carry the doctor; and after
it had gone on I said to Miss Tina:

'And where are they now—the things that were
in the trunk?'

'In the trunk?'

'That green box you pointed out to me in her
room. You said her papers had been there; you
seemed to mean she had transferred them.'

'Oh, yes; they're not in the trunk,' said Miss
Tina.

'May I ask if you 've looked?'

'Yes, I 've looked—for you.'

'How for me, dear Miss Tina?   Do you mean
you 'd have given them to me if you had found
them?'—and I fairly trembled with the question.

She delayed to reply and I waited. Suddenly
she broke out: 'I don't know what I 'd do—what
I wouldn't!'

'Would you look again—somewhere else?'

She had spoken with a strange, unexpected emotion,
and she went on in the same tone: 'I can't—I can't
—while she lies there.   It isn't decent.'

'No, it isn't decent,' I replied gravely. 'Let the
poor lady rest in peace.'   And the words on my

lips were not hypocritical, for I felt reprimanded and shamed.

Miss Tina added in a moment, as if she had guessed this and were sorry for me, but at the same time wished to explain that I did push her, or at least harp on the chord, too much: 'I can't deceive her that way. I can't deceive her—perhaps on her death-bed.'

'Heaven forbid I should ask you, though I've been guilty myself!'

'You've been guilty?'

'I've sailed under false colours.' I felt now I must make a clean breast of it, must tell her I had given her an invented name on account of my fear her aunt would have heard of me and so refuse to take me in. I explained this as well as that I had really been a party to the letter addressed them by John Cumnor months before.

She listened with great attention, almost in fact gaping for wonder, and when I had made my confession she said: 'Then your real name—what is it?' She repeated it over twice when I had told her, accompanying it with the exclamation: 'Gracious, gracious!' Then she added: 'I like your own best.'

'So do I'—and I felt my laugh rueful. 'Ouf! it's a relief to get rid of the other.'

'So it was a regular plot—a kind of conspiracy?'

'Oh, a conspiracy—we were only two,' I replied, leaving out, of course, Mrs. Prest.

She considered; I thought she was perhaps going to pronounce us very base. But this was not her way, and she remarked after a moment, as in candid, impartial contemplation: 'How much you must want them!'

'Oh, I do, passionately!' I grinned, I fear to admit. And this chance made me go on, forgetting my compunction of a moment before. 'How can she possibly have changed their place herself? How can she walk? How can she arrive at that sort of muscular exertion? How can she lift and carry things?'

'Oh, when one wants and when one has so much will!' said Miss Tina as if she had thought over my question already herself and had simply had no choice but that answer—the idea that in the dead of night, or at some moment when the coast was clear, the old woman had been capable of a miraculous effort.

'Have you questioned Olimpia? Hasn't she helped her—hasn't she done it for her?' I asked; to which my friend replied promptly and positively that their servant had had nothing to do with the matter, though without admitting definitely that she had spoken to her. It was as if she were a little shy, a little ashamed now, of letting me see how much she had entered into my uneasiness and had me on her mind. Suddenly she said to me without any immediate relevance:

'I rather feel you a new person, you know, now that you 've a new name.'

'It isn't a new one; it 's a very good old one, thank fortune!'

She looked at me a moment. 'Well, I do like it better.'

'Oh, if you didn't I would almost go on with the other!'

'Would you really?'

I laughed again, but I returned for all answer'

'Of course if she can rummage about that way she can perfectly have burnt them.'

'You must wait — you must wait,' Miss Tina mournfully moralized; and her tone ministered little to my patience, for it seemed, after all, to accept that wretched possibility. I would teach myself to wait, I declared nevertheless; because in the first place I couldn't do otherwise, and in the second I had her promise, given me the other night, that she would help me.'

'Of course if the papers are gone that's no use,' she said; not as if she wished to recede, but only to be conscientious.

'Naturally. But if you could only find out!' I groaned, quivering again.

'I thought you promised you'd wait.'

'Oh, you mean wait even for that?'

'For what, then?'

'Ah, nothing,' I answered rather foolishly, being ashamed to tell her what had been implied in my acceptance of delay—the idea that she would perhaps do more for me than merely find out.

I know not if she guessed this; at all events she seemed to bethink herself of some propriety of showing me more rigour. 'I didn't promise to deceive, did I? I don't think I did.'

'It doesn't much matter whether you did or not, for you couldn't!'

Nothing is more possible than that she wouldn't have contested this even hadn't she been diverted by our seeing the doctor's gondola shoot into the little canal and approach the house. I noted that he came as fast as if he believed our proprietress still in danger. We looked down at him while he disembarked and then went back into the *sala* to meet him. When he came up, however, I naturally left Miss Tina to go off with him alone, only asking her leave to come back later for news.

I went out of the house and walked far, as far as the Piazza, where my restlessness declined to quit me. I was unable to sit down; it was very late now though there were people still at the little table in front of the cafés: I could but uneasily revolve, and I did so half a dozen times. The only comfort, none the less, was in my having told Miss Tina who I really was. At last I took my way home again, getting gradually and all but inextricably lost, as I did whenever I went out in Venice: so that it was considerably past midnight when I reached my door. The *sala* upstairs was as dark as usual, and my lamp as I crossed it found nothing satisfactory to show me. I was disappointed, for I had notified Miss Tina that I would come back for a report, and I thought she might have left a light there as a sign. The door of the ladies' apartment was closed; which seemed a hint that my faltering friend had gone to bed in impatience of waiting for me. I stood in the middle of the place, considering, hoping she would hear me and perhaps peep out, saying to myself too that she would never go to bed with her aunt in a state so critical; she would sit up and watch—she would be in a chair, in her dressing-gown. I went nearer the door; I stopped there and listened. I heard nothing at all, and at last I tapped gently. No answer came, and after another minute I turned the handle. There was no light in the room; this ought to have prevented my entrance, but it had no such effect. If I have frankly stated the importunities, the indelicacies, of which my desire to possess myself of Jeffrey Aspern's papers had made me capable I needn't shrink, it seems to me, from confessing this last indiscretion. I regard it as the worst thing I did, yet there were extenuating circumstances. I was deeply though doubtless not disinterestedly anxious for more news of Juliana, and Miss Tina had accepted from me, as it were, a rendezvous which it might have been a point of honour with me to keep. It may be objected that her leaving the place dark was a positive sign that she released me, and to this I can only reply that I wished not to be released.

The door of Miss Bordereau's room was open and I could see beyond it the faintness of a taper. There was no sound—my footstep caused no one to stir. I came further into the room; I lingered there, lamp in hand. I wanted to give Miss Tina a chance to come to me if, as I couldn't doubt, she were still with her aunt. I made no noise to call her; I only waited to see if she wouldn't notice my light. She didn't, and I explained this—I found afterwards I was right—by the idea that she had fallen asleep. If she had fallen asleep her aunt was not on her mind, and my explanation ought to have led me to go out as I had come. I must repeat again that it didn't, for I found myself at the same moment given up to something else. I had no definite purpose, no bad intention, but felt myself held to the spot by an acute, though absurd, sense of opportunity. Opportunity for what I couldn't have said, inasmuch as it wasn't in my mind that I might proceed to thievery. Even had this tempted me I was confronted with the evident fact that Miss

Bordereau didn't leave her secretary, her cupboard, and the drawers of her table gaping. I had no keys, no tools, and no ambition to smash her furniture. None the less it came to me that I was now, perhaps alone, unmolested, at the hour of freedom and safety, nearer to the source of my hopes than I had ever been. I held up my lamp, let the light play on the different objects as if it could tell me something. Still there came no movement from the other room. If Miss Tina was sleeping she was sleeping sound. Was she doing so—generous creature—on purpose to leave me the field? Did she know I was there and was she just keeping quiet to see what I would do—what I *could* do? Yet might I, when it came to that? She herself knew even better than I how little.

I stopped in front of the secretary, gaping at it vainly and no doubt grotesquely; for what had it to say to me after all? In the first place it was locked, and in the second it almost surely contained nothing in which I was interested. Ten to one the papers had been destroyed, and even if they hadn't the keen old woman wouldn't have put them in such a place as that after removing them from the green trunk—wouldn't have transferred them, with the idea of their safety on her brain, from the better hiding-place to the worse. The secretary was more conspicuous, more exposed in a room in which she could no longer mount guard. It opened with a key, but there was a small brass handle, like a button as well; I saw this as I played my lamp over it. I did something more for the climax of my crisis; I caught a glimpse of the possibility that Miss Tina wished me really to understand. If she didn't so wish me, if she wished me to keep away, why hadn't she locked the door of communication between the sitting-room and the *sala*? That would have been a definite sign that I was to leave them alone. If I didn't leave them alone she meant me to come for a purpose—a purpose now represented by the super-subtle inference that to oblige me she had unlocked the secretary. She hadn't left the key, but the lid would probably move if I touched the button. This possibility pressed me hard and I bent very close to judge. I didn't propose to do anything, not even—not in the least—to let down the lid; I only wanted to test my theory, to see if the cover *would* move. I touched the button with my hand—a mere touch would tell me; and as I did so—it is embarrassing for me to relate it—I looked over my shoulder. It was a chance, an instinct, for I had really heard nothing. I almost let my luminary drop and certainly I stepped back, straightening myself up at what I saw. Juliana stood there in her night-dress, by the doorway of her room, watching me; her hands were raised, she had lifted the everlasting curtain that covered half her face, and for the first, the last, the only time I beheld her extraordinary eyes. They glared at me; they were like the sudden drench, for a caught burglar, of a flood of gaslight; they made me horribly ashamed. I never shall forget her strange little bent, white, tottering figure, with its lifted head, her attitude, her expression; neither shall I forget the tone in which as I turned, looking at her, she hissed out passionately, furiously:

'Ah, you publishing scoundrel!'

I can't now say what I stammered to excuse

myself, to explain; but I went toward her to tell her I meant no harm. She waved me off with her old hands, retreating before me in horror; and the next thing I knew she had fallen back with a quick spasm, as if death had descended on her, into Miss Tina's arms.

IX

I LEFT Venice the next morning, directly on learning that my hostess had not succumbed, as I feared at the moment, to the shock I had given her—the shock I may also say she had given me. How in the world could I have supposed her capable of getting out of bed by herself? I failed to see Miss Tina before going; I only saw the *donna*, whom I entrusted with a note for her younger mistress. In this note I mentioned that I should be absent but a few days. I went to Treviso, to Bassano, to Castelfranco; I took walks and drives and looked at musty old churches with ill-lighted pictures; I spent hours seated smoking at the doors of cafés, where there were flies and yellow curtains, on the shady side of sleepy little squares. In spite of these pastimes, which were mechanical and perfunctory, I scantily enjoyed my travels: I had had to gulp down a bitter draught and couldn't get rid of the taste. It had been devilish awkward, as the young men say, to be found by Juliana in the dead of night examining the attachment of her bureau; and it had not been less so to have to believe for a good many hours after that it was highly probable I had killed her. My humiliation galled me, but I had to make the best of it, had, in writing to Miss Tina, to minimize it, as well as account for the posture in which I had been discovered. As she gave me no word of answer

I couldn't know what impression I made on her.
It rankled for me that I had been called a publishing
scoundrel, since certainly I did publish and no less
certainly hadn't been very delicate.   There was a
moment when I stood convinced that the only way
to purge my dishonour was to take myself straight
away on the instant; to sacrifice my hopes and
relieve the two poor women for ever of the oppression of my intercourse.   Then I reflected that I had
better try a short absence first, for I must already
have had a sense (unexpressed and dim) that in
disappearing completely it wouldn't be merely my
own hopes I should condemn to extinction.   It
would perhaps answer if I kept dark long enough
to give the elder lady time to believe herself rid of
me.   That she would wish to be rid of me after
this—if I wasn't rid of her—was now not to be
doubted; that midnight monstrosity would have
cured her of the disposition to put up with my
company for the sake of my dollars.   I said to
myself that after all I couldn't abandon Miss Tina,
and I continued to say this even while I noted that
she quite ignored my earnest request—I had given
her two or three addresses, at little towns, *poste
restante*—for some sign of her actual state.   I would
have made my servant write me news but that he
was unable to manage a pen.   Couldn't I measure
the scorn of Miss Tina's silence—little disdainful as
she had ever been?   Really the soreness pressed;
yet if I had scruples about going back I had others
about not doing so, and I wanted to put myself on
a better footing.   The end of it was that I did
return to Venice on the twelfth day; and as my
gondola gently bumped against the place steps a fine

palpitation of suspense showed me the violence my
absence had done me.

I had faced about so abruptly that I hadn't even
telegraphed to my servant. He was therefore not
at the station to meet me, but he poked out his
head from an upper window when I reached the
house. 'They have put her into earth, *quella vecchia*,'
he said to me in the lower hall while he shouldered
my valise; and he grinned and almost winked as if
he knew I should be pleased with his news.

'She 's dead!' I cried, giving a very different
look.

'So it appears, since they 've buried her.'

'It 's all over then? When was the funeral?'

'The other yesterday. But a funeral you could
scarcely call it, signore: *roba da niente—un piccolo
passeggio brutto* of two gondolas. *Poveretta!*' the
man continued, referring apparently to Miss Tina.
His conception of funerals was that they were mainly
to amuse the living.

I wanted to know about Miss Tina, how she might
be and generally where; but I asked him no more
questions till we had got upstairs. Now that the
fact had met me I took a bad view of it, especially
of the idea that poor Miss Tina had had to manage
by herself after the end. What did she know about
such arrangements, about the steps to take in such
a case? *Poveretta* indeed! I could only hope the
doctor had given her support and that she hadn't
been neglected by the old friends of whom she had
told me, the little band of the faithful whose fidelity
consisted in coming to the house once a year. I
elicited from my servant that two old ladies and
an old gentleman had in fact rallied round Miss Tina

and had supported her—they had come for her in a
gondola of their own—during the journey to the
cemetery, the little red-walled island of tombs which
lies to the north of the town and on the way to
Murano. It appeared from these signs that the
Misses Bordereau were Catholics, a discovery I had
never made, as the old woman couldn't go to church
and her niece, so far as I perceived, either didn't,
or went only to early mass in the parish before I
was stirring. Certainly even the priests respected
their seclusion; I had never caught the whisk of
the *curato's* skirt. That evening, an hour later, I
sent my servant down with five words on a card to
ask if Miss Tina would see me for a few moments.
She was not in the house, where he had sought her,
he told me when he came back, but in the garden
walking about to refresh herself and picking the
flowers quite as if they belonged to her. He had
found her there and she would be happy to see me.

I went down and passed half an hour with poor
Miss Tina. She had always had a look of musty
mourning, as if she were wearing out old robes of
sorrow that wouldn't come to an end; and in this
particular she made no different show. But she
clearly had been crying, crying a great deal—simply,
satisfyingly, refreshingly, with a primitive, retarded
sense of solitude and violence. But she had none of
the airs or graces of grief, and I was almost surprised
to see her stand there in the first dusk with her
hands full of admirable roses and smile at me with
reddened eyes. Her white face, in the frame of her
mantilla, looked longer, leaner than usual. I hadn't
doubted her being irreconcilably disgusted with me,
her considering I ought to have been on the spot to

advise her, to help her; and, though I believed there
was no rancour in her composition and no great
conviction of the importance of her affairs, I had
prepared myself for a change in her manner, for
some air of injury and estrangement, which should
say to my conscience: 'Well, you 're a nice person
to have professed things!' But historic truth com-
pels me to declare that this poor lady's dull face
ceased to be dull, almost ceased to be plain, as she
turned it gladly to her late aunt's lodger. That
touched him extremely and he thought it simplified
his situation until he found it didn't. I was as kind
to her that evening as I knew how to be, and I
walked about the garden with her as long as seemed
good. There was no explanation of any sort between
us; I didn't ask her why she hadn't answered my
letter. Still less did I repeat what I had said to her
in that communication; if she chose to let me suppose
she had forgotten the position in which Miss Bordereau had surprised me and the effect of the discovery on the old woman, I was quite willing to take
it that way: I was grateful to her for not treating
me as if I had killed her aunt.

We strolled and strolled, though really not much
passed between us save the recognition of her bereave-
ment, conveyed in my manner and in the expression
she had of depending on me now, since I let her
see I still took an interest in her. Miss Tina's was
no breast for the pride or the pretence of independence; she didn't in the least suggest that she
knew at present what would become of her. I forbore to press on that question, however, for I certainly
was not prepared to say that I would take charge
of her. I was cautious; not ignobly, I think, for

I felt her knowledge of life to be so small that in
her unsophisticated vision there would be no reason
why—since I seemed to pity her—I shouldn't somehow look after her. She told me how her aunt had
died, very peacefully at the last, and how everything had been done afterwards by the care of her
good friends—fortunately, thanks to me, she said,
smiling, there was money in the house. She repeated that when once the 'nice' Italians like you
they are your friends for life, and when we had gone
into this she asked me about my *giro*, my impressions,
my adventures, the places I had seen. I told her
what I could, making it up partly, I'm afraid, as in
my disconcerted state I had taken little in; and
after she had heard me she exclaimed, quite as if
she had forgotten her aunt and her sorrow: 'Dear,
dear, how much I should like to do such things—
to take an amusing little journey!' It came over
me for the moment that I ought to propose some
enterprise, say I would accompany her anywhere
she liked; and I remarked at any rate that a pleasant
excursion—to give her a change—might be managed:
we would think of it, talk it over. I spoke never
a word of the Aspern documents, asked no questions
as to what she had ascertained or what had otherwise happened with regard to them before Juliana's
death. It wasn't that I wasn't on pins and needles
to know, but that I thought it more decent not to
show greed again so soon after the catastrophe.
I hoped she herself would say something, but she
never glanced that way, and I thought this natural
at the time. Later on, however, that night, it
occurred to me that her silence was matter for
suspicion; since if she had talked of my movements,

of anything so detached as the Giorgione at Castelfranco, she might have alluded to what she could easily remember was in my mind. It was not to be supposed that the emotion produced by her aunt's death had blotted out the recollection that I was interested in that lady's relics, and I fidgeted afterwards as it came to me that her reticence might very possibly just mean that no relics survived. We separated in the garden—it was she who said she must go in; now that she was alone on the *piano nobile* I felt that (judged at any rate by Venetian ideas) I was on rather a different footing in regard to the invasion of it. As I shook hands with her for good night I asked her if she had some general plan, had thought over what she had best do. 'Oh yes, oh yes, but I haven't settled anything yet,' she replied quite cheerfully. Was her cheerfulness explained by the impression that I would settle for her?

I was glad the next morning that we had neglected practical questions, as this gave me a pretext for seeing her again immediately. There was a practical enough question now to be touched on. I owed it to her to let her know formally that of course I didn't expect her to keep me on as a lodger, as also to show some interest in her own tenure, what she might have on her hands in the way of a lease. But I was not destined, as befell, to converse with her for more than an instant on either of these points. I sent her no message; I simply went down to the *sala* and walked to and fro there. I knew she would come out; she would promptly see me accessible. Somehow I preferred not to be shut up with her; gardens and big halls seemed better places to talk. It was a splendid morning, with something

in the air that told of the waning of the long
Venetian summer; a freshness from the sea that
stirred the flowers in the garden and made a pleasant
draught in the house, less shuttered and darkened
now than when the old woman was alive. It was
the beginning of autumn, of the end of the golden
months. With this it was the end of my experiment—or would be in the course of half an hour,
when I should really have learned that my dream
had been reduced to ashes. After that there would
be nothing left for me but to go to the station; for
seriously—and as it struck me in the morning light
—I couldn't linger there to act as guardian to a
piece of middle-aged female helplessness. If she
hadn't saved the papers wherein should I be in-
debted to her? I think I winced a little as I asked
myself how much, if she *had* saved them, I should
have to recognize and, as it were, reward such a
courtesy. Mightn't that service after all saddle me
with a guardianship? If this idea didn't make me
more uncomfortable as I walked up and down it
was because I was convinced I had nothing to look
to. If the old woman hadn't destroyed everything
before she pounced on me in the parlour she had
done so the next day.

It took Miss Tina rather longer than I had expected to act on my calculation; but when at last
she came out she looked at me without surprise.
I mentioned I had been waiting for her and she
asked why I hadn't let her know. I was glad a few
hours later on that I had checked myself before
remarking that a friendly intuition might have told
her; it turned to comfort for me that I hadn't
played even to that mild extent on her sensibility.

What I did say was virtually the truth—that I was too nervous, since I expected her now to settle my fate.

'Your fate?' said Miss Tina, giving me a queer look; and as she spoke I noticed a rare change in her. Yes, she was other than she had been the evening before—less natural and less easy. She had been crying the day before and was not crying now, yet she struck me as less confident. It was as if something had happened to her during the night, or at least as if she had thought of something that troubled her—something in particular that affected her relations with me, made them more embarrassing and more complicated. Had she simply begun to feel that her aunt's not being there now altered my position?

'I mean about our papers. *Are* there any? You must know now.'

'Yes, there are a great many; more than I supposed.' I was struck with the way her voice trembled as she told me this.

'Do you mean you've got them in there—and that I may see them?'

'I don't think you can see them,' said Miss Tina, with an extraordinary expression of entreaty in her eyes, as if the dearest hope she had in the world now was that I wouldn't take them from her. But how could she expect me to make such a sacrifice as that after all that had passed between us? What had I come back to Venice for but to see them, to take them? My joy at learning they were still in existence was such that if the poor woman had gone down on her knees to beseech me never to mention them again I would have treated the proceeding as a bad joke. 'I 've got them but I can't show them,' she lamentably added.

'Not even to me? Ah, Miss Tina!' I broke into a tone of infinite remonstrance and reproach.

She coloured and the tears came back to her eyes; I measured the anguish it cost her to take such a stand which a dreadful sense of duty had imposed on her. It made me quite sick to find myself confronted with that particular obstacle; all the more that it seemed to me I had been distinctly encouraged to leave it out of account. I quite held Miss Tina to have assured me that if she had no greater hindrance than that——! 'You don't mean to say you made her a death-bed promise? It was precisely against your doing anything of that sort that I thought I was safe. Oh, I would rather she had burnt the papers outright than have to reckon with such a treachery as that.'

'No, it isn't a promise,' said Miss Tina.

'Pray what is it, then?'

She hung fire, but finally said: 'She tried to burn them, but I prevented it. She had hid them in her bed.'

'In her bed——?'

'Between the mattresses. That's where she put them when she took them out of the trunk. I can't understand how she did it, because Olimpia didn't help her. She tells me so, and I believe her. My aunt only told her afterwards, so that she shouldn't undo the bed—anything but the sheets. So it was very badly made,' added Miss Tina simply.

'I should think so! And how did she try to burn them?'

'She didn't try much; she was too weak those

last days. But she told me—she charged me. Oh, it was terrible! She couldn't speak after that night. She could only make signs.'

'And what did you do?'

'I took them away. I locked them up.'

'In the secretary?'

'Yes, in the secretary,' said Miss Tina, reddening again.

'Did you tell her you'd burn them?'

'No, I didn't—on purpose.'

'On purpose to gratify me?'

'Yes, only for that.'

'And what good will you have done me if after all you won't show them?'

'Oh, none. I know that—I know that,' she dismally sounded.

'And did she believe you had destroyed them?'

'I don't know what she believed at the last. I couldn't tell—she was too far gone.'

'Then if there was no promise and no assurance I can't see what ties you.'

'Oh, she hated it so—she hated it so! She was so jealous. But here's the portrait—you may have that,' the poor woman announced, taking the little picture, wrapped up in the same manner in which her aunt had wrapped it, out of her pocket.

'I may have it—do you mean you give it to me?' I gasped as it passed into my hand.

'Oh, yes.'

'But it's worth money—a large sum.'

'Well!' said Miss Tina, still with her strange look.

I didn't know what to make of it, for it could scarcely mean that she wanted to bargain like her

aunt. She spoke as for making me a present.
'I can't take it from you as a gift,' I said, 'and
yet I can't afford to pay you for it according to
the idea Miss Bordereau had of its value. She
rated it at a thousand pounds.'

'Couldn't we sell it?' my friend threw off.

'God forbid! I prefer the picture to the money.'

'Well, then, keep it.'

'You 're very generous.'

'So are you.'

'I don't know why you should think so,' I returned;
and this was true enough, for the good creature
appeared to have in her mind some rich reference
that I didn't in the least seize.

'Well, you 've made a great difference for me,'
she said.

I looked at Jeffrey Aspern's face in the little
picture, partly in order not to look at that of my
companion, which had begun to trouble me, even
to frighten me a little—it had taken so very odd, so
strained and unnatural a cast. I made no answer
to this last declaration; I but privately consulted
Jeffrey Aspern's delightful eyes with my own—they
were so young and brilliant and yet so wise and so
deep; I asked him what on earth was the matter
with Miss Tina. He seemed to smile at me with
mild mockery; he might have been amused at my
case. I had got into a pickle for him—as if he
needed it! He was unsatisfactory for the only
moment since I had known him. Nevertheless, now
that I held the little picture in my hand I felt it
would be a precious possession. 'Is this a bribe to
make me give up the papers?' I presently and all
perversely asked. 'Much as I value this, you know,

if I were to be obliged to choose the papers are what
I should prefer. Ah, but ever so much!'

'How can you choose—how can you choose?'
Miss Tina returned slowly and woefully.

'I see! Of course there's nothing to be said if
you regard the interdiction that rests on you as
quite insurmountable. In this case it must seem to
you that to part with them would be an impiety of
the worst kind, a simple sacrilege!'

She shook her head, only lost in the queerness of
her case. 'You'd understand if you had known her.
I'm afraid,' she quavered suddenly—'I'm afraid!
She was terrible when she was angry.'

'Yes, I saw something of that, that night. She
was terrible. Then I saw her eyes. Lord, they
were fine!'

'I see them—they stare at me in the dark!' said
Miss Tina.

'You've grown nervous with all you've been
through.'

'Oh, yes, very—very!'

'You mustn't mind; that will pass away,' I said
kindly. Then I added resignedly, for it really
seemed to me that I must accept the situation:
'Well, so it is, and it can't be helped. I must
renounce.' My friend, at this, with her eyes on me,
gave a low soft moan, and I went on: 'I only wish
to goodness she had destroyed them; then there
would be nothing more to say. And I can't understand why, with her ideas, she didn't.'

'Oh, she lived on them!' said Miss Tina.

'You can imagine whether that makes me want less
to see them,' I returned not quite so desperately.
'But don't let me stand here as if I had it in my

soul to tempt you to anything base. Naturally,
you understand, I give up my rooms. I leave
Venice immediately.' And I took up my hat, which
I had placed on a chair. We were still rather
awkwardly on our feet in the middle of the *sala*.
She had left the door of the apartments open behind
her, but had not led me that way.

A strange spasm came into her face as she saw
me take my hat. 'Immediately—do you mean
to-day?' The tone of the words was tragic—they
were a cry of desolation.

'Oh, no; not so long as I can be of the least
service to you.'

'Well, just a day or two more—just two or three
days,' she panted. Then, controlling herself, she
added in another manner: 'She wanted to say something to me—the last day—something very particular.
But she couldn't.'

'Something very particular?'

'Something more about the papers.'

'And did you guess—have you any idea?'

'No, I've tried to think—but I don't know. I've
thought all kinds of things.'

'As for instance?'

'Well, that if you were a relation it would be
different.'

I wondered. 'If I were a relation——?'

'If you weren't a stranger. Then it would be
the same for you as for me. Anything that 's mine
would be yours, and you could do what you like.
I shouldn't be able to prevent you—and you 'd have
no responsibility.'

She brought out this droll explanation with a
nervous rush and as if speaking words got by heart.

They gave me an impression of a subtlety which at first I failed to follow. But after a moment her face helped me to see further, and then the queerest of lights came to me. It was embarrassing, and I bent my head over Jeffrey Aspern's portrait. What an odd expression was in his face! 'Get out of it as you can, my dear fellow!' I put the picture into the pocket of my coat and said to Miss Tina: 'Yes, I 'll sell it for you. I shan't get a thousand pounds by any means, but I shall get something good.'

She looked at me through pitiful tears, but seemed to try to smile as she returned: 'We can divide the money.'

'No, no, it shall be all yours.' Then I went on: 'I think I know what your poor aunt wanted to say. She wanted to give directions that her papers should be buried with her.'

Miss Tina appeared to weigh this suggestion; after which she answered with striking decision: 'Oh, no, she wouldn't have thought that safe!'

'It seems to me nothing could be safer.'

'She had an idea that when people want to publish they 're capable——!' And she paused, very red.

'Of violating a tomb? Mercy on us, what must she have thought of me!'

'She wasn't just, she wasn't generous!' my companion cried with sudden passion.

The light that had come into my mind a moment before spread further. 'Ah, don't say that, for we *are* a dreadful race.' Then I pursued: 'If she left a will that may give you some idea.'

'I 've found nothing of the sort—she destroyed it. She was very fond of me,' Miss Tina added with an effect of extreme inconsequence. 'She wanted me to be happy. And if any person should be kind to me—she wanted to speak of that.'

I was almost awestricken by the astuteness with which the good lady found herself inspired, transparent astuteness as it was and stitching, as the phrase is, with white thread. 'Depend upon it, she didn't want to make any provision that would be agreeable to *me*.'

'No, not to you, but quite to me. She knew I should like it if you could carry out your idea. Not because she cared for you, but because she did think of me,' Miss Tina went on with her unexpected, persuasive volubility. 'You could see the things— you could use them.' She stopped, seeing I grasped the sense of her conditional—stopped long enough for me to give some sign that I didn't give. She must have been conscious, however, that though my face showed the greatest embarrassment ever painted on a human countenance it was not set as a stone, it was also full of compassion. It was a comfort to me a long time afterwards to consider that she couldn't have seen in me the smallest symptom of disrespect. 'I don't know what to do; I'm too tormented I'm too ashamed!' she continued with vehemence. Then, turning away from me and burying her face in her hands, she burst into a flood of tears. If she didn't know what to do it may be imagined whether I knew better. I stood there dumb, watching her while her sobs resounded in the great empty hall. In a moment she was up at me again with her streaming eyes. 'I'd give you everything, and she'd understand, where she is—she'd forgive me!'

'Ah, Miss Tina—ah, Miss Tina,' I stammered for all reply. I didn't know what to do, as I say, but at a venture I made a wild, vague movement in consequence of which I found myself at the door. I remember standing there and saying: 'It wouldn't do, it wouldn't do!'—saying it pensively, awkwardly, grotesquely, while I looked away to the opposite end of the *sala* as at something very interesting. The next thing I remember is that I was downstairs and out of the house. My gondola was there and my gondolier, reclining on the cushions, sprang up as soon as he saw me. I jumped in, and to his usual '*Dove commanda?*' replied, in a tone that made him stare: 'Anywhere, anywhere; out into the lagoon!'

He rowed me away and I sat there prostrate, groaning softly to myself, my hat pulled over my brow. What in the name of the preposterous did she mean if she didn't mean to offer me her hand? That was the price—that was the price! And did she think I wanted it, poor deluded, infatuated, extravagant lady? My gondolier, behind me, must have seen my ears red as I wondered, motionless there under the fluttering *tenda* with my hidden face, noticing nothing as we passed—wondered whether her delusion, her infatuation had been my own reckless work. Did she think I had made love to her even to get the papers? I hadn't, I hadn't; I repeated that over to myself for an hour, for two hours, till I was wearied if not convinced. I don't know where, on the lagoon, my gondolier took me; we floated aimlessly and with slow, rare strokes. At last I became conscious that we were near the Lido, far up, on the right hand, as you turn your

back to Venice, and I made him put me ashore.
I wanted to walk, to move, to shed some of my
bewilderment. I crossed the narrow strip and got
to the sea-beach—I took my way toward Malamocco.
But presently I flung myself down again on the
warm sand, in the breeze, on the coarse, dry grass.
It took it out of me to think I had been so much
at fault, that I had unwittingly but none the less
deplorably trifled. But I hadn't given her cause—
distinctly I hadn't. I had said to Mrs. Prest that
I would make love to her; but it had been a joke
without consequences and I had never said it to my
victim. I had been as kind as possible because I
really liked her; but since when had that become
a crime where a woman of such an age and such an
appearance was concerned? I am far from remembering clearly the succession of events and feelings
during this long day of confusion, which I spent
entirely in wandering about, without going home,
until late at night; it only comes back to me that
there were moments when I pacified my conscience
and others when I lashed it into pain. I didn't
laugh all day—that I do recollect; the case, however
it might have struck others, seemed to me so little
amusing. I should have been better employed perhaps in taking the comic side of it. At any rate,
whether I had given cause or not, there was no
doubt whatever that I couldn't pay the price. I
couldn't accept the proposal. I couldn't, for a bundle
of tattered papers, marry a ridiculous, pathetic, provincial old woman. It was a proof of how little she
supposed the idea would come to me that she should
have decided to suggest it herself in that practical,
argumentative, heroic way — with the timidity,

however, so much more striking than the boldness, that her reasons appeared to come first and her feelings afterward.

As the day went on I grew to wish I had never heard of Aspern's relics, and I cursed the extravagant curiosity that had put John Cumnor on the scent of them. We had more than enough material without them, and my predicament was the just punishment of that most fatal of human follies, our not having known when to stop. It was very well to say it was no predicament, that the way out was simple, that I had only to leave Venice by the first train in the morning, after addressing Miss Tina a note which should be placed in her hand as soon as I got clear of the house; for it was strong proof of my quandary that when I tried to make up the note to my taste in advance—I would put it on paper as soon as I got home, before going to bed—I couldn't think of anything but 'How can I thank you for the rare confidence you 've placed in me?' That would never do; it sounded exactly as if an acceptance were to follow. Of course I might get off without writing at all, but that would be brutal, and my idea was still to exclude brutal solutions. As my confusion cooled I lost myself in wonder at the importance I had attached to Juliana's crumpled scraps; the thought of them became odious to me and I was as vexed with the old witch for the superstition that had prevented her from destroying them as I was with myself for having already spent more money than I could afford in attempting to control their fate. I forgot what I did, where I went after leaving the Lido, and at what hour or with what recovery of composure I made my way back to my

boat. I only know that in the afternoon, when the
air was aglow with the sunset, I was standing before
the church of Saints John and Paul and looking
up at the small square-jawed face of Bartolommeo
Colleoni, the terrible *condottiere* who sits so sturdily
astride of his huge bronze horse on the high pedestal
on which Venetian gratitude maintains him. The
statue is incomparable, the finest of all mounted
figures, unless that of Marcus Aurelius, who rides
benignant before the Roman Capitol, be finer; but
I was not thinking of that; I only found myself
staring at the triumphant captain as if he had an
oracle on his lips. The western light shines into all
his grimness at that hour and makes it wonderfully
personal. But he continued to look far over my
head, at the red immersion of another day—he had
seen so many go down into the lagoon through the
centuries—and if he were thinking of battles and
stratagems they were of a different quality from any
I had to tell him of. He couldn't direct me what
to do, gaze up at him as I might. Was it before this
or after that I wandered about for an hour in the
small canals, to the continued stupefaction of my
gondolier, who had never seen me so restless and yet
so void of a purpose and could extract from me no
order but 'Go anywhere—everywhere—all over the
place'? He reminded me that I had not lunched
and expressed, therefore, respectfully the hope that
I would dine earlier. He had had long periods of
leisure during the day, when I had left the boat
and rambled, so that I was not obliged to consider
him, and I told him that till the morrow, for reasons,
I should touch no meat. It was an effect of poor
Miss Tina's proposal, not altogether auspicious, that

I had quite lost my appetite. I don't know why it happened that on this occasion I was more than ever struck with that queer air of sociability, of cousinship and family life, which makes up half the expression of Venice. Without streets and vehicles, the uproar of wheels, the brutality of horses, and with its little winding ways where people crowd together, where voices sound as in the corridors of a house, where the human step circulates as if it skirted the angles of furniture and shoes never wear out, the place has the character of an immense collective apartment, in which Piazza San Marco is the most ornamented corner and palaces and churches, for the rest, play the part of great divans of repose, tables of entertainment, expanses of decoration. And somehow the splendid common domicile, familiar, domestic and resonant, also resembles a theatre with its actors clicking over bridges and, in straggling processions, tripping along fondamentas. As you sit in your gondola the footways that in certain parts edge the canals assume to the eye the importance of a stage, meeting it at the same angle, and the Venetian figures, moving to and fro against the battered scenery of their little houses of comedy, strike you as members of an endless dramatic troupe.

I went to bed that night very tired and without being able to compose an address to Miss Tina. Was this failure the reason why I became conscious the next morning as soon as I awoke of a determination to see the poor lady again the first moment she would receive me? That had something to do with it, but what had still more was the fact that during my sleep the oddest revulsion had taken place in my spirit. I found myself aware of this almost as soon as I opened my eyes: it made me jump out of my bed with the movement of a man who remembers that he had left the house-door ajar or a candle burning under a shelf. Was I still in time to save my goods? That question was in my heart; for what had now come to pass was that in the unconscious cerebration of sleep I had swung back to a passionate appreciation of Juliana's treasure. The pieces composing it were now more precious than ever and a positive ferocity had come into my need to acquire them. The condition Miss Tina had attached to that act no longer appeared an obstacle worth thinking of, and for an hour this morning my repentant imagination brushed it aside. It was absurd I should be able to invent nothing; absurd to renounce so easily and turn away helpless from the idea that the only way to become possessed was to unite myself to her for life. I mightn't untie myself, yet I might still have what she had. I must add by the time I sent down to ask if she would see me I had invented no alternative, though in fact I drew out my dressing in the interest of my wit. This failure was humiliating, yet what could the alternative be? Miss Tina sent back word I might come; and as I descended the stairs and crossed the *sala* to her door—this time she received me in her aunt's forlorn parlour—I hoped she wouldn't think my announcement was to be 'favourable.' She certainly would have understood my recoil of the day before.

As soon as I came into the room I saw that she had done so, but I also saw something which had not been in my forecast. Poor Miss Tina's sense of failure had produced a rare alteration in her, but

I had been too full of stratagems and spoils to think of that. Now I took it in; I can scarcely tell how it startled me. She stood in the middle of the room with a face of mildness bent upon me, and her look of forgiveness, of absolution, made her angelic. It beautified her; she was younger; she was not a ridiculous old woman. This trick of her expression, this magic of her spirit, transfigured her, and while I still noted it I heard a whisper somewhere in the depths of my conscience: 'Why not, after all—why not?' It seemed to me I *could* pay the price. Still more distinctly, however, than the whisper I heard Miss Tina's own voice. I was so struck with the different effect she made on me that at first I wasn't clearly aware of what she was saying; then I recognized she had bade me good-bye—she said something about hoping I should be very happy.

'Good-bye—good-bye?' I repeated with an inflection interrogative and probably foolish.

I saw she didn't feel the interrogation, she only heard the words; she had strung herself up to accepting our separation and they fell upon her ear as a proof. 'Are you going to-day?' she asked. 'But it doesn't matter, for whenever you go I shall not see you again. I don't want to.' And she smiled strangely, with an infinite gentleness. She had never doubted my having left her the day before in horror. How *could* she, since I hadn't come back before night to contradict, even as a simple form, even as an act of common humanity, such an idea? And now she had the force of soul—Miss Tina with a force of soul was a new conception—to smile at me in her abjection.

'What shall you do—where shall you go?' I asked.

'Oh, I don't know. I've done the great thing. I've destroyed the papers.'

'Destroyed them?' I waited.

'Yes; what was I to keep them for? I burnt them last night, one by one in the kitchen.'

'One by one?' I coldly echoed it.

'It took a long time—there were so many.' The room seemed to go round me as she said this, and a real darkness for a moment descended on my eyes. When it passed, Miss Tina was there still, but the transfiguration was over and she had changed back to a plain, dingy, elderly person. It was in this character she spoke as she said: 'I can't stay with you longer, I can't'; and it was in this character she turned her back upon me, as I had turned mine upon her twenty-four hours before, and moved to the door of her room. Here she did what I hadn't done when I quitted her—she paused long enough to give me one look. I have never forgotten it and I sometimes still suffer from it, though it was not resentful. No, there was no resentment, nothing hard or vindictive in poor Miss Tina; for when, later, I sent her, as the price of the portrait of Jeffrey Aspern, a larger sum of money than I had hoped to gather for her, writing to her that I had sold the picture, she kept it with thanks; she never sent it back. I wrote her that I had sold the picture, but I admitted to Mrs. Prest at the time—I met this other friend in London that autumn—that it hangs above my writing-table. When I look at it I can scarcely bear my loss—I mean of the precious papers.

EVERYMAN'S LIBRARY

A LIST OF THE 990 VOLUMES
ARRANGED UNDER AUTHORS

Anonymous works are given under titles

*Anthologies, Composite Volumes, Dictionaries, etc., are
arranged at the end of the list*

LONDON: J. M. DENT & SONS LTD.

NEW YORK: E. P. DUTTON & CO. INC.